THE CASE OF THE LLAMA RAISING LIBRARIAN

BUTTERCUP BEND MYSTERIES
BOOK THREE

DEBBIE DE LOUISE

In honor of my readers and those who have yet to try my books but have given this one a chance. I hope you enjoy my efforts. I write for you and look forward to your feedback.

CHAPTER ONE

Cathy sat by the window in Gran's kitchen watching the snowflakes fall. She wasn't the only one observing this winter activity. Her six-month-old kittens, Harry and Hermione, whom she'd gotten for her birthday in October, gazed wide-eyed nearby.

"Are you bored, Catherine?" Florence asked, as she entered the room.

"No, Gran. There's plenty to do. I'm just taking a break and watching the kittens."

Florence smiled. "They are cute to watch. But you've been hanging around the house since college break started. I'm beginning to worry about you. Steven and Michael have called, and you haven't even been available to see or at least talk with them. What's wrong?"

Cathy shrugged, but she didn't face her grandmother. "I'm fine. I only want some time alone." She couldn't tell her or even her best friend Nancy that she'd received a marriage proposal from Steve at Christmas and another from Michael at New Year's. She'd been putting off giving them an answer.

She hadn't expected Steve to invite her to his house on Christmas Eve and ask her to reach into a stocking with her name on it where she pulled out a ring box while he got down on one knee. The following week, Michael had invited her over to toast the New Year and slipped a ring next to her champagne glass. Although the two men were friends, she suspected that they wouldn't have shared their proposal with the other, nor the fact that she had put them off.

The doorbell rang. Florence went to answer it. Cathy prayed it wasn't Steve or Michael. Both had come to the house a week after their proposals, but she told her grandmother to make an excuse that she wasn't home and stayed upstairs in her room. She also avoided going to Rainbow Rescues, the pet rescue center she owned with her brother, because Michael, their vet, might be checking the animals. When her gardener, Steve, came to shovel the snow at Gran's house and Rainbow Gardens, her pet cemetery, she wouldn't join him when Gran served him hot chocolate afterwards. She also avoided Nancy, her friend who worked at the detective agency for Howard Hunt, her grandmother's boyfriend. After she'd helped Nancy and Howard solve the murder of her anthropology professor in October, she'd accepted a position at the agency but hadn't spoken to Nancy or Howard since the holidays. Nancy had all but broken down Florence's door trying to talk with her, but Gran insisted that it would be better to leave her alone.

As Cathy heard voices from the living room, her heart beat fast as she tried to figure out who was visiting. Michael, Steve, and Nancy hadn't come by for a few days. And, while she was relieved, she felt guilt and regret at how she was treating them. The voices grew louder as they approached. Her grandmother was speaking with a woman. It wasn't Nancy or her sister-in-law, Becky. The voice belonged to someone older. She recognized it as Gran led Mildred Hastings, the librarian, into the kitchen.

"Look who's here, Catherine? Mildred wants to ask you something. I'll put on tea and be right back."

Cathy turned to face the librarian. Was she here on Michael, Steve, or, more likely, Nancy's behalf to find out what was going on with her? She took a breath as the woman smiled, glanced at her through bifocals, and brushed flakes of snow from her gray, curly hair. Her brown eyes behind the thick lenses of her glasses held friendliness but a hint of sadness. "Hello, Cathy. I'm sorry I didn't call, but I wanted to speak with you in person. I need your help."

Cathy thought the librarian was asking for help with her studies. Like Cathy, she'd gone back to college in the fall. "Sure, Mildred. Are you working on something for school?"

"No." Mildred stepped closer and the kittens, wary of strangers, skittered away. "So sorry to frighten your cats. Hobo is used to me, so when I visit Nancy, he doesn't run away."

Hobo was the marmalade tabby her friend adopted from Rainbow Rescues last spring. He lived in Nancy's downstairs apartment in the house that Mildred owned.

Cathy had hoped that the help Mildred needed was academic, so she was disappointed. "That's okay, Mildred. What do you need? Nancy didn't send you, did she?"

Mildred shook her head. "To be honest, she knew I was coming and asked me to see how you were doing, but that's not the reason I'm here."

Before Mildred could explain the purpose of her visit, Florence returned with a tray of tea and cookies. She placed them on the table. "Mildred, please have a seat. I'll leave you two to talk. If you need anything else, let me know."

"I'd like you to stay. I think you should hear what I have to ask Cathy."

Florence raised a gray eyebrow. "That sounds mysterious." As Mildred took a seat at the table, Florence slipped into a chair next to her. Cathy joined them.

"It is actually mysterious," Mildred began, as Florence passed her and Cathy mugs. "I don't know if either of you remember Doris Grady who used to work at the library with me. She retired five years ago when Cathy and Doug first moved in here with you, Florence."

Cathy had a vague recollection of another librarian who once read to her and Doug in the library's children's corner when they visited Gran as kids. Florence nodded. "I remember Doris. She moved to a town near Hyde Park. I attended her retirement party."

"I forgot that you were there." Mildred blew on her mug and then took a sip of tea. She turned to Cathy. "I didn't say anything to Nancy about what I'm about to ask you. She thinks I'm visiting to find out why you're avoiding her. I know you're going through something, but this may be just what you need to take your mind off it."

Cathy gripped her teacup as the librarian continued. She had no idea what was coming. Was she suggesting therapy? Did she want to stage an intervention? Was this Gran's idea, even though her face held puzzlement?

"I'll cut to the chase, dear." Mildred took another sip of tea and then placed her cup back on the coaster Gran had provided. Her next words were a shock. "Doris is dead. Her daughter thinks she was murdered. I'm hoping you'll help me find her killer."

CHAPTER TWO

Cathy was too shocked to speak, but Florence had plenty to say. "What makes you think your friend was murdered? How did she die? Aren't the local police looking into it?"

Mildred gazed down at the checkered tablecloth. "I'm afraid not. You see, they termed her death a heart attack, but I, and her daughter, Danielle, think it was murder. Danielle called me after she read in the paper about how the Hunt, Meyers, and Carter Detective Agency assisted the sheriff in making the arrest in Dr. Bodkin's murder."

Cathy found her voice. "She asked you to hire Howard to investigate her mother's death?"

"Yes, but I suggested speaking with you first. I know you're now part of the agency." She looked into Cathy's eyes. "I trust that Danielle has a good reason to suspect Doris was killed but, if she hired Howard and it turns out she's wrong, it might stir up too much negative publicity for her business. I felt that you, as a business owner yourself, would take a subtler approach to the investigation."

"I appreciate your confidence in me, but I'm new at HMC. I haven't even worked on my first case. They gave me credit for helping solve my professor's murder, but I didn't do much at all. It was mostly Nancy and Howard."

Florence interrupted. "Excuse me, but what business is Danielle in? I know that Doris mentioned a family farm."

Mildred reached for one of the biscuits and added it to her plate. "That's correct. Oaks Landing Farms was first owned by Doris' grandfather and passed down the family line. Doris' sister, Mavis, was running the farm along with Danielle and her husband until Doris moved back. Their mother also still lives there, but she was diagnosed with dementia a few years ago."

"Is Danielle's husband the only man on the farm?" Florence asked, as she also took a biscuit for her plate.

"Doris' ex lives nearby and lends a hand. They also hire farmhands."

"What type of farming do they do?" Cathy asked. She waved away a biscuit Gran offered. She was trying to avoid extra calories.

"That's the interesting part." Mildred smiled. "It's a fiber farm. They raise llamas and alpacas and sell their wool. I've been invited there by Danielle and was hoping you'd join me to check things out on the qt."

Cathy thought about Steve and Michael and how she'd left them hanging for a week and still couldn't decide what to tell them. Maybe a trip would clear her mind. Before she could reply to Mildred's offer, Florence said, "I think it might be a good thing for Cathy to get away from Buttercup Bend for a while, but I worry that she might be in danger if you're right about Doris being murdered."

"I understand your concern, but I'll be with Cathy. If I sense any trouble, I'll notify the Hyde Park police."

Cathy felt a stirring of excitement at Mildred's words, the same she'd felt when investigating Maggie Broom and Barry Bodkins' murders. She wasn't afraid of facing danger. To her, it was less scary than facing her emotions for the two men she was dating. "When do you want to go?" she asked.

"I'd like to leave at 9 tomorrow morning. I'll call Danielle tonight to tell her we're coming but not to say anything to anyone else on the farm. I'll ask her to tell her relatives that you and I are being hired to fill in the gap that Doris left by helping with the farm's chores and other activities. I've been there before, so they know me as Doris' co-worker, but I'd like to introduce you as my daughter if that's okay."

Cathy liked that idea and agreed. It would help keep her identity as a detective secret. When she asked about the people she'd be meeting, Mildred promised to fill her in on their way to the farm. Since Mildred had an old car and didn't use it much, preferring to walk to work because the library was within blocks of her house, Cathy offered to drive.

Florence asked, "How long do you expect to be away?"

"I took a two-week vacation from the library, but we'll be back sooner if we solve the case or find out there's nothing to solve."

Cathy noticed how Mildred included herself in the investigation. She didn't mind because she was used to working with Nancy, and it always helped to have a partner.

After Mildred left, Cathy helped Florence put away the few uneaten biscuits and the empty teacups. "Are you sure about this, Catherine?"

"Yes, Gran. I think you're right that getting away from town will do me good. I hadn't expected that Mildred would want to leave so soon, but I can be ready by tomorrow. Will you take care of Harry and Hermione while I'm gone? I'll miss them." Cathy was used to the kittens sleeping with her, and she'd grown fond of their silly antics.

"Don't worry about that. I will take good care of them. Should I tell anyone you'll be away?"

Cathy considered a moment and then said, "You can tell Doug and Becky if you want, but I think most of my friends have felt I've been away even though I've been here at home."

Gran walked over to her and gave her a hug. "Oh, Catherine. I certainly hope you're able to come to terms with what you're facing. I'm sorry you haven't been able to confide in me, but it's obvious it has to do with Michael and Steven. I won't give you advice because you're a grown woman now. This change of scenery may help as long as you don't see it as an escape. You'll have to come home eventually."

Cathy smiled. Her grandmother was a wise woman. "You're right, Gran. I'm taking a breath, but I know I'll have to exhale at some point. What should I pack?"

Florence smiled. "For a farm in January? I'd bring jeans, boots, and warm clothing."

Up in her room, Cathy took her suitcase from her closet and tossed it on her bed. When she opened it, Hermione, her female kitten, jumped into it. Harry, Hermione's brother, followed. "Do you guys want to come with me?" she asked, gently lifting them out of the case. She wished she had her phone or camera handy to take a photo of them when they were in the case. It would make her laugh and help her remember them while she was away, but she already had tons of pictures of them in her phone's photo gallery.

As she went through her drawers, she was careful to shut them after she took out clothes because she was used to the kittens going inside them, too. But when she laid her jeans and sweaters across her bed, Hermione jumped on them and began to knead her paws through the soft sweaters. "Hermione, no. You'll pull a thread." Although Gran was very good at clipping nails with Cathy's assistance, the kittens' claws grew quickly. She was glad that New York State now banned declawing. Rainbow Rescues, her shelter, had recently hired a groomer to clip the nails of the pets, but Gran clipped Harry and Hermione's as well as Doug and Becky's German shepherds, Max and Millie.

She carefully pulled Hermione off her favorite pink sweater and placed her on the floor. She noted how big the kitten had grown after three months and only imagined how large she and her brother would be when she came back from the llama farm.

After she was packed, Cathy sat on her bed petting her kittens. She'd placed the cases by the door after Harry and Hermione had sniffed them and rubbed against them.

"Don't worry, guys, Gran will take good care of you while I'm away." She imagined they were looking at her with sad eyes. Hermione's green ones were open wide. Harry's gold eyes were half closed.

"Saying your goodbyes?" Cathy hadn't heard Florence come up the stairs. She'd left her door open, and Gran stood there next to her cases.

"I'm not leaving yet, but they know I'm going. They tried to hide in my suitcase while I was packing."

Florence laughed. "Cats are very intuitive, and they like enclosed spaces such as boxes. Their cat tunnel is one of their favorite toys."

"I hope I'm doing the right thing, Gran. I know you'll take care of the kittens, but I'm not even saying goodbye to anyone. It feels wrong."

Florence joined Cathy on the bed displacing Harry and Hermione who went back to examine the suitcases.

"Sometimes it's better to let things rest, dear. Steven and Michael got your message and are giving you space. Nancy hasn't quite accepted your absence, but she'll understand."

Cathy looked into her grandmother's wise eyes. "I know, Gran, but she won't be too happy if she finds out I'm investigating a murder without her."

Florence smiled. "You don't know it's a murder yet, and Mildred was the one who chose you to check out things with her."

Cathy sighed. "You're right, as usual. Part of me is looking forward to this adventure. I've never been to a llama farm, and the only time I've been to Hyde Park was when you took me and Doug one summer to see the Vanderbilt Mansion." Cathy smiled at the memory.

"That was such an enjoyable time. You were ten and Doug was twelve, I believe."

"I wrote a story about it for school and got an "A." Dad was proud of me. Mom said we should all go back one day." Cathy gazed down at her bedspread, noticing a few pulled threads where Hermione had kneaded the covers. She felt sad thinking about her parents who'd died in a car accident in which she'd been injured six years ago but survived with only a fading scar on her cheek and a deeper one in her heart. "I wish we would've made that trip. There are so many things I wish I'd done with them before..."

"Stop, Catherine. You can't think like that. I felt the same way after William died, but the memories I have of him are special. I hold on to those." She got off the bed. "Why don't you get some sleep now? You have a big day ahead of you tomorrow. Mildred wants to start early."

As Florence left, she switched off the lights and gently

closed the door halfway behind her to allow the kittens to leave if they wanted. They were used to the house now but spent most of the night in Cathy's room.

As soon as Gran was gone, Hermione jumped back on the bed and curled up next to Cathy. Harry lay at her feet. She fell asleep to the purrs of the kittens and thoughts of what the next day would bring.

CHAPTER THREE

The next morning, Cathy rose to bright sunshine. The temperature had gone up to the forties, and the snow from the day before was melting. She could hear water dripping off the roof. The kittens heard it, too, and were alert to the sound. They jumped on her headboard which was by the window and peered out. She yawned and stretched and then checked the clock on her nightstand. The glowing numbers indicated it was 7 o'clock. She'd arranged to pick up Mildred at nine, and the librarian was always prompt. "Come on downstairs with me, kitties, and I'll feed you before I leave."

Florence was already awake and cooking at the stove when she entered the kitchen with Harry and Hermione behind her.

"Good morning, Catherine. I thought you'd like something to tide you over before your trip to the farm. I'm making scrambled eggs with bacon. We can share if you'd like."

Cathy sniffed the air, and her stomach did a flip. "It smells delicious, Gran. I'll have a small plate after I feed the cats. Thank you." She got out two small cans of cat food from the pantry and scooped them into the bowls in the corner of the kitchen they'd set aside for Harry and Hermione who hungrily dove into them.

Florence smiled as she turned to see the kittens eating. Cathy put out fresh water for them and then went over to assist her grandmother with breakfast. When they were seated at the table, Florence said, "You must be excited. Your cheeks are flushed this morning. I'm so glad you're acting more like your old self. You seemed depressed this past week."

Cathy took a sip of coffee and a forkful of scrambled eggs that were perfectly cooked and contained chopped red and green peppers and onions. After taking a bite and swallowing, she nodded. "This is delicious, Gran. And, yes, I'm excited. I like to travel, although I don't do it often. I've also never been to a llama farm."

"I don't think that's the only reason for your cheerful mood, Catherine."

"The weather's nice. It's been days since we've seen sunshine."

"No, dear. That's not the reason either. You're going to investigate a mystery. That's what you enjoy doing and are good at. That's why Howard asked you to join the detective agency with him and Nancy."

Cathy had nothing to say to that because it was true, so she continued to eat. Her grandmother knew her well. There was no sense in denying her attraction to mystery. She'd hidden it for years even from herself, while Nancy had flaunted her interest in solving them. It was only when she'd gotten involved in Maggie Broom's murder that she'd realized that part of her nature.

At a quarter to nine, Cathy, dressed in jeans, a red and white checked blouse, and a pair of brown cowboy boots that she thought might be appropriate for visiting a farm, loaded her suitcases in her car. She made sure to leave room in the trunk for Mildred's cases.

Florence saw her off after she'd given the kittens kisses. They stood in the doorway watching. She felt bad but knew her grandmother would take loving care of them.

"Good luck, Catherine, and be careful. Drive safely. The roads may still be icy."

"Don't worry, Gran. It's not far. We should be there in a little over an hour." Cathy wanted to convince herself as well as her grandmother that the trip would be easy. It had taken some time after the car crash she'd been in with her parents for her to get behind the wheel again. She still felt nervous driving but took some deep breaths and got into the car. "I'll call you as soon as we get there and are settled. You have the farm's phone number that Mildred gave you."

Florence spoke to her through the car window. "I won't use it unless it's an emergency. I can always call you on your cell. Don't forget to keep it charged."

"I won't. I'm using it for directions and have it plugged into the car charger."

"Good. Enjoy your time at the farm and keep me posted."

As Cathy started the car, Florence waved and walked back to the house. Harry and Hermione were still watching from the windows.

CHAPTER FOUR

Cathy wasn't picking up Mildred at her house. Because Nancy might suspect something, they'd arrange to meet by the library. Mildred told Nancy that she was visiting her sister upstate on her vacation. Her co-workers were aware that Mildred would be leaving her car in the library parking lot while she was away and that she'd be taking a nearby bus to her sister's house. She was standing next to her car as Cathy entered the lot, suitcases by her side.

Cathy parked next to her and got out. Since it was Sunday, the library was closed.

"Good morning, Mildred. I hope I haven't kept you waiting?"

"Not at all. I got here early, but it's a nice morning. I enjoyed getting some fresh air."

Cathy helped her with her bags. The two cases fit snugly against Cathy's in the trunk. Mildred got into the passenger's seat. "I love your car, Cathy. It still smells new, and I know it runs better than mine."

"It's not brand new, Mildred, but I'm happy with it." The

car had been her purchase for transportation to college. Before that, she was dependent on using Gran's car.

"Are you ready for our adventure?" The librarian's brown eyes held a hint of excitement.

Cathy started the car. "I think so, but I don't know what to expect."

"Neither do I, but isn't that what makes adventures fun?"

Cathy laughed. "Not always, but I guess we'll find out." She reached into her glove compartment and took out the address Mildred had given her. After she'd recited it into her iPhone that was attached to her dashboard, Mildred said, "You don't need your phone to get to the farm. I can direct you."

"When were you there last?"

"I visited Doris right after she moved to Oaks Landing. That was five years ago, so I suppose it's good you use a digital map. My memory isn't what it used to be."

Cathy smiled. Mildred was as sharp as when she read to Cathy and Doug in the library fifteen years ago.

As they drove, Cathy was glad her excitement overcame her driving anxiety. When they were on the parkway headed south, she said, "You promised to fill me in on the people I'll be meeting. We have about an hour for you to do that."

Mildred was gazing out the passenger side window. She turned and glanced at Cathy. "I thought about that. Even though you should know the character list, it's much better for you to form your own opinions of everyone. That will help us solve the mystery."

Cathy found it funny how the librarian termed the people they were meeting, as if they were characters in a book. "You're right, Mildred. Go ahead, list the characters."

Mildred smiled. The mechanical voice of Cathy's phone told her to take the next exit. As she turned, Mildred said, "We'll start with Doris' daughter. Her full name is Danielle

Diaz. She's a little older than you. I think thirty. Her husband is Dylan. He's Peruvian. They met when she took a trip there seven years ago. They came back here to marry and had their daughter Sheri. Doris' sister is Mavis Taylor. She's in her mid-fifties and never married. Their mother, Betty, I told you has dementia."

Cathy asked, "Is Betty's last name Taylor?"

"You caught that. It's short for Elizabeth."

"Was she named after Elizabeth Taylor?"

"No, but she believes she's Elizabeth Taylor. It's part of her dementia. She was quite with it until five years ago. Then, according to Danielle, she woke up one morning and insisted she was the famous actress. But I shouldn't be telling you all this. As I said, you need to see it for yourself."

"Yes, but I need to be prepared. That sounds strange. Do they all live at the farm?"

"Danielle and Dylan live in the farmhouse with their daughter. Mavis lives with her mother there, too. When Doris moved back, she also lived in the main house. I believe that's where I'll be staying, and Danielle said they have a guest room for you. I confirmed our visit with her last night."

"What about the farmhands do they live on the property?"

"Some. A few commute. I don't know their names, but I'm sure Danielle will introduce us." She paused. "There's one other person living on the property. Doris' ex, Chris Grady. He has his own place."

Cathy was surprised. "Didn't that cause tension?"

"I don't think so. Doris and Chris' divorce was amicable. They remained friends, and Danielle tells me he's great with animals. I met him when I helped Doris move back to the farm. He reminds me of an older Michael."

At the vet's name, Cathy felt her anxiety return. She'd hoped to leave it behind in Buttercup Bend. "Is he a vet?"

"He doesn't have formal training, but he's conferred with the local vet many times and knows enough to help out in a pinch. If you're wondering, they also have a gardener. Older than Steve, according to Danielle. She says he lives on the property, too."

"Wow! How big is the farm?"

"I don't know the exact acreage. Danielle has those figures, but it's pretty big. It was a dairy farm before Doris' grandfather bought it and passed it down to her and Mavis. Doris didn't have a knack for farming, so she went away to library school and then moved to Buttercup Bend."

Cathy tried to picture it in her mind. She imagined cute llamas romping in a large field with a barn and a rustic-looking house. "So, I guess Doris changed her mind about the farm when she retired?"

"She told me that she missed it. She wanted a quieter life. Not that it's very hectic in Buttercup Bend, but we have had murders as you know."

Cathy was well aware of that since she'd been involved in two of them in the last year. "It would be ironic then if Danielle is right and Doris was murdered."

"That it would. I hope she's wrong, but I'm glad we're both getting a vacation out of it."

Cathy silently agreed. The farther they drove, the more relaxed she felt. The decision she needed to make about Steve and Michael would wait until she returned. She had something different to occupy her mind, and she'd also be able to show Howard and Nancy that they'd made the right choice in hiring her at their detective agency.

CHAPTER FIVE

C athy's envisioning of the farm was close but not exact. When they arrived, Mildred told her she could bypass the visitor's parking lot and drive up to the house. Danielle had given them permission to do so.

Since it was winter and not yet ten thirty, there were no cars in the parking lot. "They give farm tours and llama hikes seasonally," Mildred explained. "They still offer these now, weather permitting, but they aren't as popular. If people sign up, it's later in the day when it's warmer."

"How much do they charge for the tours and hikes?" Cathy had her eyes on the winding road leading up to the house. The trees that flanked it were bare against the partly cloudy winter sky.

"I don't know, but it helps support the farm. It isn't cheap to run one. And, although they sell the llama and alpaca's wool, there's not much of a profit in that."

"Really? I always wondered what the difference was between alpacas and llamas. Do you know?" Cathy maneuvered around a red truck, and a barn came into view. It was large and sat next to a pen where Cathy saw several llamas grazing.

"Of course I do. I'm a librarian. The main differences are their sizes and ears. You might consider them cousins. Alpacas are smaller than llamas and have T-shaped ears, while llamas have banana-shaped ears. They're both gentle and friendly animals."

"Interesting." Cathy pulled into a space between the house and the barn. The spots weren't marked, and the lot wasn't paved, but there were two cars parked there. A small blue Mazda and a pickup truck.

Mildred checked her watch. "We're a little early. We made great time. Maybe you want to walk around with me a bit before we go up to the house."

"That's a good idea. I'm eager to see the animals." Cathy got out, and Mildred joined her. They headed for the barn and the llama pen. As they passed the barn, Cathy exclaimed, "Oh, my gosh, Mildred. Cats! Those two look like Harry and Hermione, only older, but the calico one doesn't have Hermione's white undercoat and paws."

"They must be barn cats," Mildred said. "They usually have them on farms to keep the mice and other small rodents in check. The calico is a tortoiseshell. Notice the brown markings."

Cathy walked slowly toward the cats. She saw a gray one behind them. The black cat came right up to her. She extended her hand, and the cat sniffed it. "You look like my Harry," she said. "I bet you enjoy living here."

Mildred laughed. "I love how you talk to animals. C'mon, let's see the llamas."

"I'll be happy to show those to you since you've already met Rascal, Piper, and Cricket," said a voice from behind them.

Cathy turned to see a dark-haired man standing outside the

20

barn. He was dressed in jeans and a brown tweed coat. Work boots covered his feet. He strode over to them with a careless swagger and extended his hand. "My name's Dylan. I assume you're the ladies who have come to work with us? Cathy and Mildred? My wife told me to expect you, and I see our barn cats have greeted you."

Mildred shook his hand, but Cathy held back. He seemed friendly enough, but she was still shy around new people and didn't want to appear too eager. Mildred told her that Danielle hadn't shared the true reason for their visit with anyone. She wondered if that extended to her husband. She merely nodded and said, "Nice to meet you, Mr. Diaz."

He laughed, and she noticed the short mustache above his lips and his dark eyes. She judged him to be in his mid-thirties. "Please don't call me that. I'm Dylan, not your boss. Danielle is the one who hired you. She was up early this morning planning for your arrival. She's a great cook, so you'd better be hungry." He patted his stomach which was flat. Cathy imagined working on the farm burned a lot of calories.

"I'll bring you to the house now if you don't mind waiting to meet the llamas. I promise to give you a llama tour later."

Danielle greeted them as they walked up the porch steps to the front door. The farmhouse was just as Cathy imagined it as she stepped inside, rustic and cozy with a fireplace burning in the main room and thick paneled walls. "I see my husband found you," Danielle said. She wore a long, multicolored skirt over brown boots and an ivory cable-knit sweater. Her dark, straight hair fell to her waist. "It's a little early for brunch, but I know you must be hungry, and Sheri is almost eating the table, so please come into the dining room, and I'll introduce you to everyone. Granny is having a difficult day today, so she won't be joining us, but I'll take you up to say hello to her later."

Cathy had hoped that she and Mildred would be able to speak with Danielle privately before meeting the family. She still didn't know how her mother had died or why she suspected it was murder. Reluctantly, she followed Danielle, Mildred, and Dylan into the dining area where two people and a young girl were seated. When they entered, the girl jumped up and ran to Danielle. "Mommy, Mommy. Can we eat now?"

Danielle laughed and rubbed the girl's head. Cathy was surprised to note that the child's hair, worn in braids, was a golden blonde in contrast to her parents. "Yes, Sheri. Daddy found our guests, so we're all set. Can you help Mommy bring in the food?"

Sheri nodded her head "yes" and excitedly ran with her mother into the kitchen. Mildred faced the man and woman at the table. "Good morning. I'm Mildred Hastings. I don't know if you remember me, and this is my daughter, Cathy." Mildred really had a daughter who'd lived in the apartment Nancy now occupied until she married and moved away, so the lie wasn't far from the truth.

The woman stood up. She had short, curly hair that looked rusty. Cathy thought the color was caused by a poor red dye job. There was also gray at the roots. She offered a half smile when she said, "I do recall you, Mildred. For your daughter's sake, I'll introduce myself. I'm Mavis Taylor, Danielle's aunt." She paused and then added, "and this is Chris Grady, her father." The man beside her was drinking from his glass and hadn't bothered to get off his chair. Cathy knew he was Doris' ex who was still living on the farm's property. He had the same sandy blond hair as Steve but a more mature face. She figured Sheri had inherited his light hair. She judged him to be in his sixties. "Welcome to The Farm at Oak's Landing. Danielle has asked me to show you around later and explain the jobs you'll be helping us with. I'm in charge of the llama hikes. We still give them in the winter, so I hope you've brought warm clothing."

Cathy was surprised that he gave the hikes. She imagined Dylan, the younger man, would be more up for that. Mildred continued to smile. "It's nice to meet you all again."

It was then that Danielle and Sheri returned with bowls and plates of food that they placed on the table. Dylan, who was also helping them, carried a few dishes. Sheri had been trusted with the syrup, sugar, butter, and milk servers. There were pancakes, muffins, and a platter of scrambled eggs and bacon.

"Didn't I tell you that my wife cooks up hearty food?" Dylan said. "Have a seat, you two, and dig in."

Cathy wanted to wait until everyone sat, but Mildred took the chair closest to Mavis and nodded at Cathy to take the one next to her on the right. Dylan sat next to Cathy. Danielle sat at the head of the table with Sheri between her and her husband.

"I see you've all met one another," Danielle said. "We're not so busy this time of year, but Mother was in charge of a lot of the activities and classes we give to the public to help support the farm. It'll be helpful to have two other hands with those."

Cathy heard the note of sadness in Danielle's voice when she mentioned Doris. She was familiar with that type of pain, as she still carried the loss of her own parents in her heart and knew that the loss for Danielle was more recent. Mildred said that Doris died in early December, just a month ago. She imagined how difficult Christmas must've been for the family and the challenge it presented to Danielle and Dylan to keep the holiday a happy one for young Sheri.

"We're glad to be able to help," Cathy said.

Mavis said, "I really didn't expect Danielle to hire someone so soon." She looked down the table at her niece. "Tell me again why you made that decision, Danny."

Danielle was passing around the food bowls. She handed one to Sheri who grabbed it eagerly. "Be careful, honey." She turned to Mavis. "As you know, Mildred was a friend of Doris' when she worked at the library. When I called to tell her the sad news, she offered to come and help with her daughter."

So, the story Danielle had concocted was based loosely on truth.

"If they were such good friends, how come they weren't at the funeral?" Cathy worried that Mavis suspected something with all her questions.

Danielle seemed a bit flustered when she replied, "I didn't call until after that. I hadn't thought of them. I'd only met Mildred when she helped Mom move back to the farm. It was some time since I'd seen her. But I was going through Mother's address book and found her name. I figured she'd want to be informed."

"I see." Mavis reached for the egg and bacon platter and took a heapful on her plate and then passed it to Mildred. Before she could ask another question, Mildred said, "I'm glad you let me know, Danielle, and agreed to have us help with the farm. I have a two-week vacation from the library, and Cathy's on break from college. She's never been to a llama farm, so I'm sure she'll enjoy it. She's already seen your barn cats, and Dylan told us he'd introduce us to the llamas."

Chris said, "I can do that. In fact, I'll take you on a hike if you're up to it. I have some things to attend to today, but tomorrow would work, and it's not supposed to be too cold."

Mildred said, "That sounds like fun, but my knees aren't the best."

"Oh, don't worry. The hikes aren't strenuous. I'll take you on the beginner's one. You'll get a tour of the farm, too."

"While that sounds wonderful, I'd rather skip it for now. You go ahead with Cathy."

Chris didn't insist, and they continued their meal discussing other topics.

After they ate, Mildred offered to help Danielle clean up, and Cathy joined her. She knew Mildred wanted a moment in private with Danielle, but Sheri was tagging along. "Honey, why don't you go with daddy? I'll ask you to help me bring food up to Grammy later."

"Okay, Mommy." She ran off to her father who was still seated at the table speaking with Mavis and Chris.

When the three were in the kitchen together, Danielle turned on the sink and spoke in a low voice. "Thank you both for coming. You have to excuse Mavis. She's suspicious by nature, and she doesn't like having me run things."

Cathy knew the farm was family owned. She figured it was in Danielle's grandmother's name, but since she was suffering from dementia, it was likely that Mavis had taken over. Danielle verified this fact by saying, "When Grammy started to be ill, Mavis asked for her power-of-attorney and had her sign over the farm, but I don't feel I need her permission to make decisions."

Mildred asked, "When did this happen, Danielle? Wasn't your mother, as the oldest sibling, next in line?"

"Yes, but she didn't want the farm. That's why she left all those years ago."

"But she came back."

Danielle placed some dishes in the dishwasher and turned to Mildred. "She wanted to be with family. That's why she returned. She had no interest in the farm. I mean, she was happy enough to help out, but it wasn't as important to her as it was to Mavis."

Mildred stepped closer to Danielle and said, "Tell us why you think your mother was murdered."

Danielle was about to answer when Sheri ran back into the room. "Mommy! Can we go up to feed Grammy now? Daddy is going out with Grandpa, and Auntie M. is too busy to watch me."

Danielle sighed, turned off the water, and closed the dishwasher. "Sure, honey. Give me a minute." She turned to Mildred and Cathy. "I'll fill you both in later. Come with me. I'll introduce you to Grammy Betty."

Sheri carefully balanced the tray that her mother gave her to bring upstairs to her great grandmother. Cathy admired how skillful the young girl was, although Danielle walked behind her in case she slipped or dropped the food. Cathy and Mildred were in back of them.

At the top of the stairs, Sheri stopped at a closed door. Danielle stepped in front of her and tapped on the wood. "Grammy, can we come in? I've brought our guests, the ones I told you were coming today."

A faint voice replied, "You may enter."

Cathy didn't know what to expect. She'd never had experience with anyone suffering dementia. While her grandmother had a few lapses of memory, they were normal signs of aging.

The woman sitting up in bed had a full head of dark hair that Cathy knew came from a bottle but what surprised her most was her large violet eyes. Danielle had explained that her grandmother thought she was Elizabeth Taylor, but Cathy couldn't help but notice that she looked like the film star, too or made herself up to look like her.

Sheri brought the tray over to the bed. "Here's your food, Grammy."

"Thank you. What a sweet girl. Where is the pie?"

"No pie, Grammy, but I helped Mommy make the muffins."

Betty suddenly grabbed the tray and tossed it across the room. It hit the door with a loud crash, and the food spattered everywhere. Everyone jumped back, and Sheri began to cry. She ran to her mother who put an arm around her. "It's okay, honey. We'll clean it up."

"Why is Grammy mad? Is it because she wanted pie?"

"No. She's not feeling well." Danielle turned to Mildred. "Can you please take my daughter downstairs? And, Cathy, would you mind getting some rags and paper towels from the kitchen?"

Mildred put an arm on Sheri. "Come with me, sweetie." Sheri followed her from the room. Cathy, shocked from what had happened, said, "I'll get what you need, but is she okay?"

Danielle had gone to her grandmother's side. The woman's eyes were wide. "Where is the pie? What have you done with him?"

Him? Cathy knew the woman was confused but giving food a gender was too strange. Danielle turned to her. "Please excuse my grandmother. She's talking about the horse in *National Velvet,* Elizabeth Taylor's film."

"Don't talk about me when I'm in the room. I was great in that film. It was one of my favorites."

As Danielle tried to calm down her grandmother, Cathy slipped out to get the cleaning supplies. She needed to watch her step, as the egg splatter blocked part of the doorway.

"What a mess," she thought. *"literally."* She felt bad for Danielle and even worse for Sheri. She heard the girl still crying when she got downstairs. Mildred was trying to comfort

her with cookies. As Cathy grabbed a roll of paper towels and some dishcloths, Dylan and Chris came in.

"What's going on?" Dylan asked, rushing over to his daughter. Mildred explained what happened upstairs, and he said, "Danny shouldn't have brought her. She knows Betty was doing poorly today."

"But I wanna see Grammy."

"You can see her when she's better." Dylan turned and saw Cathy holding the towels. "I'll go and help Danny clean up. I'm sorry you had to experience this on your first day with us."

Cathy didn't know how to reply. She merely handed over the towels. As Dylan headed to the stairs, he called back, "Chris, can you take care of Sheri?"

"No problem," Chris said. "I like to spend time with my granddaughter. Wanna go play with Lulu?"

Sheri's face brightened, and she wiped her tears away with her sweater. "I love Lulu. Yes, please let's go."

Cathy wondered who Lulu was. She hadn't seen any other children on the farm, but maybe some lived nearby.

As Chris and Sheri put on their coats, Chris said, "Hey, you two. Want to join us? Cathy, I know I promised you a hike tomorrow, but you can meet our star llama today."

"Thanks, but I wouldn't want to intrude on Sheri's playdate with her friend."

He laughed. "You won't because Lulu, the llama, is the friend I'm taking Sheri to play with."

CHAPTER SIX

"You can all go," Mildred said. "I can meet Lulu another time. Danielle may need me here."

"Danny is fine." But just as Chris said that, Cathy heard Dylan arguing with his wife. His voice was raised so loud that she could hear it from downstairs.

"You know that your grandmother is ill, and you keep bringing Sheri up here. What's wrong with you?"

"I'm sorry. I thought it would be good for them to be together. She's not always this bad."

"Not always, but most of the time. You know I think she should be in a home."

"Please, Dylan. She's my grandmother. Mother would never have put her away."

"Why would your mother care? She left the farm and our family and then thought she could just come back here and take up where she left off."

"Don't say that. She did care, and it's my family and my farm, not yours."

Cathy heard Danielle's voice choke. But Dylan didn't seem

to have any sympathy for his wife's tears. "Excuse me. I'm part of the family even if you don't consider me a member, and the farm is Mavis' not yours. You tend to forget that."

As the argument progressed, Chris said, "Let's go. They'll work it out. They always do."

Cathy took her coat, but Mildred still seemed reluctant. "I'll stay. I'm tired from the trip and know where my room is. I'll take a nap and then start to unpack."

"Up to you." Chris turned. "You coming, Cathy?"

Cathy nodded. She knew it was best to get Sheri away while her parents were fighting. She also wanted to see Lulu the llama.

Outside, Chris hoisted Sheri onto his shoulders. Cathy was amazed it was such an effortless move. It again reinforced her opinion that he was in great shape for his age. "Into the truck you go, my dear." He carried her to the passenger seat and tied her seat belt. Turning to Cathy, he said, "You don't mind riding in back, do you?"

Cathy hadn't even expected them to be taking the truck since the llama pen near the barn seemed so close. "No, but I thought we'd walk. The llamas are right over there." She glanced toward the pen.

Chris laughed. "Those are the male llamas. Lulu is with the females up by my house. It's not a long drive, but it's a bit chilly today, and Danny gets nervous about Sheri catching a cold."

"I love to ride in the truck," Sheri said. "It's bouncy."

Chris rolled his eyes. "That, too."

As they drove, Chris gave Cathy some facts about the farm and llamas. "We're a fiber farm which means that our main product is wool. The best type comes from our alpacas, although we also shear the llamas. We have a store where we sell a variety of products. I'll show you that, too. It's closed now, but Danny wants to ask you or Mildred to take some shifts there."

"Can we have ice cream?" Sheri asked, interrupting her grandfather.

"I usually take Sheri to my house after visiting Lulu. I keep her favorite ice cream in my freezer," he explained.

Sheri's face lit up. "I love blue raspberry. Do you want some, too, Miss Hastings?"

Cathy forgot that she was using Mildred's last name. "Sure, if there's enough for all of us."

Chris said, "I have plenty, but I don't partake. I'm watching calories, but I have other flavors if you prefer."

Cathy was sorry the conversation got off the farm because they were already rounding a bend in the road where she could see sheep and goats grazing. In the distance was another farmhouse similar to the main house and a barn. As they pulled closer, she spotted the llamas in a fenced-in area.

Chris parked the truck by the house, and Sheri didn't wait for him to help her down. She excitedly ran ahead. Chris chuckled. "I like to see her so happy." Cathy wondered at that comment if he meant that Sheri wasn't typically happy. Was the girl's sadness from her grandmother's recent death or the conflict Cathy had overheard between Danielle and Dylan?

Sheri was already at the llama pen's gate. "Hold up, honey!" Chris exclaimed as he and Cathy approached. Cathy noticed that there were smaller animals in the pen with the llamas. She recalled Mildred's explanation of the differences between llamas and alpacas. As they caught up with Sheri, Chris said, "We keep the female alpacas and llamas together unless we're breeding them. You'll notice the size difference. Sheri grew up with them, but when we have school visits, some of the kids are frightened by how large the llamas are. Full grown ones can weigh up to five hundred pounds."

"Wow!" Cathy said. "Where's Lulu? How can you tell them apart?"

"Lulu has spots. She's a paloosa."

Chris corrected her. "That's appaloosa. Spotted llamas are called the same as spotted horses."

Sheri was hopping from one foot to the other as if ready to jump the fence. "Can we go in now, grandpa?"

Chris opened the gate. "Go ahead. You might want to make a stop in the barn to get hay later if you want to feed her."

"She's munching on the grass," Sheri pointed out, and Cathy watched as the young girl ran to the spotted llama. She counted five other llamas in the pen and twice that of alpacas.

"You can pet one if you want. They're quite gentle," Chris said. Sheri was already petting Lulu. The llama regarded her with big brown eyes. Cathy walked over to them. "This is Lulu," Sheri said, introducing the llama. "Lulu, this is Miss Hastings. She's going to be working at the farm with her mommy."

Cathy laughed. "You can call me Cathy. And you, too, Lulu," she added.

"Wanna pet her, Cathy? She's very soft."

"The alpacas are softer," Chris said, "their fiber is lighter and warmer than wool."

Cathy found that interesting. "I don't knit or crochet, but my grandmother does."

Chris smiled. "You can pick up some skeins in the shop. I won't charge ya." He winked.

Cathy placed her hand on Lulu's back and moved it down as if she was stroking her kittens. The llama didn't purr, but her eyes widened. "She's friendly," Cathy said.

"They all have different personalities," Chris pointed out. "Lulu is a sweetheart."

"How long have you had her?"

Sheri answered. "She's five like me. Mommy said daddy brought her back from Peru the year I was born."

"That's right," Chris said. "Lulu was just a baby or "cria," as baby llamas are termed, when she came to the farm. It's not easy to bring livestock back to the U.S. There are all sorts of red tape requirements. She was raised here for her wool unlike some of the South American llamas that are mostly raised as work and guard animals."

As Sheri continued petting and talking with Lulu, Cathy stood by the gate with Chris. "Mildred said that Danielle met Dylan in Peru. Was she looking for llamas?"

Chris smiled. "Looking for llamas and found a husband. She met Dylan on her first trip to Peru. She'd gone to visit some of the farms. According to her, it was love at first sight when she met Dylan. He handed the farm over to his brother and made plans to move to Oaks Landing."

"Sounds like a whirlwind romance to me." Cathy lowered her voice, "but they don't sound so happy now."

"That happens with couples sometimes, but they love one another. I think there's a lot of pressure with Betty's condition, and Doris' death didn't help matters."

Cathy wanted to ask why he'd divorced Doris, but Sheri was running back to them. "Can we have ice cream now, Grandpa? Lulu seems tired. She wants to take a nap."

Cathy thought Sheri was the one who was tired because the girl's eyelids were drooping, and she let out a long yawn.

Chris laughed. "Sure, if you promise you won't fall asleep in the ice cream bowl."

Sheri looked serious when she said, "Oh, no. I won't do that. It would mess up my hair, and Mommy would be mad."

. . .

They walked over to Chris' house. It was smaller but featured the same brick exterior. It was also rustic inside with a large fireplace in the main room. Sheri raced ahead of them into the kitchen. She seemed to have gotten her second wind. She grabbed a stool from the corner and tried to reach the freezer. "Be careful, honey," Chris said, standing behind her. He helped her bring two containers of ice cream to the table. She hopped off the stool and sat in one of the wooden chairs as he took spoons and an ice cream scooper from the silverware drawer and then brought two bowls over to the table. "Don't forget to use a napkin," he told Sheri. Turning to Cathy, he said, "I hope you like vanilla."

"Yes, but only one scoop, please."

"Sheri will do the honors." He handed his granddaughter the red ice cream scooper that matched the table's plaid placemats that featured roosters.

Sheri opened the ice cream containers and plopped three scoops of the blue-colored ice cream in her bowl. She then wiped off the scooper and placed one scoop of vanilla in the other bowl that she pushed across the table to Cathy.

"Thank you."

"You should've served our guest first," Chris said, but Sheri was already licking her spoon. "Sorry, Grandpa. I'm hungry."

A few minutes later, after helping Chris clean up, Sheri's eyelids began to droop again. Cathy was surprised the sugar hadn't kept her going, but Chris seemed to expect this. He picked her up and carried her to the living room couch. The moment her head hit the throw pillow her grandfather placed under it, she was asleep.

"She still takes afternoon naps," he explained. "She won't be out long. Would you like coffee or something else while we wait?"

Cathy shook her head. "No, thanks, but I'd like to hear

more about the farm." What she actually wanted to hear was more about the people on it.

He hesitated slightly but then shrugged. "Sure. Have a seat by the fire. I'll start it up." She watched as he stoked the logs and started a low blaze. Cathy took the chair near the fireplace, and he took the one across from it. "So, what would you like to know?"

Cathy knew she shouldn't start with a question about Doris, but she couldn't help herself. "Mildred didn't know too much about what happened to your ex. She mentioned a heart attack. Did she have a weak heart?"

Chris gazed at the fire as he replied, "Not that we knew of. It was sudden, right after dinner. We usually all eat together at the house. Danielle and Mavis share the cooking. Doris wasn't much of a cook." A short smile lifted the corners of his mouth, and Cathy noticed the age lines around it. "At the farm, we like a hearty meal. Mavis had made a crockpot stew. She likes to experiment with recipes and use different spices." He paused. "When Doris collapsed after eating, we thought it was a reaction to something in the food, although she wasn't known to be allergic to anything. Danielle called for help, and I tried CPR, but it didn't do any good. Doris was already gone when they arrived." His voice was flat, his eyes still staring into the fire. He suddenly turned and looked directly into Cathy's. "Danielle had a funny notion that her mother was poisoned. She insisted that the food and drinks be checked, but the coroner ruled Doris' death a heart attack."

"Why do you think Danielle suspected that Doris was murdered? "

He seemed to ponder that a few minutes and then his eyes returned to the fire. "I have no idea. Doris wasn't the easiest person to get along with. She and Mavis were never on great terms. Betty favored her, so when Doris moved to your town,

Mavis hoped she would gain her mother's favor, but that didn't happen. Even so, Betty wrote Mavis into her will to get the farm. It only made sense because Doris had no interest in it."

Cathy found the nerve to ask, "Would you mind telling me why you and Doris divorced?"

He brought his eyes back to her. "I would, but it won't stop me. We simply grew apart. I loved the farm the moment I sold my house and moved here with Doris. When she told me she wanted to go back to school to become a librarian, I supported her, even though it meant she had to move away because the nearest school was in Albany. Today, she might've been able to take remote classes. In any case," he waved his hands, "she got the job in Buttercup Bend and never came back to the farm. She asked me to join her, but I asked for a divorce instead. I realized we weren't in sync. That's the only way I can explain it."

"Where did you two meet and how long were you married?"

When Chris drew a breath and looked toward Sheri who had begun to stir on the couch, Cathy thought he wouldn't answer, but he did. "We met at a party that Mavis gave for her mother's fiftieth birthday at the farm. We dated only a brief time and were married here, too. That lasted about twenty years, but it was pretty much over by the time Danielle was born."

"But you stayed on the farm?"

"It was my home, and I do my share of the work."

Cathy wanted to ask more questions, but Chris stood up and turned down the fire. "Sheri is waking. We need to get back."

CHAPTER SEVEN

When they got back to the house, Chris glanced at his watch and said, "I hope you enjoyed meeting Lulu. Mavis has been bugging me about seeing the accountant, so I have an appointment with him shortly. I'll catch you both later." He bent down and gave Sheri a hug and then walked over to his truck. Cathy noticed one of the other cars was missing. She took Sheri's hand and walked her to the door. She hoped the argument with her parents was over and was relieved to hear silence as they entered.

Although the place seemed empty, Danielle sat alone on the living room couch. Seeing Cathy and her daughter, she spoke quietly. "Welcome back. I hope you had fun with Lulu, Sheri. Where's Grandpa?"

The girl, wide awake now, ran to her mother. "I had a fun time, Mommy. Grandpa gave me ice cream at his house."

"I see." She touched the blue ring around the girl's mouth.

Danielle glanced at Cathy. "Where did Dad go?"

"He said he was seeing the accountant." She noticed the redness around Danielle's eyes. "Is Mildred in her room?"

"Yes. She asked me to tell you to come upstairs when you returned." She paused. "I'd like to talk with you both later, after Sheri goes to bed. I need to fill you in on your duties and ... other things. Dinner is at six. Mavis went into town to pick up groceries." Even though Cathy didn't ask, Danielle added, "Dylan's upstairs in his office. He's working on his book."

"Dylan writes?" Cathy wondered if their blowup had given him inspiration, but Danielle said, "Nothing you'd be interested in reading. He writes articles for a farm magazine, but he also started a book. He won't tell me what it's about." She turned to her daughter. "Honey, would you like to watch T.V.?" When Sheri nodded, Danielle got up. "Come. Let's go to the den. We should clean you up first. See you at six, Cathy. Mildred's room is the second one on the left upstairs. Your room is next to it. Dylan brought your bags up there."

Mildred was sitting on the bed when Cathy knocked. Her suitcase was open, but a few things hadn't been unpacked.

"You're back. Good. I have something important to show you. Close the door."

Cathy did as she asked. She wondered why Mildred wanted privacy.

"I found a note in one of the drawers as I was putting some of my things inside," she explained. "As you know, this was Doris' room."

Cathy looked around. The walls were peach-colored, the bed a four-poster with a lace bedspread. The oak bureau contained four drawers. Mildred stood up and opened the top drawer where she pulled out a folded piece of paper. The sheet was slightly crumpled. "It was wedged between the drawers. I think she was considering sending it but didn't want to leave it out for someone to find."

Cathy walked over to the bureau. "What does it say?"

Mildred unfolded the paper, cleared her throat, and read it aloud.

"Dear Mavis. I know you've resented me from the time I returned to Oaks Landing. We've never gotten along because we are such different people, but you have nothing to fear from me. I'm not after the farm, and I have no plans to reunite with Chris. I only want what's rightly mine and Danielle's. I hope you realize that..."

Mildred looked up from reading. "That's where it ends, but it looks like she was planning to write something else because there's an ink mark at the end, and she didn't sign it. Before you ask, it's undated, so I have no idea when she wrote it."

Cathy considered. "Danielle promised to speak with us after Sheri is asleep. Maybe that will clarify this."

"I don't know. There's a lot going on here, Cathy. After you left, Dylan stormed out of Betty's room, went into a room down the hall, and slammed the door. I was just coming upstairs. Danielle was in a state. She tried not to show me, but she was quite upset."

"I know. When I spoke with her, her eyes were red." Cathy paused. "I found out some things when Chris brought me and Sheri to his house." She filled Mildred in on what Chris told her about Doris' death, his relationship with her, and her relationship with Mavis.

When she was done, Mildred sighed. "We have our work cut out for us. It sounds like Danielle may be right that her mother was murdered." She took Doris' note and put it away in a drawer under her clothes.

"So, you suspect Mavis? But how did she do it? They ruled Doris' death a heart attack."

Mildred walked back to the bed and sat next to Cathy. "You should know as well as I that there are poisons that are undetectable. Mavis cooked that night. It's possible she put something in Doris' food."

Cathy recalled how, back in May, a similar murder had occurred when the killer added nightshade to the victim's drink. However, the poison was detected. They eventually caught the killer, although there were many suspects since the plant was commonly grown in the town's gardens.

"But what's the motive?" Cathy asked. "You don't just kill someone because you dislike them."

Mildred smiled. "If that were true, Sheriff Miller would've put me behind bars a long time ago. I'm thinking it has to do with the farm. Even though Doris wrote in her letter that she wasn't interested in it, she was the older sister. Mavis may have been threatened that her mother would've left it to her."

"I don't think that's the case, but I'm interested in what she said about not reuniting with Chris. Mavis never married, but do you think she was interested in Doris' ex?" Cathy suddenly remembered that Chris mentioned he'd been introduced to Doris at her mother's fiftieth birthday party at Oaks Landing and that Mavis had invited him. She told Mildred what he'd said.

"We have to keep an eye on them and see. If Mavis is interested in Chris, I'm not sure he returns those feelings, but I want to hear what Danielle has to tell us."

Cathy knew that it didn't really matter if someone returned your feelings. It would still hurt if someone else took them away. She thought of Steve and Michael and how she would feel if she made them wait too long and they looked elsewhere for wives.

. . .

Dinner was quiet. It gave Cathy an opportunity to observe the family. She felt the coldness between Danielle and Dylan as they moved their chairs as far away as possible and barely glanced at one another. Danielle kept her eyes on Sheri and helped her cut up her chicken. Mavis asked Chris about his meeting with the accountant, but he said he didn't want to talk business at dinner and would fill her in later. They left together after Danielle served dessert, a moist carrot cake with walnuts and cream-cheese frosting. "This was my mother's recipe," Danielle said. "It was passed down to her from Grandma."

Cathy didn't know when Danielle had the opportunity to bake it, but it was delicious. Sheri dug in with vigor. Her mother said, "Slow down. I think you've had too many desserts today, honey." The girl smiled, a smattering of cream cheese on her lips. Danielle wiped them with a napkin. "After you're done, please help me clean up." That's when Mavis and Chris left. Cathy thought it was rude that they hadn't bothered to bring their dishes into the kitchen. She offered to help, too, but Danielle said, "Thank you, but Sheri and I can manage. I'll speak with you and Mildred after I've put her to bed." Cathy imagined she'd also be bringing Betty her dinner after her daughter was asleep. She and Mildred took a seat in the living room near the fireplace and waited. Dylan joined them.

"Do either of you ladies play chess?" he asked.

Cathy found that an odd question. Her father had taught her, but she hadn't played in years. Mildred replied, "We have a chess club at the library. I run it."

"Super. Would you like to play? I can bring out the chess set."

Mildred shook her head. "I'm not really in the mood." She looked over at Cathy. "We're waiting for Danielle. She wanted to speak with us."

Dylan's expression remained neutral. "That will take time. Sheri isn't the easiest kid to put to bed. We take turns reading to her. It's Danielle's turn tonight." He flopped down on the couch. "I should go back to my writing, but I need a break. I haven't really spoken to you since you arrived." He paused. "I apologize for what you heard. Danielle and I," he glanced down at his hands that he was unconsciously wringing, "we don't see eye to eye about her grandmother. Danielle thinks she's protecting her, but I'm concerned about her safety. She's slipped too far from reality. It's only a matter of time before..." He looked up. "Sorry. I shouldn't burden you with our family problems."

"What about Doris?" Mildred asked. "I'm sure Danielle is still grieving for her. You need to go easier on her about Betty."

He gave a crooked smile. "Danielle and Doris weren't all that close. They used to be, but when Doris left, Danielle was a teen. She was at a sensitive age. Chris practically raised her himself."

"I heard you met her in Peru," Cathy said.

"That's where I'm from. She took a trip to our farm to see the animals, the llamas and alpacas in particular." His dark eyes softened. "She was so beautiful. She still is, and I still love her very much. It may not seem that way, but I'm afraid I have a bad temper. It must be my Latin heritage. When things go wrong, I pick it out on her but never Sheri. She's my little angel." He swallowed and continued. "When Doris came back, Danny was so happy. Don't get me wrong. Doris visited us from time to time, but when she moved back, it meant a lot to Danny. She was pregnant at the time with Sheri, and she needed her mother. Mavis isn't the maternal type."

"Was Mavis also happy that Doris came home?" Mildred asked.

Instead of answering, Dylan got up. "I should get back to my book. The only way to beat writer's block is to work it out."

"You didn't answer my question."

Dylan's eyes were dark again when he said, "No. Mavis wasn't happy at all when Doris returned, mainly because she thought she would be taking Chris away from her again."

CHAPTER EIGHT

After Dylan went upstairs, Mildred said, "Sounds like you're right, Cathy. There was something between Mavis and Chris."

"Yes, and there still is." Cathy and Mildred turned toward the staircase where Mavis was standing looking down at them. She continued her descent and took the seat that Dylan had vacated. "For new employees, you two should really keep your noses out of the household's personal affairs, but since you have made a true assumption, I might as well fill you in. Chris is talking with Dylan, so I have a few moments before I go home with him."

Cathy watched as Mavis regarded them through her green eyes. They weren't the color of her mother's, but they had a similar intensity. "Please tell us," Mildred urged.

Mavis smiled and leaned back against the couch cushions. "I was dating Chris when we celebrated Mother's fiftieth birthday here at the farm. We weren't exclusive at the time, but I thought we were headed in that direction. We met in college in a business class. I regret that I asked him to attend the party. He spent most of the night speaking and dancing with Doris. In the next few weeks, he hardly called me. Doris told me he was now seeing her."

"That must've upset you," Cathy said.

Mavis gave a short laugh. "What do you think? Wouldn't you be upset if your sister took your boyfriend away? But what could I do? I had no claims on him, and he was in love with her."

"But they divorced," Mildred pointed out.

Mavis' smile widened, but Cathy saw that it was stiff. "She asked for the divorce. She wanted her freedom, hated the farm, and wanted to leave."

This was a different story than what Chris had told them. "I thought he left her because she went back to college, and he didn't want to move away."

"Nope." Mavis wrapped a finger around a red curl and twirled it. "He would've followed her anywhere, but there were other factors. They weren't a good match. She left her daughter with him. What mother would do that? Danny was fifteen. I helped Chris raise her, but she forgot all that when Doris came home after she retired from the library. Danny welcomed her back with open arms." Mavis' voice had risen and become sharp as she told the tale. "Chris did, too. It was a slap in my face. He said they were only friends, but I was driving around the farm one night and saw her car at his house. It was late. I waited, but she never came home."

"When was this?" Cathy thought of the letter Mildred found in Doris' room that said she wasn't interested in reuniting with Chris.

"Recently. I don't know. It could've been going on since she returned. He became distant to me. All the time she was gone, I expected him to propose, but I guess I wasn't good enough for him." She took a breath. "I'm hoping things will be different now that he's finally free of her."

"Danielle thinks Doris was murdered," Mildred said. She met Mavis' eyes. "It sounds like you would have a motive to kill her."

Mavis gave her curl a yank and lowered her finger. "I imagine I would, but I didn't. She had a heart attack." She stood up. "I'm going to see what's keeping Chris. Nice speaking to you ladies. Have a good night."

Cathy wondered, as Mavis headed for the stairs, why she would think things would change between her and Chris now that Doris was dead when they hadn't all the years she'd been away from the farm. Emotions were strange, she decided, and hope could cloud one's view of reality. She was shaken out of her daydream by Danielle who walked by with Sheri. The girl was hopping as she followed her mother. "I'm putting Sheri to bed," she told them. "I'll meet you back here in a little while."

While they waited, Mavis and Chris came down. "See you tomorrow, Cathy," Chris said. "Remember our hike. We'll go right after breakfast."

Cathy had nearly forgotten that he'd offered to take her on the hike. She hoped Lulu would be the llama they'd be walking with. She smiled and nodded. "Looking forward to it." Chris opened the door for Mavis, and they walked out together. Cathy saw him pull her into a hug and thought that Mavis' faith in their relationship wasn't imaginary. She also thought it odd that Chris would jump into a relationship with Mavis when his ex was only dead a month. Then she reminded herself that Mavis and Chris were seeing one another when Doris entered the picture. Did Chris finally feel free from her as Mavis suggested?

Mildred asked, "Cathy, have you checked in with your

grandmother yet? She might be worried that you haven't called."

"I should've done that. Thanks for the reminder." Cathy took her cell from her pants pocket and tapped Florence's contact. The phone rang twice before Florence answered. "Catherine. How are you? Did you have a nice trip? I was hoping you would call."

"Sorry I didn't call sooner. All is well, Gran. Mildred and I made it here safely, and we've met the family. Danielle's been busy, but she'll be speaking with us after she puts her daughter to bed. I even met the llamas. It's a beautiful farm."

"I'm glad you're enjoying it, but don't forget to be careful. The kittens are fine. I've been giving them plenty of attention, but they miss you. They've been sleeping together on your bed."

Although Cathy was sure Harry and Hermione knew she was gone, she thought her grandmother was the one who missed her the most. "I'll be back before you know it, Gran." She paused. "Has Nancy or anyone else asked about me?"

"Nancy called, and Steven and Michael came by again. I told everyone you'd taken a vacation. I hope this trip away will clarify your feelings and not serve as a distraction for them."

Cathy didn't know how to respond to that. She was saved by replying when Danielle said, "I'm here. Dylan offered to finish putting Sheri to sleep. Oh, sorry. I didn't realize you were on the phone."

"I was just finishing my call." Cathy spoke back into her cell. "I have to go, Gran. I'll call you tomorrow."

Danielle walked over to them. "This isn't the most private place for us to talk. Let's go into the den."

Cathy and Mildred followed her down the hall to a room they hadn't yet seen. She ushered them in ahead of her and then closed the door. Cathy looked around. There was a large screen TV where she assumed Sheri watched cartoons and kid shows and Dylan viewed sports. The walls were lined with bookshelves featuring a variety of authors and genres. The bottom shelf was filled with children's books. A red wrap-around couch looked inviting. Danielle invited them to sit and took the space between them.

"First, I want to thank you both for coming. I'm sorry you overheard the argument between me and Dylan about my grandmother. It hasn't been easy since Mom died. She's really gone downhill. I understand Dylan thinks putting her somewhere for care is best, but I can't bring myself to do it."

Cathy thought of her grandmother and knew that, if she were in that situation, she would have a tough time doing the same.

"We understand," Mildred said. "Chris told Cathy about what happened to Doris, but we'd like to hear your side of the story."

"Of course." Danielle pushed back a long strand of her dark hair and said, "We were all eating together in the dining room that night which isn't always possible with everyone's schedules. Even one of our farmhands, the landscaper, and our veterinarian joined us. Dr. Savella had been by to give our llamas their monthly injection, so Mavis invited her to dine with us."

"Monthly injection? Is that a vaccination?" Cathy asked. She was thinking of the shots that her pets and the rescue center animals received, but none were given on a monthly basis.

"Yes. Llamas are prone to parasites. The most common one is the meningeal worm, or brain worm as it's sometimes called. If infected, a llama only has a ten percent chance of survival, so the shots are important to protect them."

"Interesting," Mildred said. "I believe I read about that in one of the library books I browsed to prepare for our visit here."

"Who else was at the dinner?" Cathy asked. While she found this fact interesting, she knew they needed a complete list of suspects.

"Just the family. Me, Mavis, Doris, of course, Dylan, Sheri. Oh, and Betty was there, too. She wasn't taking her meals upstairs then. I really wish she had been because she witnessed her daughter's death. After that, she really declined."

"Chris said that Doris collapsed at the table," Cathy said. "He tried to give her resuscitation while you waited for the paramedics."

"That's right." Danielle lowered her eyes. Cathy saw a tear slide down her cheek. She took a breath. "Stacy, Dr. Savella, also tried to revive her. She had her medical kit with her. Some of the same meds for people are used on animals."

"But nothing helped," Mildred prompted.

Danielle shook her head. "No. It was very quick. One minute, she was talking with us and the next she was gone."

There was silence for a moment as the grandfather clock in the corner chimed the hour and then Danielle continued. "They ruled her death a heart attack, but I never believed that. Since Mother's been back on the farm, she's woken up at 4 a.m. each morning, gone horseback riding, taken visitors on hikes. There's no heart disease in our family, and she was the healthiest person I knew."

Mildred spoke gently. "That can happen sometimes. My husband was never sick a day in his life and then he dropped dead at his desk. He was only fifty-five."

Cathy had known Mildred was a widow but didn't know how her husband had died.

"I'm sorry." Danielle wiped her face with the back of her

sweater sleeve. "Dylan thinks I'm not accepting Mother's death. He believes my looking into other causes is my way of keeping her in my thoughts. He says I read too much crime fiction." She gazed across the room at a shelf lined with mystery books. Cathy recognized Agatha Christie titles and other popular mystery writers.

Mildred asked, "Why do you think your mother was murdered, and who do you suspect?"

Danielle turned to her. "I have my suspicions, but I don't want to point a finger at anyone or sway your impressions. I'm hoping the two of you can find evidence, some reason why my mother's life was ended, so justice can be done, and she can rest in peace." She stood up. "I should bring Grandma her food now. We'll talk again soon. I still have to fill you in on your duties, but I know you need time to get adjusted."

CHAPTER NINE

After their meeting with Danielle, Cathy and Mildred went upstairs. Mildred invited Cathy into her room. On their way, they passed an open door and heard Dylan reading a story to his daughter. Cathy recognized "The Three Little Pigs." The sound of Sheri's laughter echoed down the hall as Dylan deepened his voice to imitate the wolf. Whatever failings he had as a husband, it was clear he was a good father.

In Mildred's room, they took a seat on the bed. "What do you think of what Danielle told us tonight?" Mildred asked.

"I doubt that she's right about her mother's death. Do you have the same feeling?"

"I can't say yet. I need to know more. Even if it turns out that Doris' death was natural, I think we'll both enjoy our stay here. Are you ready for your hike tomorrow?"

Cathy laughed. "I hope I make it. I'm not in good shape right now." She thought about the days she'd spent inside this past week. She'd been so depressed by her indecision about Steve and Michael that she hadn't even had the energy to take photos for Pauline at the newspaper. She missed those walks through Buttercup Bend.

"You're in better shape than me, honey."

Cathy wasn't sure about that. Although Mildred was over thirty years older than she was, the librarian was quite spry. It was only her knees that held her back. Florence had confided in Cathy that she thought it would do Mildred wonders if she had a knee replacement.

"So where do we start?" Cathy asked. "Danielle wants us to find evidence."

Mildred got up and walked to her open suitcase. She pulled out a few clothes and began placing them in the bureau. As she worked, she answered Cathy. "As a member of Hunt, Myers, and Carter's Detective Agency, you should know that motive is the most important factor in a murder case. We haven't met all the suspects who were at that fatal dinner. While you're hiking with Chris tomorrow, I'll set up a meeting with the vet, landscaper, and farmhand that Danielle mentioned. I'll make sure we both go because I need your impressions of them."

As Cathy considered Mildred's suggestion, she eyed a painting on the wall. It featured a younger Mavis and Doris who held a baby on her lap. Mildred noticed her looking at it. "That was painted shortly after Danielle was born. Do you recognize Doris?"

"Yes, but I only have a vague memory of her. She read to me and Doug once at the library when you were out sick. She looks different in the painting." Cathy remembered a tall woman with short dark hair who wore glasses. But the woman in the photo holding the baby had long hair similar to Danielle's. She was an exotic-looking beauty with pale skin with deep blue eyes. Mavis also had long locks, a real red in contrast to her bottled color. Cathy wondered who'd painted the portrait and then noticed it was signed with the initials "ET." Could the artist have been Betty?

Mildred closed the drawer and came back to the bed. "What do you think of my plan about speaking with all the guests who came to that dinner?"

Cathy didn't believe it was posed as a question. "It makes sense, but how are you going to make those appointments? What if they aren't available to talk with us? You need to include Betty, even though it'll be a challenge."

"I thought of that. It'll be difficult, but maybe we can catch her when she's having one of her lucid days. As far as talking with the non-family members, I'm sure Danielle will help us. She wants to find out what happened to her mother."

"Does she?" Cathy wasn't so sure. Even though Danielle had hired them to find answers, if it turned out she was wrong in her belief that Doris was murdered, would that give her the closure she sought?

Cathy and Mildred spoke a little longer and then Mildred yawned, and they called it a night. Cathy went into the room next door, unpacked, and got into bed. She missed her furry friends who slept with her but knew her grandmother was taking loving care of them. As she turned off the lights, she heard a muffled voice from a few doors down and realized it was Dylan still reading to his daughter. Danielle was right that the girl didn't fall asleep easily. She wondered if that was because she still took afternoon naps.

Cathy woke suddenly. The room was dark, and there was no light coming through the window's curtains. A noise outside her door alerted her. She crawled out of bed, slipped on a robe, and walked silently on her bare feet into the hall. She jumped and nearly screamed when a shadow grabbed her arm. She turned around and faced Betty. In the dim light, the old woman seemed ethereal in her long white nightgown, her dark hair loose and falling over her shoulders. "Come with me. We must talk. I know who killed her."

Cathy followed Betty to her room. "Close the door." Cathy noticed her voice sounded strong, younger than her years. It was different from the one she'd used earlier when they first met.

"Have a seat." Betty indicated a chair by the bed as she closed the door.

Cathy hesitated. Should she call Danielle or Mildred? She decided to listen to what the woman had to say first.

"I was watching them all that night," she began. "I saw her add the poison to Doris' drink."

"Who?" Cathy asked. "Who did you see?" She wondered why Betty hadn't come forth sooner with this information or at least told her granddaughter.

"It was her, but I think he was in on it, too."

"Betty, do you mean Mavis and Chris?" Cathy prompted.

She paused, her violet eyes wide. "I'm not Betty. I'm Nancy. Nancy Drew, and I'm going to solve this crime."

Cathy realized that Danielle's grandmother had slipped into the young female sleuth's persona. She decided to humor her. "I'm sure you will, Nancy. I apologize for not recognizing you. Can you tell me more?"

But the spell was broken. As if removing a mask, Betty said, "Who's Nancy? I'm Elizabeth, Elizabeth Taylor. What are you doing in my house?" As she stood up from the bed, she was nearly half a foot taller than Cathy.

"I'm Cathy Carter. Don't you remember meeting me? Danielle brought me up earlier with your lunch."

Betty shook her head. "I didn't have lunch today. Someone took my tray away, and The Pie, too." She was back in *National*

Velvet. Her voice took on an agitated tone. Cathy stepped toward the door, placing her hand on the knob.

"Where are you going? Why did you come into my room?"

Cathy knew this had been a mistake. The woman was ill and could alternate between characters in movies and books. Nothing she'd say could be trusted and angering her might result in danger. She opened the door and quickly rushed into the hall. As she did, a body collided with hers.

"Cathy, what's going on?" It was Dylan. He was still dressed in his day clothes and must've just finished putting his daughter to bed. He looked toward Betty who was standing there, an angry expression on her face. "You're the one," she said, pointing a finger at Dylan. Cathy heard the change in her voice. She was Nancy again. "You did it with her."

"Calm down, Betty. Did you have a nightmare?"

"I'm not Betty. I'm Nancy, and I'm going to report you to the police."

Dylan took her by the arm and gently led her back into her room. "You go back to sleep now, Nancy. You're safe here. No one committed any crimes."

Betty didn't resist. Her shoulders slumped, and she sounded like an old woman as she said, "I'm sorry, Dylan. I woke up with a headache. Was I sleepwalking again?"

Cathy realized that Betty was now herself. Both Nancy Drew and Elizabeth Taylor were gone.

Dylan nodded. "No worries. Did you forget your sleeping pills tonight?"

"I don't like to take them."

He walked toward the bed where Cathy saw a glass of water and a bottle of pills. He took out two pills and handed them to her. "You'll feel better with a good night's sleep."

Betty took the pills and swallowed them with a gulp of

water. Then she slipped into bed. Dylan covered her with the patchwork blanket. "There you go."

Betty turned and looked toward the door. "I'm sorry if I scared you or said something strange, young lady. I have these memory lapses."

Cathy felt sorry for her. "That's okay, Mrs. Taylor. I hope you feel better."

As Dylan turned off the lights and closed the door behind them, he said, "This is why I suggested to Danielle that she be put into a care facility. I worry that she'll hurt someone or herself. Sheri is only a few doors away."

"She thought she was Nancy Drew. She told me she knew who killed Doris."

Dylan's face changed. A flicker of emotion passed through his dark eyes, but Cathy couldn't tell whether it was fear or anger. "You can't believe what she says in that state, and Doris had a heart attack. Danielle planted that seed in her mind, so she's come up with suspects and decided she could solve the case as Nancy Drew." He paused. "Can you do me a favor and not tell anyone about this episode? I'll speak with Danielle privately. She has to make sure Betty takes her pills at night. She should watch her take them."

Cathy wondered why he wanted to keep what happened secret when, surely, the family was aware of it. Then she remembered Mildred who was investigating Doris' death. She crossed her fingers behind her back as she said, "I won't tell anyone."

He smiled. "Then have a good night. I'm sorry she woke you."

CHAPTER TEN

Cathy was in the middle of a strange dream where Betty was riding a horse. Mavis and Chris, also on horseback, were chasing after her. Danielle stood at the finish line waving a flag with Sheri, while Dylan, armed with a rifle, aimed a gun at the riders and fired. The noise spooked the horses, and they reared up, knocking their occupants to the ground. She woke with a start. Someone was banging at her door.

"Cathy, get up." It was Mildred. She was dressed in a gray pantsuit that Cathy had never seen her wear and wondered if she'd bought it for this trip.

She opened the door. "What time is it?"

"Eight o'clock. They're already cooking breakfast downstairs. Can you smell it?"

Cathy whiffed the air. A scent of bacon filled her nose. "I'll get dressed, but I have to tell you something first."

Mildred walked in. "Did you find a clue?"

"You might say that." Cathy drew in a breath. "I woke up last night because I heard something in the hall. It was Betty."

She told Mildred what happened including what Dylan said afterwards.

Mildred cocked an eyebrow. "You know what this means, Cathy? Doris was really murdered."

"Not necessarily. Betty isn't in her right mind."

"Even so. There might be something to what she told you, and it's very strange that she said Dylan was in on it. That might mean Danielle poisoned Doris."

"That's crazy. Danielle called us here to investigate her mother's death. If she killed her, why would she do that?"

"Good point." Mildred gazed around the room as if searching for something. She turned back to Cathy. "If it's not Danielle, it has to be Mavis."

"She is the likeliest suspect, but we haven't met the other people who were present at the dinner that night. You were planning to ask Danielle to introduce us."

"That's right, and you'll be with Chris on the hike this morning. You can get more details from him, especially about his break with Doris. We can't rule him out."

"We can't rule anyone out, Mildred, despite what Nancy Drew said." Cathy gave a short laugh. "Let me get dressed now. I'll meet you downstairs. We'll talk more after I get back from the hike."

When Cathy walked into the kitchen, Danielle, Chris, and Mildred were sitting around the table talking. "Here she is now," Chris said, looking up from his platter of scrambled eggs and bacon as she entered.

"Talking about me?"

"About our upcoming hike. Are you ready?" He looked at her. "I would trade those sneakers for boots and wear a warm coat. It snowed overnight. Did you notice?"

She hadn't. She walked over to the window and glanced out. The lawn and road were covered with a blanket of pristine snow. "It's beautiful."

"Wait until you see the farm. I plan to show you that before our llama walk." He speared some egg on his fork and took a bite.

Danielle stood up. "Please, sit down, Cathy. I'll get you some breakfast."

Cathy noticed her eyes were still red-rimmed. Either she didn't sleep well or was upset by what Dylan told her about her mother's episode. She noticed he wasn't around, and neither was Sheri or Mavis.

"Thanks, Danielle." She took the seat next to Mildred.

Placing a plate of food in front of Cathy, Danielle said, "It should still be warm. I can heat it a few seconds in the microwave if it isn't."

Cathy took a bite of the eggs. "They're fine."

Danielle smiled, but she still looked sad and tired. "I'll get you coffee. In case you're wondering, Dylan took Sheri out early this morning to gather eggs from the chickens. You might run into them on your hike. Mavis sleeps late and often skips breakfast."

Cathy wondered if Mavis was still at Chris' house or whether he brought her back to sleep in her own room.

Mildred asked, "Can you fill us in on our duties, Danielle?"

"Oh, yes." Danielle brought Cathy her coffee and passed her small pitchers of milk and sugar. "Thanks for the reminder. I'm planning to reopen the gift shop this week. Mother was in charge of that, but I was hoping," she glanced at Cathy, "that you would take on that job for now. The hours will be ten to five with a lunch break. I'll give Chris the key, so he can show you the items we have for sale. We also sell tickets for the hikes. The store will be open Wednesday through

Sunday. We sell items online, too. Dylan is in charge of dealing with those."

Mildred asked, "What about me? What would you like me to help with?"

"I was thinking you could alternate with Cathy in the shop, but I'm also starting up our classes. `I was wondering if you're interested in teaching one. We offer painting, wind chime making, and soapmaking. Mavis is currently teaching the wind chime and soapmaking classes, but she isn't very artistic. Doris took that class over after Betty couldn't handle it anymore."

Cathy thought of the painting in Mildred's room. She saw the glint in Mildred's eyes and recalled the beautiful murals she'd painted in the library.

"I think I can manage that," Mildred said. "What days are the classes?"

"Dylan is adding the online registration today. They won't start until next week, but it'll give you time to get whatever supplies you need and to outline the class."

"Did your mother or Betty keep a syllabus?"

Danielle shook her head. "I'm afraid not, but that may make it easier for you. You can teach whatever you want. Doris taught watercolor, while Betty specialized in oils. The classes generally run for six weeks, but I realize you're not here that long, so we'll offer a one-week course, a few hours a day, Monday to Friday. If we don't get enough registrants, I'm sure there's something else you can help with around the farm."

"Sounds good." Mildred glanced at Cathy. She knew that any spare time Mildred had would be devoted to the investigation.

Chris, having finished his meal, stood up and cleared his place. Returning to the table, he said, "I'll meet you by my truck, Cathy, but we won't be driving, so don't forget to change into boots."

. . .

Cathy had brought brown, fur-lined boots with her. They matched her imitation lambskin coat. Although she knew she wouldn't need money, she also took her purse. She wanted to bring her camera to take shots of the snow but decided that would be rude, so she planned to go out alone at another time and photograph the farm.

Chris was waiting by his truck as he promised, leaning against it smoking a cigarette. He stubbed it out in a patch of snow when he saw her. "Nasty habit. Doris was always after me to quit. It's one of the things she didn't like about me. She made sure I never lit up in the house." He walked toward her. "We can start here and do a circle of the farm. I heard you already met our greeters, Piper, Rascal, and Cricket." He waved a hand toward the barn where the three cats stood. As they walked by, the trio came over.

"I think they want to be fed," Cathy said.

"Sheri and Dylan already took care of that this morning, but that doesn't stop them from begging. You'd think the field mice around here and other critters would satisfy them, but they're more like house cats than barn cats. Visitors constantly give them treats."

"They're very friendly." Cathy bent down and petted the black cat who reminded her of Harry. "Hi, Rascal," she said. The cat rubbed his head against her hand and purred. Behind him, the calico looked on. The gray cat stood further back. She seemed a bit wary of strangers.

"You have cats?" Chris asked.

"Two of them. Kittens. I lost my older cat last summer."

"Sorry. It's hard when you get attached to them. Jodi is still all broken up over Honey."

Cathy was petting Piper. "Who's Jodi?"

61

"One of our farmhands. She lives on our property. We're passing that way, so I'll introduce you."

Cathy had a thought. As she moved on to Cricket, approaching her slowly, she asked, "Was Jodi at the dinner when..." She didn't have to finish her sentence. "Yes. She was there."

Cricket backed away as Cathy moved closer. "She's shy. Maybe if I had some cat treats."

"She'll come around," Chris said. "Let's get going. I have an appointment with the accountant before lunch."

"Again? Is there a problem?"

He shrugged. "Nothing you'd be interested in. Say goodbye to the kitties. We have a long walk, and I want us to have time for the llama hike."

Cricket finally allowed Cathy to touch her, but she scampered away afterwards. Piper and Rascal followed her back into the barn.

"Not much to see in there," Chris said. "We have horses and hay, a typical barn." He strode down the road, his black boots disappearing into the ankle high snow. Passing the male llama and alpaca pen, he said, "I could introduce you to these guys, but we can do that another day."

Cathy glanced at the animals and noticed that there wasn't much difference between them and the ones near Chris' house. "How can you tell between the male and female llamas and alpacas?" she asked.

He laughed. "The usual way, and males tend to be a little larger."

They continued on their way through the snow-blanketed farm. She thought Mildred would enjoy painting the scene and teaching it to her class if the snow was still around or if they got another snowfall.

They came to a small building. Cathy saw Sheri standing

outside holding a basket of eggs. "That's the hen house," Chris pointed out as Sheri ran to him. "Grandpa. Check out all the eggs Henny laid today."

He smiled. "Where's your dad?"

"Right here." Dylan walked out of the building. "I see you're giving Cathy a tour of the farm."

"Yes, and we're going on a llama hike later. Danielle gave me the key to the shop. Cathy will be working there on Wednesday."

"Danielle mentioned that. Is Mildred set with the painting class?"

"She seems enthusiastic about it."

Dylan glanced at Cathy. She read a warning in his eyes and remembered he'd asked her not to mention what happened last night. "I heard you fed the barn cats. Piper and Rascal were friendly, but Cricket was a bit wary of me."

Dylan smiled, the warning look gone from his eyes. "Danielle usually does that, but she asked me since I was taking Sheri to gather eggs today. You must be a cat lover to remember their names."

"I own a pet rescue, remember?"

"Ah, yes. Danielle mentioned that, too. You should speak with Jodi. I think it's time she adopted another pet."

"Can we see Jodi?" Sheri asked. "I miss her."

"Sorry, honey. We need to get back home with the eggs. We'll visit her another day."

Dylan turned to Chris. "If you drop by there, let me know how she's doing and when she'll be up to coming back. She still hasn't been answering Danielle's calls."

Cathy wondered what the story was about this farmhand and why she was ignoring Danielle. She knew Mildred would be interested, too, since Jodi had been at the dinner the night Doris died.

She tried to get the information from Chris as they walked toward his house. "What's the story with Jodi? Isn't she still working on the farm?"

Chris paused, as if considering what to tell her. "She's still employed with us, but she's on a leave since Doris died. As I told you, she was there that night. She hasn't been back to work since."

"I imagine it must've been a frightening experience for her."

"That's not the reason." Chris took a cigarette and a pack of matches from his pocket. "Mind if I smoke? I promise I won't blow it your way. I take it you don't."

"No, but you can if you want." Cathy wondered whether Chris was a nervous smoker, that he'd been upset by what she'd asked, and was trying to drum up the courage to tell her about Jodi.

After he lit up and blew out a ring of smoke that disappeared into the frosty air, he answered her question. "Jodi is an orphan. She lost her parents in a fire a few years ago. She was out with some friends that night and, when she returned, the house was in flames and firefighters were searching for her parents. It was too late."

"How awful." Cathy recalled how Doug broke the news about their parents by her hospital bedside after the accident. It was the worst day of her life.

"She started working for us shortly after that. She needed a place to live, so we agreed to let her take one of the cabins rent free in exchange for her work. She only worked a few days a week helping with some farm chores and leading hikes. The other days she attended college and helped Stacy at the veterinary hospital. She's training to be a veterinarian."

Cathy thought of Brody who was still working with

Michael as a vet tech back in Buttercup Bend. "So, what happened? Why is she on leave?"

Chris took another puff of his cigarette, exhaled, and said, "Back in November, Doris went to visit Jodi. She'd been good friends with her since she returned from Buttercup Bend. Danielle usually went with her and took Sheri along, but Doris decided to go by herself that day. She drove over there because her knees were bothering her. She had the same issue as your mom, and that's why her work around the farm was limited to the shop and classes." He paused, tossed his cigarette by the side of the road, and stubbed it out. "Jodi had a cat named Honey that she'd adopted right after her parents' death. She couldn't have one when they were alive because her mother was allergic. She's an only child and has no relatives in the area. That cat meant the world to her."

Cathy had a feeling what was coming, but she waited for the whole story.

"Honey was an indoor cat, but that day she ran out when Jodi opened the door to Doris. They looked around but couldn't find her. Doris promised her that she would look near the main house when she got home. She ended up finding her but, unfortunately, Honey was hiding near the barn with the barn cats. When Doris drove up to the house, Honey ran into her path. Danielle called the vet right away, but they couldn't save the cat."

"Jodi must've been devastated," Cathy said.

"She was. She asked me to bury Honey near the cabin. She made a garden there."

"I bet Doris felt horrible, but it doesn't sound like it was her fault."

He shook his head. "It was an accident, but she was still very upset by it."

"But Jodi came to the dinner. Why? I would think she would've taken her leave after she lost Honey."

"She wanted to keep working. She said she didn't blame anyone for what happened, but when Doris died and Danielle started saying she was murdered, Jodi was afraid that she suspected her."

"Why would she think that?" When she and Mildred had questioned Danielle about who she suspected, she hadn't named anyone.

"Danielle said some things that night that she regretted. She was overcome with grief and anger at her mother's death. She tried to explain to Jodi later that she didn't mean to accuse her, but Jodi hasn't talked to her since. Dylan thinks she's not coming back and that she's only staying to have a place to live. Her parents didn't leave her much money, only enough to pay for her school and other living expenses. But it's a matter of time before Mavis evicts her."

As they approached a small cabin, Chris said, "There's her place now. I'm going to check on her as Dylan asked."

Cathy followed him toward Jodi's home, thinking of what Mildred said about uncovering the motive for Doris' murder in order to solve it. Was Jodi avoiding the family because she didn't like the idea that Danielle considered her a suspect, or was she guilty of killing Doris? The death of her beloved cat might qualify as a motive, especially for a girl who'd lost so much in her young life.

CHAPTER ELEVEN

Cathy stood behind Chris as he knocked on the cabin door. He waited a few minutes and then knocked again and called her name. "Jodi, are you there? It's Chris. Can you open the door? I'd like you to meet someone."

After no response, he turned to Cathy. "She might be at school or gone out somewhere. The shop is nearby. I'll show you that, and we can stop by again later to see if she's back."

As Cathy was about to follow him, the cabin door opened. "Wait, Chris. She's there."

The girl who stood in the doorway had shoulder length dusty brown hair, a spatter of freckles around her nose, and large almond-shaped eyes. She wore an oversized cream sweater that fell to her knees which were partially visible through her ripped blue jeans. Cathy thought she was pretty in a plain way.

Chris turned around. "Hello, Jodi. May we come in? This is Cathy Hastings from Buttercup Bend. She and her mother are working at the farm for two weeks. She's going to help out at the shop, and her mom, Mildred, will be teaching an art class."

Jodi's face remained expressionless. Cathy had the feeling she was going to close the door on them, but she opened it wider instead. "You can come in," she said in a flat voice. "But I hope Danielle hasn't sent you."

They walked inside. The cabin was small but neat. Cathy noticed the unlit fireplace despite how chilly it was in the house. After what she'd learned about Jodi's family, she understood why no fire burned in it.

"I'm not here because of Danny. I was just showing Cathy around the farm and thought I'd stop by."

Jodi shrugged. "Whatever."

"How have you been? How's school?"

Jodi was looking at Cathy when she replied to Chris' questions. "I'm fine and so is college."

Cathy saw the painting of an orange tabby with green eyes that stood above the fireplace. She figured it was Honey and wondered if Betty had painted her. "That's a beautiful painting," she said and was sorry she had because tears sprang to the girl's eyes. She wiped them away with the sleeve of her sweater. "That's my Honey. Most orange cats are male, so she was rare. She came to my door one day. I couldn't find her owner. It was right after..." She paused. "It was fate. She helped me get through so much and then..." she sniffled.

Chris said, "Cathy works at a pet rescue. She may be able to set you up with another cat."

Jodi's voice broke and grew high as she looked at him. "If that's why you brought her here, you've wasted your time." She turned to Cathy. "Nice meeting you, Miss Hastings. Enjoy your tour of the farm." It was a dismissal.

Cathy saw Chris was about to say something, but she

stopped him. "Let's go, Chris. I know you have an appointment later."

He nodded. "Okay." As he walked to the door, he added, "Have a nice day, Jodi."

"I feel bad for her," Cathy said, as they were back on the path passing Chris' house. "But at least she let us in. You shouldn't push too hard. Dylan can bring Sheri over. She said she misses Jodi. Maybe Jodi misses her."

"She won't want to see Dylan because of Danny."

"What about Mavis?"

He gave a short laugh. "Mavis never had a good relationship with her. Danny was the one who took her in which is ironic in a way."

Cathy wondered if Chris was the only one Mavis got along with. "I could bring Sheri," she offered.

"That may not be a good idea. You mentioned the painting, so that's already a mark against you. Jodi is sensitive. That's why she still won't talk with Danny even after she's apologized dozens of times."

"Girls at that age can be sensitive. What about the vet, Dr. Savella? Is she still friends with Jodi?"

Chris gave another half smile. "Stacy may not be working for the farm much longer. Before Doris died, she went over the books and told Mavis that she thought Stacy's services were too expensive for us to afford. Mavis usually ignored Doris' suggestions about the farm, but she began looking into other vets."

Cathy was surprised. "Did Stacy know what Doris told Mavis?"

"Yes. They'd discussed her fees, and Stacy insisted that because of her specialty with llamas she wouldn't lower her prices. Llamas and alpacas are Ruminants, a group of animals such as sheep, goats, and cows. Few vets are trained in caring for them."

Cathy found that interesting and wondered if Michael had that training because she knew he had experience with livestock which was one of the reasons he was able to deliver Becky and Doug's baby when she went into labor during a storm. "If Stacy, Dr. Savella, knew Doris had been persuading Mavis to fire her, why did she still go to the dinner?"

"I think she was hoping Mavis would change her mind and, so far, another vet hasn't been hired. I'm not sure that would've been the case if Doris was still around. My ex-wife could be very persistent when she wanted to be. Danny takes after her."

Cathy still wasn't clear about the farm's hierarchy. "Didn't Betty have any say in anything when she was well?"

They'd passed Chris' house and come upon a cabin similar to Jodi's. "Betty was in charge and did a good job, but when she began to decline, Mavis had her sign a power-of-attorney and also gave her ownership of the farm."

"When was this?"

Chris took the key Danielle gave him from his pocket. "Right before Doris moved back. It was as if Mavis was psychic and knew her sister would return and claim her right to Oaks Landing."

"But you said that Doris left because she didn't want anything to do with the farm. Why would she be upset that Mavis got it?"

Chris turned to her. "You ask a lot of questions, Cathy. I'm not in the mood to talk about this right now. We can speak another time. I'd like to show you the shop." He inserted the key into the door's lock and turned it.

CHAPTER TWELVE

C hris switched on the lights. As Cathy's eyes adjusted, she saw shelves filled with a variety of items, skeins of different colored wool, children's toys, souvenirs with the Oaks Landing logo – a cartoon depiction of a llama standing under an oak tree. There were racks of T-shirts, sweatshirts, and hoodies also bearing the logo. The window, which she noticed hadn't been washed in some time, featured items, too. There was a film of dust over everything, and a few cobwebs hung from the ceiling.

"How long has this been closed?" she asked.

Chris walked over to the register. "Since the summer. Dylan has been concentrating on our online store."

"But I thought Doris worked here and that's why I've been asked to take over. Also, isn't this where the hike tickets are sold?"

He nodded, taking a handkerchief from his pocket, and wiping down a counter. "When we closed the store, we started selling tickets at the main house. About Doris," he paused. "We had night hours in the summer, and she had, ah, a bad experience here a few nights, so she quit."

"What happened?" Danielle hadn't said anything about this to Cathy or Mildred.

"Mavis insisted she was being silly, but Doris swore that someone was hanging around outside watching her. She thought they were going to rob the place. Mavis said that if she was so frightened, she could go back to working days, but she gave up altogether. Mavis worked a few shifts to make up for it and never heard or saw anything, but we weren't getting many customers, so she decided to close the shop and asked Dylan to sell stuff online."

Cathy thought of the online shop Doug was in charge of for Rainbow Rescues and how well it was doing raising funds for their pet rescue. "Then why did you decide to reopen the physical shop? Surely, you won't get much business in the winter."

Chris shrugged. "That was Danny's decision, and Mavis isn't happy with it, but the shop will be open limited days and hours. It could be an experiment. We'll see how it goes. I suggest that you bring a book when you work here." He smiled and added, "and a dust cloth."

Cathy figured that Danielle had to have jobs for her and Mildred and that was the reason she decided to open the shop. She found the story about Doris thinking someone was watching her interesting and knew Mildred would, too, when she told her about it.

Chris showed her the register and the price sheet next to it that listed the cost of the merchandise. Then he went to the door. "Ready for the llama hike?"

Cathy followed him out, and he locked the door. They followed the trail to the area she'd seen previously when Sheri was with them. The llamas and alpacas were standing in their fenced-in area, their hooves covered in snow.

"Don't they get cold?" Cathy asked.

"Not really. They adapt quite well to their conditions. When Lulu came back from Peru, we had a bad winter here, and she went through it like a trooper." He opened the gate and walked over to the spotted llama. Cathy noticed he was carrying a lead. He must've had it under his coat. "You can walk Lulu. She knows the route well. Doris always insisted on her when she gave hikes. When I gave them, I usually took a second llama, but we're using the short course today. Come here."

Cathy joined him by Lulu, and he handed her the lead that he'd attached to the llama. "Let's go."

As he promised, Lulu seemed to know where they were headed. She walked slowly, so Cathy didn't have any trouble keeping up with her. She only stopped a few times to shake the snow off her hooves.

Cathy knew they were heading back to the house. Seeing the property from the other side, she again wished she'd brought her camera and planned to come back soon to photograph this area of the farm.

"You can ask more questions if you'd like," Chris said, as they turned toward his house. "I'm sorry I cut you off before."

"Don't be. My Gran says I'm too inquisitive."

"Your Gran? I didn't know that Mildred's mother was still alive." Chris looked surprised, and Cathy worried that she'd slipped up. "I'm talking about my father's mother."

"Ah." He seemed to accept that explanation.

Cathy decided to ask him questions since he'd given her the go ahead. Her first one was something that was on her mind since he told her that Doris had seen the farm's books and hadn't been happy about their expenditures.

"Is the farm in financial trouble?" she asked. "Is that why

you've been seeing the accountant and why Mavis is considering letting people go?"

"A little. It's expensive to run a farm. There's the cost of the animal feed and other expenses including salaries. That's why we're hoping the sales from the store, the classes, and the hikes will keep us afloat, but when we lost Doris..."

"Things sounded bad before then."

Chris nodded. "Yes. They were headed in that direction but have gotten worse. That's why Mavis was upset when my daughter hired you and Mildred, but Danny said she'd pay you through her own funds. She used to work part-time at the town's flower shop. Dylan had her quit after Doris died, but she had some money saved."

Cathy knew that she and Mildred weren't being paid except for food and board at the farm and helping Danielle investigate her mother's death.

When they'd finished their hike and brought Lulu back, they returned to the house. "Thanks for the tour and llama hike," Cathy said, "and for showing me the shop."

Chris nodded and walked to his truck. "You're welcome." He glanced at his watch. "Gotta run now. I'll catch you later."

Mildred was standing in the doorway. "How was the hike?" she asked. "I wish I could've come, but I have some news for you. Don't take off your boots."

"The hike was fun, and I loved seeing the farm in the snow. I'm going out again some time with my camera to take photos. I also saw the shop. Why should I keep my boots on?"

"Danielle is taking us into town to meet Dr. Savella and Henry Harris."

Cathy stepped into the house. "Who's Henry Harris?"

"The farm's landscaper. Danielle is upstairs. She'll be down in a minute to take us."

"How did you convince her to introduce us to them?"

Mildred smiled. "I told her we wanted to see all the people who attended that dinner last month. She'll do anything to help us with the investigation."

Cathy looked around. "Where is everyone else?"

"Dylan took Sheri out to a friend's house, and Mavis had a beauty salon appointment."

Cathy thought of Mavis' poor dye job and wondered what she was paying her stylist for it.

"Did you get anything out of Chris? I saw him drive away in his truck. Where is he headed?"

"To the accountant. The farm's not doing well." Cathy filled Mildred in on everything including her visit with Jodi and the scare at the gift shop that caused Doris to quit.

"Great job, Cathy. I'm glad you met Jodi. She was the one person Danielle said we'd have difficulty seeing. Now I know why." She paused. "But about what Doris said happened to her at the gift shop, what if it wasn't a figment of her imagination? If someone were stalking her and planning to kill her back in the summer, it couldn't have been Jodi because the accident with the cat happened more recently."

Cathy agreed. "Yes, unless Jodi had another motive, but I really don't see that. It would also clear the vet, since she didn't know they were considering letting her go at that time. While people have committed murder after being fired, Dr. Savella must have many other patients, especially since she specializes in Ruminants which is one of the reasons that Mavis is having a problem replacing her for someone who charges less."

"True and even though we don't know if the gardener has a motive, I think it's more likely a member of the family."

Cathy thought of Betty, acting as Nancy Drew, when she pointed her finger at Dylan and said that he was the accomplice to the woman who poisoned her daughter.

CHAPTER THIRTEEN

Cathy's thoughts and her conversation with Mildred were interrupted when Danielle came downstairs in her coat. "You're back, Cathy. Good. I guess Mildred told you we're going into town."

"Yes. Thank you for setting up a meeting with the vet and landscaper." Cathy held back from mentioning the things she'd learned from Chris. Even though she didn't suspect Danielle, she had to keep a clear mind about the case and couldn't trust anyone who might be involved.

They drove in Danielle's blue Mazda. Cathy let Mildred sit in front and took the back seat. "Nice car," Mildred commented.

"Thanks. Check out the heated seats. Sorry, Cathy, they're only in the front."

Cathy wondered how Danielle could afford a new car when the farm was in trouble.

Mildred said, "Very spiffy. Did you sell Doris' car?"

Danielle turned on the ignition. "Yes. Even though it was

old, she kept it in good shape. It didn't have much mileage on it. I made the sale, but I gave Mavis the money to use for the farm. I already had this one. Dylan bought it for me for our tenth anniversary. We only had one car before that, and he said I needed my own to take Sheri places. He only uses his around the farm."

Cathy pondered that. She remembered what Chris told her about Dylan asking Danielle to quit her part-time job after Doris died. As they drove off the farm, she said, "Chris told me you used to work at a florist shop."

Danielle stopped at a light. "I loved it. My boss said I could come back whenever I wanted. I like having time with Sheri and working on the farm but earning a little pocket money for myself. Meeting townspeople was also rewarding." She sounded wistful.

"Why did you leave then?" Mildred inquired. Cathy hadn't shared that information with her.

"Dylan asked me to quit after Doris died. He made a deal with me. If I wanted to keep my grandmother at home, I would need to be around to care for her." Danielle's voice rose, and Cathy heard the anger in it. "Even though I did as he asked, it's still a battle between us." She made a sharp turn, and only her seatbelt saved Cathy from sliding to the other side of the car.

"Sorry. I shouldn't burden you two with this. We're visiting with Henry first. He's the landscaper. I told him that I wanted to introduce you because you might run into him around the farm. He doesn't work many hours in the winter, but he does snow removal for us."

"Thank you," Mildred said. "Is there anything we should know about him?"

Cathy was still thinking of Dylan and how unreasonable he'd been to give his wife an ultimatum and not stick to his word.

"Only one thing." Danielle pulled in front of a small ranch home. "He's been a widower for a long time, and he proposed to my mother the night before she died."

CHAPTER FOURTEEN

"Did she accept?" Mildred wanted to know. So did Cathy.

"No. She told me that she wasn't ready to commit to another man. She thought he took it well, and she said they would remain friends. But then she died the next night after he attended the dinner."

"Do you suspect him?" Cathy asked.

Danielle finished parking. "I already told you that I'm not pointing a finger at anyone. I don't want to sway either of you against anybody."

"But you accused Jodi," Mildred said.

Danielle took the key out of the ignition. "That was a mistake. I wasn't thinking straight. I regret it and wish I could make up for it. Believe me, I've tried."

"Does anyone else know that Mr. Harris proposed to Doris?" Cathy thought about Mavis and her belief that Doris was still romantically interested in Chris.

"She only confided in me and made me promise not to say

anything. They were very discreet. I never suspected a thing, and I don't think anyone else was aware of their relationship." She opened the car door. "Why don't you meet him now and see what you think."

As Cathy got out of the back seat, she saw the door to the house open. A man stood there waiting for them.

The front walk was clear of snow. What remained on the lawn and in the street was melting as the temperatures rose.

"Good afternoon," Henry Harris said, opening the door. He was taller than Chris and a few years older. Cathy judged him to be in his late sixties. His gray hair was thinning but still covered his head. Glasses, similar to Mildred's, sat slightly low on the bridge of his nose. If she didn't know he was a gardener, Cathy would think he was a teacher or professor.

"Please come in, young ladies," he directed. "I just put on tea, and I baked biscuits this morning."

Mildred smiled to be included in the "young" category. She and Cathy followed Danielle into the house. It was bright and cheerful. The living room was painted a sunny yellow. A cream couch was partially covered with a granny square Afghan that Cathy thought her grandmother would admire.

"I'm afraid my kitchen is too tiny," Harris explained, "so we can talk in here. I'll bring out the tea and biscuits. Have a seat. I'll be right back."

Mildred said, "May I assist you, Mr. Harris?"

He smiled, and Cathy saw the laugh lines around his mouth. "That would be kind of you, ma'am, and please call me Henry. I apologize that I haven't made my introduction. Danielle must've told you that I'm the Oaks Landing Farm's landscaper."

Danielle said, "Yes, but I'm the one who should've introduced them. That's Cathy Hastings and this is her mother,

Mildred. They're from Buttercup Bend. Mildred worked with Doris at the library."

"Oh, really." His blue-gray eyes lit up behind his glasses, but Cathy noticed his smile had faded at the mention of Doris. "I used to work at the Oaks Landing Public Library before I retired and became a landscaper."

"You were a librarian?" Mildred seemed surprised, but Cathy wasn't. He looked more like a librarian than a landscaper. "What got you into gardening?" she asked.

"It was my family's profession. My father owned a landscaping company here. He wanted me to follow in his footsteps, and I did. It just took me some time. He passed away a few years ago."

Mildred said, "Sorry to hear that. Why don't I help you with the tea, and we can sit down and talk?"

Cathy and Danielle sat on the couch while Mildred went into the kitchen with Henry. A few minutes later, they returned with the tea and biscuits. Mildred carried the teapot, while Henry held the tray with the teacups, biscuits, and pitchers of sugar and milk. He laid the tray down on the table in front of Cathy, and Mildred placed the teapot next to it. "I can pour the tea," she offered.

A twinkle appeared in Henry's eyes. Cathy saw what Doris must've seen in him. He was gentlemanly and quite dashing for an older man. "Not at all, Mildred. You're my guest. You've helped enough. Please sit with your daughter and Danielle."

Mildred didn't insist. When she was seated, Henry passed around the tea, asking them first how they each took it. "I hope you all like Herbal. I stay away from caffeine. I brew the leaves from my garden. In the winter, I have indoor containers of herbs." He looked toward the windowsill at a few leafy plants.

"It's tasty," Mildred said. Cathy thought of the poisonous nightshade plant that had been added to a drink at her sister-in-law's baby shower last May. Although Danielle said that nothing had been found in her mother's food or drink, she wondered if the police or coroner had missed something.

"I hear you're a widower," Mildred said, taking a biscuit off the tray. "Have you lived here alone for a long time? Your house is very cozy."

"Thank you. It still has Beatrice's touch. She made it bright and shiny. I haven't changed much. She passed away three years ago around the time my dad did. It was a tough year. We were never blessed with children, so it's been me here alone since, but I keep busy."

Danielle changed the subject. She may have caught the tears clouding Henry's eyes. "Cathy's going to help us reopen the gift shop on Wednesday, and Mildred will be giving art classes next week. They're only here for two weeks, but it'll be helpful to have extra hands."

Cathy saw the change on Henry's face when he replied, "I'm sure it will be, especially since Mavis is about to give me the pink slip."

Danielle nearly spilled her tea. She grabbed a nearby napkin and wiped a few drops that had fallen into her saucer. "When did she tell you this? I had no idea."

Henry placed his teacup down and glanced at her. "I knew it was coming for some time. Mavis claims my fees are too high, but I haven't raised them since I started working for the farm five years ago. I considered lowering them, but it's time I retired for good. I'm not young anymore. She'll get a kid who will work for half my fee."

Danielle looked visibly shaken. "I'm sorry, Henry. I'll speak to her."

"Please don't bother. Like I said, I'm getting old. My back isn't what it used to be. It's for the best."

Cathy wanted to find a safe way to mention Doris. In the

quiet that followed Henry's last words, she asked, "Did you know Doris well? Mildred tells me she moved back to Oaks Landing around the time you said you started landscaping at the farm."

His eyes clouded again, but there was a spark of light in them. "Doris and I knew one another well. We grew up together. I was a few classes ahead of her in school, but my dad often took me to the farm to help him, and Doris and I spent time together." A redness appeared on his cheeks. "I sort've had a crush on her when we were teenagers, but she met Chris and married him. A few years later, I met Beatrice and we wed. Doris made us Danielle's Godparents. I was sorry when she left for Buttercup Bend, but I understood."

"How did you feel when she came back?" Mildred asked.

He took a sip of his tea and then replied. "Beatrice was still alive then but extremely sick. I didn't really get to see much of Doris. After Bea died, she came to the funeral. It was as if the years melted away." He gazed ahead at a painting of the farm that stood above a crackling fireplace that added warmth to the room. It seemed to Cathy that he was reliving that time. "I wasn't just mourning my wife. I knew that a part of me still had feelings for Doris. It's not that I didn't love Bea or that I married her on the rebound when Doris married Chris. It's hard to explain." He shrugged and looked back at them. "I knew she was divorced, so my hopes were ignited. When I worked on the farm, I made excuses to come to the house to see her. I thought she was starting to return my feelings. We went on a few dates. We kept it quiet. Mavis employed me."

Danielle said, "We never suspected anything. Doris told me you asked her to marry you, but she turned you down."

He looked away. "She never got over your father. She said we could remain friends and then..." He looked back up. "I'm so sorry she's gone." He took a handkerchief from his pocket and wiped his eyes.

Danielle said, "She cared for you very much, Henry. If she were around, she wouldn't let Mavis fire you."

He shrugged. "Does anyone want anymore tea?" Cathy knew he was done talking about Doris.

CHAPTER FIFTEEN

They stayed a while longer until Danielle stood up and said, "We have to be going now, Henry, but thank you for the tea and biscuits."

He nodded. "My pleasure but remember what I said about Mavis. There's no need to step in on my behalf."

Cathy noticed Danielle didn't make any promises as she walked to the door. She and Mildred followed, both saying their thanks and goodbyes.

Back in Danielle's car, Cathy said, "That's so sad. He seems like such a nice man, and there's no reason he would've harmed Doris."

"I'm sure you're right, Cathy, but people do strange things sometimes when they're hurt. When he came to dinner that night, he hardly spoke to anyone including my mother. While he said they were remaining friends, it didn't seem that way to me."

"How did he react when she keeled over?" Mildred asked. "Did he rush to her side?"

Danielle started the car. "I really can't say. It was such a mess. I ran to her and then Stacy helped. Henry was the one who called 911."

"Stacy is the vet, right?"

"Yes. We're visiting her next. She lives nearby and works part-time at the Oaks Landing Animal Hospital. That's where we'll be speaking with her, but she's on a retainer with the farm as their private vet. As I said, that may not be for long."

A few minutes later, Danielle parked in the parking lot of a brick and glass building that had a statue of a dog and cat outside. The doors opened as they walked through. The office was modern with a few old-fashioned touches. It was packed with barking dogs on leashes and crying cats in carriers. Owners waited patiently to be called in for exams.

Danielle walked up to the desk and addressed one of the receptionists. "Hi, Fran. We have an appointment with Stacy."

The older woman said, "Yes, Danielle. She told me you were coming this morning. We're busy but let me bring you back to her office." Cathy, Mildred, and Danielle followed Fran through a door that led to the exam rooms and then through a second door that led into the back offices. She opened the door to a small room with a computer and a desk chair. "I'll let her know you're here. She's with a patient right now. Please have a seat."

Cathy looked around but only saw one other chair. After Fran left, Danielle said, "You take the chair, Mildred. I don't mind standing."

When Mildred hesitated, Cathy said, "Go ahead, Mildred. I'm fine standing, too, and I know you have problems with your knees."

Mildred sank into the chair. "Thanks. I'm doing okay, but I

appreciate getting off my feet for a few minutes. By the look of that waiting room, we may be here a while before Dr. Savella sees us."

The wait wasn't that long. Ten minutes later, a blonde woman wearing white scrubs entered the room. Her hair was tied into a ponytail. Cathy judged her to be in her early thirties, younger than she expected. "Good afternoon," she said, smiling. "Sorry to keep you waiting. It's a zoo out there, no pun intended." She laughed lightly at her own joke.

Danielle said, "We don't need much of your time, Stacy. I just wanted to introduce you to Mildred and Cathy Hastings from Buttercup Bend. They're lending a hand at the farm for two weeks."

A shadow passed across the vet's face. "Nice to meet both of you. I'm Dr. Savella, but everyone calls me Stacy."

Mildred said. "I hear you treat Ruminants. That must be interesting."

"It can be, and challenging at times, too. I especially love llamas and alpacas."

"I was on a llama hike this morning," Cathy said. "Chris took me. I walked Lulu."

Stacy's face brightened. "Lulu is a sweetie. She's my favorite llama."

"She was Doris' favorite, too," Danielle pointed out.

The vet glanced at her wrist, even though there was a clock on the wall. "I really must go now." She turned to Danielle. "Thanks for bringing them. I have a meeting with Mavis tomorrow. I might see you then." Without waiting for a reply, she rushed from the room.

. . .

On the drive back to the farm, Mildred asked Danielle, "I know Stacy was busy, but she seemed to leave quickly when you mentioned Doris."

Danielle smiled. "That was a coincidence. What I think made her dash off was the reminder that Mavis is speaking with her tomorrow. I'm quite sure it's about her position at the farm."

"You think she's going to fire her?" Cathy asked.

Danielle turned toward the road that led to the farm. "She hasn't said anything officially to me. I didn't even know she was seeing Stacy tomorrow, but I have a feeling that's what it's about. Although Stacy only worked for us a few years after Dr. Higgins retired, she's a great vet. I don't know who they'll replace her with."

Cathy thought of Michael, but he wouldn't be interested in traveling to Oaks Landing. She didn't even know if he treated Ruminants.

Mildred must've followed that same train of thought because she said, "We have a wonderful veterinarian in Buttercup Bend, Michael Graham. I don't know if he has experience with farm animals or what he would charge, but I don't think he'd be interested in coming this far."

"We wouldn't need him that often, and Buttercup Bend is only an hour away. If you don't mind, I'll give his name to Mavis."

Cathy said, "I think Michael is busy enough, and I hate to see Stacy lose her job at the farm."

"She's on retainer with other farms in the area and works at the animal hospital, so I don't think it'll be much of a loss to her," Danielle pointed out.

That's not how Cathy saw it. Stacy didn't look pleased about her upcoming meeting with Mavis.

CHAPTER SIXTEEN

When they got back to the farm, Mavis was sitting on the couch in the living room reading. She put her book down and said, "Welcome back! How was your meeting with Henry and Stacy?"

Danielle hung up her coat. "It went well. They met Cathy and Mildred. I found out you're meeting with Stacy tomorrow, and I assume Henry at some point. Why didn't you tell me?"

Mavis shrugged. Cathy noticed her hair was a less harsh shade of red. She may have asked her hairdresser to tone down the color. She was also sporting a matching manicure. "I don't need to report to you, Danny, but if you're interested, I'm giving Stacy notice tomorrow. It shouldn't be a surprise. I'm paying her until the end of the month."

Danielle walked over to Cathy and Mildred and asked for their coats. After she'd hung them up next to hers, she turned back to Mavis. "I hope you've thought this out. Have you hired someone to replace Stacy?"

"That does present a problem. I'm not having much luck,

but I'm sure I'll be able to come up with someone by the time she leaves."

Mildred said, "I just mentioned to Danielle that Cathy and I know a great vet from Buttercup Bend. We're not sure if he has the qualifications or that he'd mind traveling here, but we could ask him."

Cathy wasn't happy that Mildred had offered up Michael, but the suggestion seemed to appeal to Mavis. She smiled and said, "Thank you, Mildred. Please give him a call and if he's interested, I'll arrange an interview."

"What about Henry? Have you found a replacement for him?" Danielle asked.

"There are several landscapers in the area who are interested and charge less. I'll be deciding that before the end of this week. Any other questions, Danny?"

"Is Chris back from the accountant's office?"

"Some time ago. He took Sheri to see Lulu. They should be back soon. He's taking me to dinner tonight if you could please cook for our guests, your daughter, and my mother, of course."

Cathy had never seen Danielle look so angry. Her dark eyes blazed as she replied, "Sure thing. I'll go shopping for the groceries now." She faced Cathy and Mildred, "Sorry to run, but it seems I've been ordered to prepare dinner tonight."

"Don't worry," Mildred said. "We'll find something to keep us occupied. C'mon, Cathy, let's go upstairs. We should make that call to Michael now."

While Cathy was relieved to get away from Mavis, she was apprehensive about Mildred contacting Michael. No one besides Gran was supposed to know that they were in Oaks Landing investigating a murder.

. . .

Mildred led Cathy into her room. "We need to talk," she said, plopping down on the bed. Cathy continued to stand. "We sure do. Mildred, why would you suggest that we contact Michael about the veterinary position here?"

"Please don't be mad, Cathy. We have no idea if he can treat Ruminants or would want the job, but I thought it would be a way to get him down here to see you. I know Florence felt that you getting away would help you face your problems, but I've always believed in confronting them head on. I think you should call Michael. Even if he won't come, you'll speak with him."

Cathy sighed. "You're my friend, Mildred. I've known you since I was a child visiting the library with Gran, but I don't agree with your plans. I won't call Michael." Without listening to Mildred's reply, Cathy stormed out of the room. She didn't slam the door, but she felt like it. Back in her own room, she grabbed her camera. She had to get out of the house, and it was likely the snow would be gone by the next day, so she wanted to take photos of the farm while it still blanketed the ground.

"There you are," a voice said, as she stepped out into the hall. She thought it was Mildred coming to her room to apologize, but then she saw Betty standing by her door.

"Oh, hi, Betty. How are you today?"

"Betty? Who's Betty? I'm Catherine. Catherine the Great, Empress of Russia, and who may you be visiting my palace?"

Cathy was surprised that Betty was now taking on personas other than movie and TV stars. She even noted a slight Russian accent to her words. She wondered why the woman was allowed to walk around on her own and began to think that Dylan had a point about putting her away. "I'm Cathy Hastings from Buttercup Bend," she replied, not sure how to answer.

Betty's violet eyes grew large. "I knew it. You're a spy." She grew agitated. "Guards," she called. "Guards, where are you?"

Cathy didn't think she should fear this diminutive old woman, but the look in her eyes terrified her. She stepped back. She was sure Mildred would hear Betty's screams and come to her aid, but Mavis arrived first. Running up the stairs, she rushed to her mother. "Mother, calm down. It's Mavis. You're Betty Taylor, and this is your house." As she spoke in a controlled voice, Betty took a deep breath and was back. "Oh, I'm so sorry," she said in her normal voice. "I was taking my afternoon nap, and I must've sleepwalked again."

Mavis took her arm. "It's okay. Why don't you go to your room and lie down again? I'll be around if you need me and then Danny will be back. She's gone grocery shopping." As she walked Betty down the hall to her room, Mavis glanced over her shoulder and gave Cathy a look that she interpreted as, "see what I mean." It was then that Mildred stepped into the hall. "Cathy, are you okay? I'm sorry I didn't come sooner. I was on the phone with Michael. I know you won't be happy, but he's agreed to come down and meet with Mavis. Believe me, I'm only doing this to help."

Cathy had no energy left to argue. "When is he coming, and what did you tell him?" she asked.

"The truth, of course. Don't worry. I made him promise not to tell anyone else. We both know he's good for his word. I gave him the farm's number, and he said he'll call Mavis in a little while to see when she's available to meet with him."

Cathy said, "Mavis is taking care of her mother. She had another, uh, episode."

"That's what I thought. The poor woman." Mildred noticed the camera strung over Cathy's shoulder. "Are you going somewhere?"

"I was about to take a walk. I want to shoot some winter photos of the farm before it gets dark."

"Nice idea. I've always found walks clear my head,

although I haven't been able to take too many since my knee problems."

"You really should have a knee replacement, Mildred."

"I'm putting it off. I don't like hospitals, and the recovery will take too long."

Cathy didn't want to force the issue. She was still upset with Mildred for contacting Michael. The urge for a walk grew stronger. "I'll be going then, Mildred."

As she turned to head downstairs, Mavis came out of Betty's room. Mildred met her halfway down the hall. Cathy didn't stay around to hear what they said to one another.

CHAPTER SEVENTEEN

Outside, Cathy took a lungful of the cold, brisk air. The barn cats scurried over to her, and she gave each a pet. Even scaredy cat, Cricket, agreed to be touched. She took a photo of the three of them standing together and was pleased that she was able to get them all to look at her. She was reminded again of Harry and Hermione and was wondering if they missed her. She made a note to herself to check in with Gran later to see how they were doing.

She continued on, following the path she'd taken earlier with Chris, stopping along the way to take shots of the snow-covered pastures, farm animals, and Jodi's house. She considered tapping on the door and seeing if the girl would talk with her but decided otherwise. As she came to the female llama and alpaca pen, she looked for Lulu. While the other llamas came to the gate for their photo shoots, she noticed Lulu napping. She called her name, but the llama continued to sleep, her chest gently rising. She took a shot of her at rest and planned to stop there again on her way back when Lulu might be up.

Rounding the corner, she passed Chris' house and took a

photo of it. Then she arrived at the gift shop. That's when she saw it. Several footsteps were visible in the snow. She recognized hers and those of Chris, but there seemed to be a set leading up to the gift shop door which stood slightly ajar. She recalled Chris locking the door after them and thought of the story that Danielle told her about Doris thinking she was being stalked by someone outside the gift shop. She suddenly felt a chill run up her back that had nothing to do with the cold temperatures and wondered if she should turn back or call Mavis on her cell phone. Instead, she placed her hand on the shop's door and slid it open. She remembered where the light was, so she flicked it on quickly. The place was silent, so she assumed any intruder had already left. Then she realized that the person who'd been there had dusted and swept the room. She laughed at herself for being scared when it had to be someone from the house. The footsteps outside weren't much bigger than hers, so it was one of the women, likely Danielle who may have stopped on her way out grocery shopping to prepare it for the opening the next day. Although Chris hadn't returned the key to Mavis, she was sure Danielle had her own. She was about to turn and leave when she noticed something new near the register, a piece of paper. She walked over to it and gasped as she saw that it was a printout from the October issue of the online archive of the *Buttercup Bugle*. The page featured her photo and the headline, "Cathy Carter joins the Hunt and Meyers Detective Agency after helping to solve Dr. Barry Bodkin's murder." Danielle wouldn't have left that, so someone else knew her real identity.

CHAPTER EIGHTEEN

Cathy grabbed the paper, folded it, and put it in her coat pocket. She closed the door behind her and left. She wasn't sure what she would do when she returned to the house. She'd share her finding with Mildred and see what she thought. It might be best to continue in the current manner instead of confronting Mavis who might've left the paper. But how she'd done that when she was in the house when Cathy returned from her hike with Chris was a big question. She also doubted that Mavis would clean up the place.

Walking back to the house, she wasn't in the mood to take anymore photos, but she stopped by the llama pen to see Lulu and was surprised that she was still napping. Did Llamas sleep a lot? Were they like cats who slept twelve to sixteen hours a day? The other llamas were still up and grazing. Could Lulu be sick? She made a note to mention that to Danielle or Chris. Stacy could take a look at her when she came the next day. Mavis said she was paying the veterinarian until the end of the month.

· · ·

Cathy was disappointed that the barn cats didn't greet her when she returned, but she had other pressing matters to deal with. She saw Danielle's car so knew she was home. Entering the house, she smelled the aroma of garlic and tomatoes.

Mildred was entertaining Sheri with a game of Hide and Go Seek. She was giggling as Mildred found her behind the couch. She looked up to see Cathy. "Miss Hastings. Want to play? You can be "It"?"

"Sorry, Sheri. I'm tired from my walk." She made the excuse, so she could speak with Danielle. She couldn't say anything in front of her daughter about the printout and didn't want to mention that something seemed off with Lulu.

Danielle was stirring the sauce for pasta when Cathy entered the kitchen. "Hi, Cathy. How was your walk? I heard you were taking photos of the farm. I'd love you to show them to Dylan if you don't mind his using some on our website."

"Of course. Where is he?"

"He's upstairs with Betty. I heard what happened when I got back from shopping. Mavis said she was in a bad state. I asked Dylan to spend some time with her."

This surprised Cathy, knowing how Dylan felt about Betty. She walked over to the stove. "Do you need any help with dinner?"

"No. I asked Mildred to keep Sheri occupied until I was done and then she'll want to help me set the table."

Cathy tried to figure out a way of broaching the subject that was on her mind. Although she knew Danielle hadn't left the paper, she said, "Danielle, thanks for cleaning up the gift shop. You did a fantastic job."

Danielle stopped stirring and faced Cathy, her dark eyes raised in puzzlement. "I didn't clean the gift shop. I was shopping, remember? I came right back here to cook."

Cathy took the *Buttercup Bugle* printout from her pocket.

"Well, somebody did, and they didn't lock the door behind them. They left this." She showed Danielle the paper.

"I'm sorry. I don't know who could've done this. Mavis promised me she wouldn't leave the house while Betty was upstairs."

"It's not Mavis. She was here with Mildred when I got back from the hike with Chris. Who else has a key to the gift shop?"

Danielle thought a moment, slowly resuming her stirring of the pot. "The only one I can think of is Jodi. Last summer, after Doris quit working at the shop, Mavis asked Jodi to help out the days she couldn't, so she gave her a copy of the key, but I can't imagine why she would clean up or leave this article about you there."

"Could it be that she still thinks you suspect her of killing your mother and that's why you had Chris introduce me and Mildred to her?"

Danielle stopped stirring again and sighed. "I suppose that's a possibility. She may want you to know that she's aware you're a detective."

"Do you think she'll tell anyone?"

"I doubt it. She's not really on good terms with any of us. But she knows I've assigned the gift shop to you and that you'd find the paper tomorrow."

"I don't like it." Cathy was uncomfortable that someone knew about her and Mildred. "I'd like to speak with her and explain that I don't consider her a suspect and neither do you."

Danielle turned off the burner and checked the one next to it that had begun to boil. Adding the spaghetti, she said, "Until I know what really happened to my mother, I'm not discounting anyone. Visiting her again isn't a great idea, but if you and Mildred want to do that, I'm not going to stop you."

"Do what? Visit Who?" Mildred, looking flushed and exhausted, was standing in the kitchen doorway. She'd heard the last part of their conversation. Sheri stood next to her. "Are we eating yet, Mommy? Millie is tired of playing with me."

Danielle said, "It's almost done, honey. You can start setting the dining room table. Since Grandpa and Mavis aren't eating with us tonight, there's six of us, but set a place for Granny, too." She looked toward Mildred. "Cathy will fill you in later."

"Betty's dining with us?" Mildred looked as surprised as Cathy felt.

"Yes. Dylan is going to bring her down." She checked the clock. "At six." It was 5:45. "I've decided it's better she dine with us again. I had Dylan give her a pill to calm her down, so there shouldn't be any problems."

"Goody! Granny's coming." Sheri began to skip.

Danielle placed the plates, bowls, glasses, and silverware on the counter. "Cathy, can you help Sheri set the table, please?"

"Sure." Cathy grabbed the pile of plates and silverware. She gave Sheri the salad bowl and glasses.

They were all seated around the table when Dylan came downstairs with Betty. Despite the fact that Danielle said she'd been given a sedative, she seemed alert. Her blue eyes looked clear as she gazed at the group. "Good evening," she said. "Thank you for inviting me."

Danielle smiled. "We're glad to have you, Betty." She began to pass around the spaghetti and sauce bowls. There was also a platter of fresh garlic bread.

Cathy's heart sank when Betty said, "I'm not Betty. I'm Julia. Julia Child, and I think you should put more cheese on my plate. Where is the cheese?"

Danielle began to pass the parmesan shaker to her grandmother when Betty reached across the table and took the salt.

"No, Granny," Sheri said, "That's the salt, not the cheese."

Betty put down the shaker and smiled. "Excuse me, young lady. My mistake."

Dylan shook his head. "See, Danny. I told you that she wasn't ready."

"It's okay," Danielle said. "Let me put the cheese on your plate, uh, Julia." As she came around to her grandmother's seat, Dylan stood up. "That's it. I'm going out. I've had enough of this. I'll pick up dinner somewhere. You can babysit her along with Sheri."

"I don't need a babysitter," Sheri said, "I want you to stay, Daddy."

"Sorry, Sweetie. I've lost my appetite." As he left, tears began to fall down Sheri's cheeks. Mildred, next to her, grabbed a tissue and wiped them. "Don't cry, honey. It's okay. Daddy will be back."

"If he's not eating, neither am I. She's Julia Child again." She pointed at Betty. "Is someone going to die?"

"Sheri!" Danielle exclaimed, dropping the cheese shaker. "No one's going to die. Grandma is just having one of her spells."

Suddenly, Betty was back. "My spell? Was I sleepwalking again?"

When everyone was settled, the dinner continued in silence. Afterwards, Mildred offered to take Betty upstairs. Danielle took her aside and asked her to give Betty her sleeping pill. "Just one tablet does the trick. Dylan's right. We can't have her roaming around alone at night. Can you also bring Sheri up to her room? I'll read to her as soon as I clean up. She can watch TV until then."

"I can read to her," Mildred offered. "I'm a librarian. I have experience reading to children in story times."

"That would be wonderful. Thank you so much." Cathy

noticed Danielle was shaky, so she followed her into the kitchen. "Are you okay? I can help with the dishes."

Danielle gave her a weak smile. "Thanks, Cathy. I'm okay but a bit shaken up. I'm afraid that if I don't do something about Betty soon, Dylan's going to divorce me."

"Why do you say that?"

"Because he's mentioned it. Besides my insistence that's my mother was murdered and Betty's "spells," he's about had it with me." Her eyes filled with tears. "I love him, Cathy, but I also love my grandmother. I don't know what to do."

"I shouldn't get involved and, with my trouble with men, I'm the last one to give advice, but I think you have to make a choice between your husband and grandmother."

Danielle took a deep breath. "You're right. I knew this would happen soon. If Dylan comes back tonight, I'm going to tell him to look into places for Betty. Mavis will be pleased."

As Cathy grabbed a dish towel and Danielle began to wash the dishes, she said, "What Sheri said tonight about someone dying. Was she referring to your mother? Does she still say that when you all eat together?"

"She did at the beginning but hasn't lately until Betty joined us. It must be because she was Julia Child."

"What do you mean?" Cathy wasn't following."

Danielle handed her a dish to dry. "Betty was Julia Child the night Mother died."

CHAPTER NINETEEN

After Cathy and Danielle were done doing dishes, Mildred came downstairs. "Sheri's asleep and so is Betty."

"I can't thank you enough," Danielle said, relief in her voice.

"You need to rest, too," Mildred said.

"I hope I can. I'm going to my room to read and wait for Dylan. We have to talk when he gets home. Help yourselves to anything you want."

After she left, Cathy asked Mildred to join her in the living room. When they were seated on the couch, she said, "We have to talk, too. Something happened on my walk. I couldn't say with everyone around. I told Danielle about it, but you should know."

Mildred raised an eyebrow. "What happened?"

Cathy showed her the printout and related her experience in the gift shop. When she was done, she added, "Danielle thinks it was Jodi. I said we should speak with her about it, make sure she doesn't tell anyone, and assure her we don't suspect her of killing Doris."

Mildred considered. "That might be the best thing to do, but we can't rule her out. Maybe she left that paper as a threat, so you won't investigate her too closely. She does have a good motive. That cat meant the world to her."

"I don't agree. Mavis has the strongest motive. You read the letter Doris wrote and see how close Mavis and Chris are now. But the biggest question is, if Doris was murdered, and we still haven't determined that, how was it done?"

Mildred squinted behind the lenses of her bifocals as if concentrating hard on the question. Then she replied, "That's what we're here to find out, Cathy. In the meantime, I have something to tell you, too. Mavis is interviewing Michael tomorrow. He'll be here in the morning."

That reminded Cathy of Lulu. "Maybe he can take a look at Lulu. She was sleeping when I passed the llama pen today. I didn't know if that was her normal rest period, but the other llamas were up and walking around."

"Did you mention that to Danielle?"

"With everything that happened tonight, I forgot, but I'll mention it to her tomorrow. I don't want to alarm Sheri either. Maybe Lulu was only tired from playing with Sheri earlier when Chris took her there."

"That's possible, but you should still tell Danielle or Mavis if you want. I think it's weird that she's interviewing Stacy's replacement on the same day that she's letting her go."

Cathy remembered something. "Tomorrow is my first day working at the gift shop, too. I might not be here when Michael arrives." She was surprised that the thought disappointed her.

. . .

Cathy was asleep when something woke her, a noise out in the hall. At first, she thought it was Betty until she heard Dylan's voice. She checked the clock and saw that it was after midnight. She couldn't make out what Dylan was saying, but she was sure he was talking with Danielle. When she finally fell back to sleep, she had a strange dream. Michael was at the farm riding a tractor, his dark wavy hair billowing in the wind behind him. As he circled the farm, Lulu appeared out of nowhere and ran out into his path. There was a terrible crash, and Cathy awoke shaking. Mildred called her name from outside her door. "Cathy, are you okay? Did you hear that sound?"

Cathy grabbed her robe and let Mildred in. "I thought it was part of my dream. Do you know where it came from?"

"Downstairs. We should go see."

Cathy put on her slippers. She noted that Mildred was in her long nightgown, fluffy slippers covered her feet. She followed her down the stairs. "What if it's a burglar?" she whispered. She hadn't noticed any alarms or locks near the doors.

"Don't worry." Mildred took a small object from the pocket of her nightgown. "I always carry pepper spray just in case."

Cathy thought that wouldn't help against a gun, but she continued down the stairs. When they were at the bottom, she heard voices coming from the kitchen. She recognized the woman's voice as Mavis speaking with Chris. "Sorry I'm so klutzy. I dropped that pan."

"I think the word you're looking for is drunk." Chris' laughter floated through the door. "I'm glad I drove you home."

"Sorry I couldn't stay. Dinner was delightful. I have two meetings in the morning, so I thought it best I sleep in my own bed. Otherwise, I won't be clearheaded for them." Her giggle sounded childlike.

"We better go back," Mildred whispered to Cathy. They quietly returned to their rooms. As Cathy opened her door, she jumped as she caught a glimpse of someone on her bed. Then she realized it was Sheri.

"What are you doing here?"

"I couldn't sleep. Don't tell Mommy. She would yell at me for coming in your room."

"Did the noise wake you?"

"No. it was Auntie Mavis. She comes home late a lot. Sometimes she stays at Grandpa's house."

"Then why couldn't you sleep?"

"I'm worried that Daddy is going to leave."

Cathy sat next to the girl and gave her a hug. "Oh, Sheri. Parents fight sometimes, but they work things out."

"What if they don't? Daddy wants to send Grammy away. I don't want her to go either."

"Your grandmother is sick, honey. She needs help, so it may be best for her to be somewhere with doctors and nurses. Sometimes, you have to let loved ones go if it's better for them." As Cathy spoke the words, she thought of Steve and Michael and how keeping them in limbo wasn't in their best interest. Was she being selfish by holding on to them?

"What's going on?" Danielle stood in the doorway, her eyes red, her dark hair strung loosely down her back. Cathy noted she was still in her day clothes. "Sheri, I've told you not to go into anyone's room at night. Cathy, I'm sorry she bothered you."

"She's not a bother at all, Danielle. She's scared. She's afraid Betty or her father will be leaving."

Danielle ran to her daughter and hugged her. "Oh, sweetie. Daddy isn't going anywhere. We had a good talk. He'll find a nice place for Grammy, and we'll all be able to visit her as much as we want. Now c'mon. I'll put you back to bed." She took her hand, and Sheri walked with her to the door.

CHAPTER TWENTY

The next morning, everyone seemed in better spirits. Cathy was able to speak with Mavis privately about Lulu. She shrugged and said, "I'm sure it's nothing. I don't know much about llamas, but I'll ask one of the vets to check her. We'll have two here today. I hear that Dr. Graham is a good friend of yours."

Cathy felt a flutter in her stomach. "Yes. He treats our pets at our animal rescue."

"I hope you can do without him if I hire him."

"I don't think that'll be necessary, but you can keep Dr. Savella on a part-time retainer. It's always good to have two vets around in case of an emergency." Cathy felt bad that Mavis was letting Stacy go. She was also worried that Michael would accept the position and move away from Buttercup Bend.

"I've thought of that, but between you and me, I never cared for her. Betty hired her originally."

"What about the gardener, Henry? Are you firing him, too?"

"Firing is the wrong word. It's about time he retired. He

can hardly pull weeds anymore." Mavis faced Cathy. "Aren't you due to open the gift shop soon? Danny said she'll come with you to get you started. I have to prepare for my meetings." With that, she strutted off in her high-heeled boots.

Leaving Sheri with Dylan who seemed to have calmed down since rushing out after dinner, Danielle walked Cathy over to the gift shop. "Mavis promised to bring Betty her breakfast this morning. I've agreed to keep her on her medications until Dylan finds a place for her."

"Are you happy with that decision?"

"I don't have a choice, Cathy. Dylan's right that she could hurt herself or someone else. She needs professional care."

Cathy agreed but she knew that, if it were Gran, it would be difficult for her and Doug to make that choice.

Although the snow had melted, dissolving the footsteps, the gift shop was still unlocked. "I see what you mean, Cathy. Somebody was here after you and Chris." Danielle switched on the lights. "I don't think you'll get many customers today, although Dylan sent out an eBlast from our website. If you get too bored, you can call the house and ask for Mildred to take over the rest of your shift. There's a direct dial on the phone, or you can use your cell."

"Don't worry. Chris suggested that I bring a book, so I brought the one I've been reading." Cathy took out a copy of Kristin Hannah's *The Winter Garden*. "I don't usually read historical fiction, but I've heard many good things about this author, and Mildred suggested I try this one. She used it at the library book club. I checked it out before I came."

"She's very good," Danielle said. "I've read several of her books." She walked over to the register and took a key from her pocket. Turning it on, she asked, "Do you know how to work this?"

"It looks the same as the one we have at our rescue center. We sell a few items there as well as what's in our website store."

"Good. I better get back to the house then. Don't forget to put up the "closed" sign when you take lunch." She indicated the two-sided sign at the front door that could be flipped.

"I won't. Thank you."

After Danielle left, Cathy walked around the shop. Now that it was spotless, she could view the items better.

The shop had only been open fifteen minutes when the windchimes at the door alerted her that she had a visitor. She thought it was Danielle coming back to remind her of something but, when she turned, she saw it was Jodi. The girl was wearing another pair of cut-up jeans and a long red sweater.

"Hello, Miss Hastings, or should I call you by your real name, Miss Carter?"

"Jodi! You placed that paper by the register yesterday and cleaned the store."

"That was me. When I saw you, I recognized you, but I had to verify that, so I did some checking online. You're investigating Mrs. Grady's murder, aren't you?"

Cathy knew she couldn't hide the truth from this inquisitive young lady. "That's right. Mildred and I were asked to do that by Danielle, but we don't have any clues yet, and I certainly don't suspect you."

"Why not? Mrs. Grady killed my cat."

"It was an accident. Danielle said you accepted it and even came to dinner with her that night."

Jodi didn't reply. She began to walk around the shop touching different items until she stopped and fingered a skein of llama wool. She turned back to Cathy. "I believe you, but I don't trust

Mrs. Diaz. I still think she wants to pin her mother's death on me. I cleaned up for you because I knew you'd be working here. It's your undercover job. But don't worry, I won't tell anyone about you. I left the note because I wanted you to know that if I could figure you out, somebody else could, too. I don't want it to be the killer. It was a warning for you to stay on your toes."

Cathy was surprised. "You think Betty, uh, Mrs. Taylor was murdered?"

"Oh, yeah. Mrs. Diaz is right about that."

"Who do you suspect?"

She let go of the wool and faced Cathy. "Mavis Taylor, of course. She's had the hots for Mr. Grady for ages. She couldn't stand it when her sister came back."

"But why would she wait five years"? While Cathy agreed that Mavis had the strongest motive, it seemed odd that she would wait so long to get Doris out of the picture.

Jodi shrugged. "I have no idea. I guess that's why you and Mrs. Hastings are here. Gotta run now." With that, she left, a tinkle of the windchimes announcing her exit.

It was almost lunchtime when Cathy prepared to close the shop. No one else had come by besides Jodi. After she flipped over the "closed" sign, she stepped out into the brisk winter day. Glancing toward the llama pen a few yards away, she saw Mavis there with Michael and Stacy. Both vets were standing by Lulu who still seemed to be sleeping. She was curled up on her stomach, legs apart on both sides of her. As if sensing that Cathy was nearby, Michael looked over and caught her eye. The look he gave her made her heart take a turn. Mavis saw her, too, and waved. "Hey, Cathy. Come join us."

Cathy tried to control her racing heart as she entered the gate.

"Hi, Cathy," Michael said. "I hear you're working in the gift shop." He glanced toward the store.

Cathy could hardly stop her voice from breaking. "Yes. It just reopened, but we haven't had much business today."

His dark blue eyes twinkled. "Maybe I'll pop in later and check what you have on sale." Cathy thought she read something else into those words.

Mavis said, "I'm impressed with your Michael. He seems very knowledgeable about animals."

Stacy gave her a glare. "If you're so impressed, why did you ask me here to look at Lulu, too?"

Mavis gave a short laugh. "I want to get the most for my money." When Stacy stepped back as if ready to leave, she added, "Just kidding. You've known Lulu longer than Michael and can tell if something's wrong."

"Very well then. I'll go first." Stacy knelt down and began examining Lulu. When she touched her, Lulu rolled over and opened her eyes. "Hey, girl. You okay?" After using the stethoscope that hung around her neck to listen to the llama's heart, Stacy got up, wiped the dirt from her pant legs, and said, "I don't think there's anything seriously wrong with her. Why don't you check her now, Dr. Graham?"

"Michael, please. May I call you Stacy? We're colleagues."

Stacy smiled. "That would be fine, Michael."

Cathy felt a tinge of jealousy as she watched the exchange. Then she reminded herself that she hadn't accepted Michael's marriage proposal.

Michael got down on his knees and performed his own exam of Lulu. When she stood up after he was done, he patted her on the head. "You're fine, Lulu." He addressed Mavis. "I concur with Stacy's findings. There's nothing wrong with your llama. If I may hazard a guess, she might be a bit under the weather, lonely, or depressed. Animals get that way, too."

Mavis shrugged. "She gets plenty of attention. My niece Sheri is wild about her."

"I don't doubt that, but you mentioned that your sister was also very close to Lulu."

"Yes, but she's been gone a month already."

"It doesn't matter. Grief can hit someone at any time after a loss. You just haven't noticed her apathy."

Stacy said, "While I agree with Michael, I think there's another factor at play here." She turned to Mavis. "Have you been trying to breed her?"

Mavis said, "Last week, I put her in a separate pen with Stewie for a few hours. I didn't tell anyone because we've had problems breeding her in the past. We never tried with Stewie, so I thought we'd give it another go. It's been so crazy here lately that it skipped my mind. Do you think she's expecting?"

Stacy nodded. "I'd say there's a good chance that's part of the reason she's acting this way."

Cathy asked, "How do you test her to find out?"

Michael answered her question. "It's a behavior test. They put her back in with Stewie and, if she spits at him and wants nothing to do with him, there'll be a baby llama, cria, in about a year."

Cathy laughed. "I never heard of that. With female cats, you simply notice changes like weight gain, increased appetite, and many seem more affectionate."

Mavis smiled. "I'll set up a spit test soon, but I don't want to say anything until we know for sure. If it's true, Sheri will be thrilled." She glanced at her watch. "It's lunchtime. Would you all like to come back to the house with me?"

Stacy shook her head. "Sorry. I have to be at the animal hospital. Thank you, anyway." Her tone indicated she wasn't thankful at all.

Michael seemed disappointed. "Sorry you can't make it,

but we understand. I took a few days off from the hospital. I called in another vet, and Brody's helping out, so I'll be at Oaks Landing until the end of the week. We can have lunch together another time and discuss what you've done at the farm."

This was news to Cathy. She thought Michael would be leaving after the interview. Mavis said, "I think that's a wonderful idea especially if I decide to hire you. I have a few more interviews, but, as I said, I'm very impressed. Have you booked a room yet? If not, I'm happy to have you stay with us. Chris has a guest room. I'm sure he'll allow you to use it."

"That's very kind, Miss Taylor. I haven't booked anything."

"The name's Mavis, Michael, and I'll speak with Chris. He's gathering eggs with Sheri but should be home by now."

"Thank you." Michael met Cathy's eyes. "I have a surprise for you back at the house, Cathy." She wondered what he meant.

CHAPTER TWENTY-ONE

When they arrived, Cathy saw Michael's car parked next to Mavis.' Chris' truck was also there along with Danielle's Mazda and Cathy's car. Mavis entered the house first, and Michael held the door open for Cathy. As soon as she stepped in, she heard voices coming from the kitchen. She followed Mavis and Michael into that room and was shocked to see Steve sitting next to Mildred, a ham sandwich on a plate in front of him. He flashed her a smile, and she saw the dimple she found so attractive. "Hi, Cat."

Michael grinned. "Here's your surprise, Cathy. When Mildred told me you were here, I asked Steve to join me. I hope you're not mad."

Cathy could hardly speak so was glad when Mavis said, "I'm happy you invited Steve. I'd like him to meet Henry. There are a lot of gardeners interested in working here, but I haven't yet chosen one. It would be interesting to hire both of you since you're such good friends." She looked toward Chris who was biting into his sandwich. "I promised Michael he could stay in your guest room, Chris. If Steve would like to stay, do you have room for him?"

Chris swallowed, wiped his mouth with a napkin, and said, "Michael is welcome, but I'm afraid I don't have enough room for two guests."

"That's okay," Steve said. "I'll find a room in town. I've taken some time off, too. Unless there's a snowstorm in Buttercup Bend, the winter is a slow season for me."

"Why don't you stay with Henry?" Mavis suggested. "He's living in his house all by himself. I'm sure he has room and would love to meet a fellow gardener."

Danielle said, "I don't know if you should impose on him, but I can give him a call. Why don't you all get seated? I'll put out more sandwiches." She glanced at Cathy, Mavis, and Michael.

When they took seats around the table, Michael said, "Cathy, you didn't answer my question. Are you upset with me for bringing Steve along?"

Cathy found her voice. "I'm not mad, Michael. It's nice to see you, Steve." She wondered how the two men who were vying for her hand could be such good friends.

Danielle took out her cell phone and left the room. Cathy heard her speaking to Henry and asking him about hosting Steve in his home. Although she couldn't hear Henry's reply, she saw by Danielle's smile when she returned that it had been a "yes."

"Good news," Danielle said. "Henry has room for you, Steve. After lunch, I can help you bring your bags over there and introduce you."

Cathy was surprised when Mildred cut in. "You're busy, Danielle. I remember where Henry lives. I can take Steve over."

Cathy had no idea why Mildred was offering to do that, but

then she remembered the look that had passed between her and the widower. Mildred had never married, but there were rumors around Buttercup Bend that she'd had quite a few boyfriends in her time but no one recently.

Steve stood up. "My bags are in Michael's car. I suggested taking my truck, but it's full of ice melt sacks right now."

Michael laughed, reached into his pocket, and handed Steve the keys to his car. "There you go. You can take drive my car if Mildred directs you."

Steve paused. "Before I leave, I want to have a word with Cathy."

"So do I," Michael said.

Cathy's heart jumped again. She knew what was coming and recalled Mildred saying that it was best to confront issues head on instead of avoiding them, so she pushed away her plate. "I'm done eating. I'll come outside and speak with both of you."

Mildred said, "I'm done, too. Mind if I come along?"

"Not at all." Cathy had a thing or two to say to the librarian, as well.

They stood on the front porch. Steve's blond head nearly reached the pot of ivy that hung from the eaves. Michael, around the same height, stood next to him, closer to the door. Mildred plopped down in the wicker rocker that reminded Cathy of the one at Florence's house. "You might want to sit, too," Steve said, gesturing to Cathy.

"I can stand. Thank you." Her heart, still racing, she waited for one of the men to start. Instead, Mildred began the conversation. "I was as surprised as you when Michael and Steve showed up together, Cathy. I was able to grab Michael and make sure that he hadn't told anyone else about our, uh, job here."

Michael said, "I apologize for breaking my promise by telling Steve, but I knew he'd want to come. We've both been worried about you, Cathy."

Steve said, "I'm glad you told me, and I haven't told anyone else. Nancy thinks I've gone to a gardening conference. I was vague enough about it, so she wouldn't do some Googling. It wasn't easy. As you know, Cathy, she's quite persistent when she wants to find out something."

"I told her that I was attending a veterinary conference," Michael said. "She grilled me about it. I hope I didn't slip up."

"Knowing Nancy, she'll find it odd that both of you are going away at the same time and are attending different conferences," Cathy pointed out, "and with me and Mildred gone, she's probably going crazy."

Mildred laughed. "Poor girl. She may be bald by the time we get back." Nancy had a habit of pulling out strands of her hair when she was nervous. "What else did you want to speak with Cathy about?"

Cathy held her breath. She wasn't ready to give either of them an answer. She was relieved when Michael said, "We're just concerned that you and Mildred are taking a risk by investigating Doris Grady's death."

"I happen to be a detective," Cathy said, "and Mildred, as a librarian, is very good at figuring out puzzles."

Mildred added, "It's unlikely we're in danger. If Doris was murdered," she lowered her voice and looked toward the windows in case anyone else was in hearing range, "it was by someone with a gripe against her, not a serial killer."

"Yes, but we know how that goes," Steve said. "If you confront a suspect, they may not appreciate your interference."

"So, you're here as our protectors?"

Michael laughed. "You could say that Cathy, and I may also have a new job."

Mildred got up from her seat. "I think we're all on the same page, so are you ready to meet Henry Harris, Steve?"

Cathy noticed that Mildred's face had reddened, and she didn't think it was from the cold. The librarian seemed eager to visit the retired gardener.

Steve nodded. "Yes. Thank you for introducing us." He walked over to Michael's car and opened the passenger door. "All set, Mildred."

When they were driving away, Michael turned to Cathy. "Fancy a walk? It's quite nice out today."

"We had snow yesterday, but it's gone already."

"It's been a warm winter so far." He stepped off the porch. Cathy followed him. They took the path that led toward the gift shop. "Do you have to get back to work?" he asked.

"I should, not that we've had any customers."

"I promised to check out the shop. I'm sure I'll find something to raise your sales statistics." He smiled, and Cathy's heart jumped again.

As they walked, she asked, "Are you seriously considering working here if Mavis offers you the job?"

Michael's hands were in his pockets. He glanced around. "I am, Cathy. I've always dreamed about working on a farm, and the animals I've seen here are incredible. I'm just sorry I'm taking the position away from Stacy. She seems like a nice woman and a competent veterinarian. Do you know why Mavis is letting her go?"

"She says because of her fees. Did she mention what she would pay you?"

Michael laughed. "That makes sense. I tried to talk her up, but it's less than what I make in Buttercup Bend."

"And you're good with that?"

He took his right hand out of his pocket and brushed back his wavy dark hair. "I told you that I've always wanted to work on a farm. I grew up in the city. Moving to Buttercup Bend was like taking a breath of fresh air, but coming here would be," he took his other hand out of his pocket and waved both hands around, "amazing."

From what Cathy had seen so far of farm life, she didn't share his enthusiasm. She remembered how Doris had left Oaks Landing because of her own lack of interest. "I didn't know you grew up in the city," she said.

He nodded. "I think we both need to know more about one another." He stopped, and Cathy nearly fell into him. He faced her. "If I'm offered the job and decide to take it, I won't leave Buttercup Bend unless you come with me."

"Michael..."

"Don't say anything, Cathy." He took a finger to her lips as if to seal them. "I know you're not ready to give me an answer, but I'm hoping that you won't keep me waiting much longer."

As Cathy tried to think of a reply, knowing she couldn't promise that, Michael resumed walking toward the gift shop.

Cathy unlocked the door and turned on the lights. "Here we are. My undercover job." She used the same term as Jodi.

Michael glanced around. "Cute shop. I think I'll browse your wares."

Cathy laughed. "Go ahead. It's not as if the place is crowded."

While Michael walked around the store, Cathy sat behind the register. She wondered how Steve was making out with Henry and whether Mildred was really interested in him.

"How much is this?" Michael asked, bringing a notepad to the desk. It featured the Oaks Landing Farm's logo of a llama standing by an oak tree.

Cathy checked her price list. "That's only a dollar, Michael."

He reached into his pocket, took out his wallet, and handed her a five.

When she went to ring it up and give him change, he waved it away. "Keep the rest. Consider it a tip."

"I can't. The books won't balance."

He laughed. "Okay. Then let me buy you dinner tonight. I saw a nice place when we were driving up here. Danielle's food is great, but I'd like more privacy for us."

Cathy tried to read the look in his eyes and found her heart flipping again. "That would be nice. Thank you."

"My pleasure. There's something else I want to mention."

She took a deep breath in an attempt to control her palpitations. "Yes?"

He slipped the notepad into his coat pocket. "I don't think Doris was murdered. It's nice of you and Mildred to come out here to help Danielle, but I doubt you'll find anything. As a veterinarian, I'm used to facts and figures. In this case, there's no evidence of foul play. Maybe you want to consider leaving sooner, coming back with me at the end of the week. Danielle may be upset, but she has to face reality. I didn't want to tell her that or say anything to Mildred, but I think you two are on a wild goose chase."

Part of Cathy agreed with him and yet she felt an undercurrent in the family. Her instincts hadn't been wrong in the past. "You don't know about the note Mildred found in Doris' old room. She was worried about Mavis thinking she was trying to get Chris back. They were together before Chris met Doris, and they're seeing one another now that she's dead."

Michael shook his head. "Mavis doesn't strike me as a killer. I wouldn't put much weight into that note. Where did Mildred find it?"

"In Doris' drawer."

"Was it a copy?"

"I don't know. It looked like it was unfinished. Maybe she thought of giving it to Mavis and then changed her mind."

"Is Mavis the only suspect you have? Who does Danielle think killed her mother?"

"She won't say. The only other person Mildred and I suspect is Jodi. She's a young farmhand who took a leave of absence after Doris died. She was dining with the family that night, but a month before, her cat was killed when Doris hit it with her car. It was an accident, but Danielle accused Jodi of seeking revenge for it. She apologized afterwards, but Jodi hasn't spoken to her since and is on leave now. Danielle says that Mavis may evict her from her house on the farm if she doesn't come back to work soon."

"Wow!" Michael's eyes widened behind his glasses. "It sounds as though Danielle can't accept her mother's death. I don't see Jodi killing Doris because her cat was killed by her accidentally."

"People have killed for less, Michael."

He shook his head. "You may be right, Cathy, but I still think Doris had a simple heart attack."

"You might be right, but I have a feeling you aren't. There's one other thing that happened the first night I was here. Betty, Doris' mother, told me something. Have you met her?"

"No, but Danielle told me she has a weird case of dementia where she thinks she's various famous people. I wouldn't believe anything she says."

"But what if there's some truth in it? She said that a woman killed Doris and that a man helped her. The woman has to be Mavis, and the man would either be Chris or Dylan."

"You're reaching, Cathy. If anyone killed Doris, there would've been more substantial clues than a mentally ill woman's words. Think about joining me when I go back to Buttercup Bend. Mavis said she'll give me my answer about the job before then." He walked to the door. "I better let you get back to work. I'll see you at the house later and will tell Danielle we won't be at dinner tonight."

CHAPTER TWENTY-TWO

After Michael left, Cathy only had one other customer, Steve. Mildred wasn't with him. "Hi, Cat."

"Hi, Steve. How did things turn out with Henry, and where's Mildred?"

"Henry's a great guy. We hit it off right away. He had no problem about my staying with him a few days. I think he's lonely. I told Mildred I'd walk back because I wanted to speak with you alone."

Cathy's heart, which had settled down, began to race again at the sight of him, his blond hair blown back by the wind. "What did you want to tell me?"

He walked up to the register. "I'm worried that you and Mildred, despite your good intentions, are off track this time. When Michael told me you came here to investigate a murder, I was concerned for your safety. But when I found out that Doris Grady's death was termed a heart attack and I met the family, I began to see that you may have come for no reason. I think you should go back with us on the weekend."

Cathy couldn't believe that Steve felt the same way as Michael because she always thought of him as more open-minded with the same type of good instincts as she had.

She was about to relate all the information she shared with Michael in the hope of convincing Steve she had a good reason to come to Oaks Landing besides avoiding giving him and Michael an answer to their proposals, when her cell phone buzzed. Glancing at the screen, she saw it was Danielle calling.

"It's Danielle, Steve." She put the phone on speaker. "Hi, Danielle."

"Hi, Cathy. Come back to the house now and bring Steve with you if he's there." She sounded excited.

"What's going on?"

"You'll see." Danielle ended the call before Cathy could ask any further questions.

"I wonder what that's about?" Steve said as they hurried back to the house where they saw flashing lights and a police car.

Danielle ran out to greet them. Despite the presence of two officers, she didn't seem upset. "I was right, Cathy," she exclaimed. "Mother was murdered."

A policeman Cathy judged to be in his fifties sported a pot belly that fell over his uniform belt. "Who are they?" he asked, glancing at Cathy and Steve.

Danielle made the introductions.

"My partner and I need to talk with both of you. Reilly is inside with the others."

"I'll be happy to answer any questions you have," Steve said, "but I only just got here today."

"Doesn't matter. I still need to question you. Come inside. Mrs. Diaz has given us a room to use upstairs."

As she and Steve followed the policeman into the house,

Cathy was shocked to see Mavis sitting on the couch crying with Chris trying to comfort her. She looked up when they entered but didn't say a word. Chris said, "Cathy, Steve. We're sorry to involve you in this family matter."

Dylan, standing by the couch, said, "I was as surprised as everyone else, but Mavis can turn off those fake tears. Everyone knows how she felt about Doris."

The policeman waved his hand. "Now, now. Be quiet, all of you." He turned to Danielle. "I'd like to speak with you upstairs first, Mrs. Diaz. I know your mother is ill, but I need to question everyone in this house."

"Even Sheri?" Danielle asked, looking toward her daughter who stood, eyes wide, next to Mildred who held her hand.

"I'm afraid so."

"Then I want to be with her."

"Okay. For now, I want you upstairs alone. Ms. Hastings can watch your daughter."

Michael, across the room, said, "Before you question any of us, we'd like to know what this is about. Steve and I just came here today, and Cathy and Mildred weren't here either the day that Mrs. Grady died.

The younger policeman, who Cathy assumed was Reilly, said that some late evidence had been found to indicate that Doris had been murdered. "We're not able to reveal the details at this point, and we're keeping the matter out of the press."

When he was done with his explanation, Reilly said, "Jones, who do you want me to question?"

"Once she's composed, I'd like you to talk with Mrs. Taylor, but wait until I come back downstairs."

Jones nodded. He looked over at Cathy and Steve. "You two might as well have a seat. This may take a few hours."

· · ·

Cathy was one of the last people questioned. When Reilly called her name, she followed him upstairs to the designated room which happened to be Danielle and Dylan's. She'd never been inside that room before, but she saw their wedding photo in a frame above the bed.

"Please sit," Reilly instructed, indicating a chair by the window.

Although she knew she wouldn't be considered a suspect, Cathy was relieved the younger policeman was talking with her instead of Jones who seemed to be playing the tough police officer.

When she was seated, Reilly faced her. "Ms. Hastings, or should I say, Ms. Carter."

Cathy gulped. "You know who I am?"

"I'm a police officer. It wasn't hard. I also know you've recently joined a detective agency in Buttercup Bend. Is that why you're here?"

Cathy knew she should tell the truth. "Yes. Doris, Mrs. Grady, was an old friend of Mildred's. Danielle, Mrs. Diaz, contacted her and asked if she and I would come here to investigate her mother's death."

"Hmm. I see. Do you know why Mrs. Diaz was so certain her mother had been murdered when the cause of death was stated as a heart attack?"

Cathy didn't know how to respond to that. She knew that Jones had already questioned Danielle, but no one had spoken with Mildred yet. "I can't say, Officer. Maybe it was a hunch. Women's intuition."

"A hunch? Okay. Did she offer you any money for your services?"

"No, but I don't see what this has to do with anything." Cathy was starting to think Reilly was actually the bad cop, or maybe both officers were.

"That's for us to decide, Ms. Carter. Did anyone else know you were here on the pretense of working on the farm?"

"Not initially, but Jodi found out."

"Who's Jodi?"

Cathy didn't realize the police weren't aware that Jodi and Henry and also Stacy were at the dinner the night Doris died.

"She's a farmhand. She lives on the farm."

He took out a pad and jotted something down. "We'll need to speak with her, too. I'll tell Jones. We're going to confer after the interviews are done." He shrugged. "That's it for now. You can come down with me." As Cathy rose from the chair, he added, "One last thing. I won't reveal your identity as long as you don't interfere with our investigation. The crime occurred in our jurisdiction, so we're in charge. Got it?"

"Yes." While Cathy agreed, she also knew that if the Oaks Landing police had taken a month to figure out that Doris had been murdered, it was likely they'd take even longer to solve the crime.

When Cathy rejoined the group, Jones took Mildred upstairs for the final questioning. Cathy wished she could talk with her first and warn her that they already knew about them investigating Doris' murder.

Michael walked over to her. "Everything alright?"

She couldn't tell him in front of the others that the cat was out of the bag about her and Mildred, so she just nodded.

"I hope dinner's still on?"

Steve, overhearing Michael, said, "What's this about dinner?"

"I invited Cathy out to that cute place we saw on the drive here. I thought she'd want a break from eating at the farm and now she could use one more than ever."

"I see. Well, I'm sure they won't keep us. We can't be considered suspects," Steve said in a flat voice. Cathy could tell he wasn't happy about her going out with Michael.

Reilly overheard them and said, "You're right. The three of you are free to go and Ms. Hastings, too, as soon as she comes back downstairs and Jones and I confer about the interviews.

A few minutes later, a smiling Mildred returned. Jones took Reilly aside, and they spoke in whispers a few feet away. Cathy only caught a few words, "Medication. Murder. Evidence." When they finished, Jones asked for everyone's attention. "Thank you for cooperating. The information you've provided will be helpful to us in solving the crime. Please refrain from traveling anywhere in the next few days, and don't talk with the press if anything is leaked about this."

Danielle said, "Thank you, Officers. Please keep us posted. If there's anything else you need, don't hesitate to call." She had her arm on Sheri who seemed about to cry.

Mavis, who'd composed herself, said, "I think we all want this solved as quickly as possible." Danielle gave her an angry look. Cathy knew she was still upset that Mavis had ignored her suspicions about Doris' death.

Jones paused. "Actually, we do need one more thing, Mrs. Diaz. We'd like to talk with Ms. Johnson, Ms. Savella, and Mr. Harris."

Cathy realized that Mildred must've mentioned that Stacy and Henry were at the house that night because she'd only told Reilly about Jodi.

"I can call them," Danielle offered. "Jodi lives on the farm, but she won't come here." She looked over at Chris. "Can you please bring the officers to Jodi's house?"

Chris stood up from his place by Mavis. "Sure. I can also take them to Henry's place and the animal hospital. I think Stacy's working there today."

"Thank you." Danielle took out her cell phone to make the calls, but Jones waved his hand. "Don't warn them. I'd rather catch them by surprise. If they're not there, we can come back."

After the policemen left, following Chris in their patrol car, Danielle said, "I'm going to take Sheri out. I think she needs fresh air."

Dylan said, "That's a good idea. I'll take her if you have other things to do. Since Lulu got a clean bill of health, thanks to Michael and Stacy," he nodded in Michael's direction, "I could take Sheri over to see her."

"Why don't I take her to Lulu? I have to go back to the gift shop, anyway," Cathy pointed out. Mavis hadn't mentioned Lulu's pregnancy because she still had to test her.

"The gift shop is closed. The officers asked me not to let anybody else on the farm until this matter is solved," Danielle explained.

"What if I take Sheri?" Mildred offered. "She seems to enjoy my company."

Sheri, as if confirming Mildred's words, smiled and began jumping up and down. "Oh, please, Mommy. I want to go with Millie."

Millie? Cathy wondered if Danielle's daughter had formed an attachment with Mildred because she wasn't allowed to spend time with her own grandmother.

Danielle agreed, took out her car keys, and handed them to Mildred. "You can take my car. I'll be here all day."

The rest of the family went in their own directions except for Danielle who joined Cathy, Michael, and Steve in the living room. "I apologize again for this disruption. I don't know if you're at liberty to say what the officers discussed with you, but

I thought you should know what Officer Jones explained to me about Doris' death."

Cathy was curious. "He didn't say anything to me. It seemed that they wanted to keep that information private."

Danielle nodded. "It wasn't easy to get it out of him, but I think he felt somewhat embarrassed that he didn't listen to me in the first place when I insisted my mother didn't have a heart attack."

Cathy thought Mavis felt that way, too, although Dylan might've been right that her tears were false, hiding her guilt.

"So, what was that late clue that led them to believe Doris was murdered?" Michael asked.

"And how was she killed?" Steve wanted to know.

Danielle looked from one man to the other. She was seated across from them in the chair by the fireplace. They were on the couch on either side of Cathy.

"It was poison, as I suspected. A quick-acting one that wasn't easy to trace."

"How did they find it after a month?" Steve asked.

"The autopsy hadn't shown it, but I requested that the food and drink that Doris consumed that night be checked. They didn't feel it was necessary, but they collected the items. Because they weren't prioritizing the matter and the lab was backed up, they didn't get to it until now." She took a breath. "I started to think they'd forgotten all about it, so I contacted them about a week ago to check and remind them. Dylan said I was crazy to keep pestering them, but I'm glad I did. I just had this feeling..."

Cathy was right. The reason Danielle was convinced her mother had been murdered was based on a hunch that turned out to be correct.

Danielle continued. "When they came today, I was shocked. I hadn't thought my call had made any difference and, even if it had, I thought they'd found nothing and wouldn't even bother letting me know."

"What type of poison did they find?" Michael asked. Cathy knew he was interested in the scientific side of things.

Danielle met his eyes. "That's what's strange. The officer said it was xylazine, a type of medication used on animals to sedate down."

CHAPTER TWENTY-THREE

"Then it could be Stacy," Cathy said. "She was there that night, and she has access to veterinary medicine."

Michael said, "Don't jump to conclusions, Cathy." He looked back at Danielle. "Do you keep any veterinary medicine on the farm?"

"Yes. Officer Jones asked me that, too. Chris has a supply stored in the barn near his house. It's for emergencies. I'm sure the police will check it out."

"Does everyone on the farm know where these medicines are?" Steve asked.

She nodded. "Yes. Henry also knew. He uses some of the tools in that barn, so we thought he should know what else was stored there."

Cathy asked, "Since you had this emergency medicine, who besides Stacy would be able to administer it properly?"

"Stacy showed me, Mavis, and Chris the medicine and explained what it was used for and how to give it. All three of us have also taken veterinary first-aid classes." Danielle stood up. "Excuse me, but I should go check on my grandmother. Although she was lucid when the police questioned her, I'm afraid it upset her."

Cathy had wondered how Betty took the questioning. "Did they allow you to stay while they spoke with her?"

"I insisted, so they did. They made an exception because of her condition."

Michael asked, "Did she say anything?"

"That's the strange part. She acted as if Doris was still alive. As I mentioned, her issues began before my mother died, but they worsened afterwards."

"I can understand that," Cathy said. "It must've been awful for her to witness her daughter's death."

Danielle nodded. "Let me go check on her. The three of you can do whatever you'd like." She glanced at Cathy. "I understand you're going to eat out tonight with Michael. I'm not in the mood to make a big dinner so that helps. I'll throw something together." She turned to Steve. "Don't worry. You're still welcome to join us."

Steve said, "Thanks, anyway, but I think I'll grab something out, too."

After Danielle went upstairs, Cathy, feeling sorry that he would be dining alone, said, "Why don't you come with us, Steve?"

She expected him to turn down the invitation, especially when Michael gave her a glare for asking. Instead, he smiled. "Thanks, Cat. I'll take you up on that."

Michael said sarcastically, "Well, if you're coming, Steve, why don't we invite Mildred, too? Make it a party. The only one missing will be Nancy."

It was at that moment that the doorbell rang. Cathy thought it might be Chris who forgot his key and was returning after bringing Reilly and Jones to see Jodi, Henry, and Stacy.

But she should've known that would've taken longer. As she went to answer it, she was shocked to see Nancy standing on the doorstep, hands on her hips, her eyes blazing, her red hair in disarray.

Michael said, "Speak of the devil."

"Nancy! How did you?" Cathy couldn't believe her eyes.

Her friend marched in. "How did I what? Find out you were here with Michael and Steve? What kind of incompetent detective do you think I am?"

Nancy turned and stared at Michael. "Sorry to interrupt your conversation about me, but I didn't come all this way to be ignored. I want answers, and I want them now."

Cathy shrank back. When Nancy was in this mood, she was a force to be reckoned with. "I'm sorry, Nance. I didn't invite Michael and Steve. Mildred called them. Actually, she called Michael, and Steve tagged along."

That didn't seem to appease her. "Why didn't you tell me about this?" she asked Michael. "I thought we were friends, but it seems you're best buddies with the man who wants your girl."

Michael didn't lose his cool. "Calm down, Nancy. I promised Mildred not to tell anyone, but Steve and I have been concerned about Cathy since New Year's. When I found out where she was, I thought he should know."

Nancy threw up her hands. "Well, that's just peachy. Where is Mildred? It looks like she's the one I should be angry with."

"It's not her fault, Nancy. She didn't want to get you involved. She's with Sheri but should be back soon." After Cathy said that she realized Nancy didn't know Sheri. She quickly explained who the little girl was.

"You'll have to fill me in on who else is on this farm and what is going on. I saw a patrol car when I drove by, and I had the hardest time convincing the two policemen to let me through. There was another guy with them. When I said I was a friend of yours, he told them to let me go."

"I'm glad Chris helped," Danielle said, entering the room. "I'm Danielle. I'll be happy to fill you in on everything."

When Danielle had finished filling in Nancy about everyone and everything at Oaks Landing, she asked if she had any questions. "I have dozens, but the most pressing one is who are those three adorable kitties I met by the barn when I arrived? They helped me cool down."

Cathy laughed to herself, wondering how it was possible Nancy could've been angrier before she'd seen Cricket, Rascal, and Piper.

"They're our farm's ambassadors, official greeters. I'm glad they calmed you. Do you have cats?"

Cathy wasn't surprised when Nancy told Danielle about Hobo. She gushed about him, her whole face lighting up and even showed her his photos on her phone. "I'm only sorry I had to leave him, but I know Florence will take great care of him."

"Florence? You left Hobo with Gran?" Cathy was worried that Nancy's cat wouldn't get along with her kittens.

Nancy guessed her concern. "Don't worry. Florence promised she'd keep Hobo away from Harry and Hermione or only let him near them when she's around, but they're six months old already and should be able to handle a guest. Hobo's also used to being around cats since he was in Rainbow Rescues so long."

That was a good point. Cathy recalled how Nancy adopted Hobo last spring from Rainbow Rescues when she finally convinced her it was time to give another cat a home after she'd lost her Popeye.

"I still don't know how you found out where I am."

Nancy smiled. "Deductive reasoning, Cat, with a little help from your grandmother and her bedroom talk with Howard."

"Nancy, no!" Cathy was shocked. "Don't tell me you stooped that low."

"Just like a reporter, a detective never reveals her sources." She winked.

A short time later, Chris returned without the policemen. Danielle introduced him to Nancy, making the excuse that she'd come to lend a hand to Cathy and Mildred. When he raised an eyebrow as if not believing that story, Nancy said, "The truth is that Cathy and I are detectives from Buttercup Bend. She came here with Mildred after Danielle asked them for help investigating Doris' death."

Cathy, instead of being mad that Nancy revealed her identity and reason for coming to Oaks Landing, was relieved. She didn't like being dishonest, and it was beginning to make her anxious.

"Well, I hope you can help us," Chris said. "I don't have much faith in those policemen."

"Did they check the barn for the veterinary medicine?" Danielle asked.

"Yep, but nothing seemed out of place. I think they're focusing on Stacy."

"That's crazy," Michael said.

Cathy again felt a sting of jealousy that he was so insistent that Stacy was innocent.

Chris said, "I know, but they brought her down to the station for further questioning."

It was then that Mildred came back with Sheri and talk about the police and Doris' murder ceased.

Cathy was glad to see that Sheri was smiling. Mildred had

done wonders to calm the young girl's fears. "We had so much fun," Sheri said. "Millie took me to see Lulu and then she asked me to show her around the farm and introduce her to the other animals. We just finished playing with the barn cats."

Danielle smiled. "Thanks so much, Mildred." She turned to her daughter. "Would you like to help me cook dinner tonight, Sheri?"

The girl's smile widened. "Yes, Mommy!" She skipped away with Danielle toward the kitchen.

Mildred looked at Nancy. "I see you've joined us, Miss Meyers."

"You're very astute for an amateur detective, Ms. Hastings." Nancy said it with an angry tone, but Cathy noticed most of the fight had gone out of her.

Before Nancy could say anything else, Cathy said, "Mildred, we're all going to dinner. Michael and Steve know a nice place nearby. We can talk about everything then."

CHAPTER TWENTY-FOUR

A statue of a cow stood outside the Farmer in the Deli restaurant. Inside, the square tables were covered with red and white checked tablecloths. A waitress wearing a white apron over a red and white dress brought them their menus and glasses of water.

"This is nice," Cathy said, glancing out the wide windows that looked over a covered patio that seated guests during nice weather. It reminded her of the Kafe in Buttercup Bend, although there were no Swedish items on the menu.

"I was worried it wouldn't be fancy enough for you," Michael said, but I Googled some reviews, and it has great ratings. People highly recommend the Steer Burger. That's what I'm ordering."

"I'd rather have the Fried Feathered Chicken," Steve said.

Mildred laughed. "That sounds funny, but I think I'll order that, too. What about you, Cathy, and Nancy?"

Cathy was having a tough time deciding, and Nancy was, too. She finally put down her menu. "I think I'll have the Porky

Pig. It's described as a shredded pork sandwich with barbecue sauce and a side of coleslaw." She looked over at Nancy who was still browsing her menu. Nancy had a habit of sampling Cathy's food when they ate out.

The waitress returned to the table to take their orders. "Do you need another minute?" she asked, glancing at Nancy. Nancy closed her menu. "No. I'll have the Ranch Platter, please." Cathy smiled to herself, realizing her friend had chosen a mix of all three dishes.

"Anything to drink?"

Cathy and Mildred said that water was fine, but Nancy asked for a spritzer. Michael and Steve wanted beers.

"Be right back." The waitress gathered their menus and walked to the kitchen to put in their orders.

When she was gone, Nancy said, "Now that I'm here, I'd like to propose a plan to solve Doris Grady's murder."

Cathy put her finger to her lips. "Speak lower, Nancy." There were several people seated at tables in their vicinity. Nancy let her voice drop. "Sorry, but I think you and Mildred have gone about this the wrong way."

Mildred, taking offense, said, "If you think so, Nancy, what do you suggest we do?"

Before she could answer, the waitress came back with a tray of their drinks. "Your food will be out momentarily," she said and stepped away again.

Michael poured his glass full of beer and took a swig, then said, "I think I speak for me and Steve when I say that we believe you ladies should leave the investigating up to the police. It's in their hands now. You can come back to Buttercup Bend with us."

Cathy said, "That makes sense, but were you offered the job here?"

"I don't know, and it doesn't matter. Mavis probably hasn't had a chance to talk with anyone else, and it's likely she won't now that the farm is closed to visitors. I'm sure I'll hear from her once this is all over."

"But weren't we supposed to stay around?" Steve asked.

"No," Mildred said. "We're in the clear. We can do whatever we want." She glanced at Nancy, "but I'd like to hear what Nancy has in mind."

Nancy sipped her water through a straw, swallowed, and then said, "Thank you, Mildred." Cathy was glad they were on good terms again. Nancy looked around the table and, in a whisper, said, "If we want to find out who done it, we need to recreate the dinner with everyone attending who was there that night."

Cathy laughed. "You read too much Agatha Christie, Nancy."

"I'm serious, Cat. I think this will work."

Mildred said, "It's not a bad idea, and I'm sure Danielle will go for it, but it's a matter of who else will agree to attend. Jodi has refused to come to the house since it happened, and Stacy might also be hesitant to come since she's the police's main suspect right now."

"What about Mavis?" Cathy asked. "She did a complete turnaround when the police notified her that her sister had been murdered, but Mildred and I have considered her a suspect since she found Doris' note that indicated Mavis was worried Doris had plans to get Chris back."

"Wait a minute. What note?" Nancy asked, and Cathy forgot that no one had told her about what Mildred found in Doris' room and the relationship between Chris and Mavis. She explained quickly.

Steve said, "I think it's worth a try, but none of us were

there that night. What do we do if we're able to get them all to reenact the scene of the crime?"

"We observe and ask questions," Nancy replied. "We'll also need a stand-in for Doris. Mildred is the obvious candidate for that." She looked across the table at her.

Mildred said, "I'm game, as long as no one kills me."

CHAPTER TWENTY-FIVE

Michael asked Steve if he wanted to be dropped off at Henry's place on the way back to the farm. "That would be good," he said. "Henry gave me a duplicate key in case he wasn't home, but I gather he doesn't go out much. Nice fellow."

"He seemed nice to us, too," Cathy said, "but he's still a suspect."

"I don't think he's involved," Mildred said.

Nancy looked over at her. "What makes you so certain? The quietest and most pleasant people often turn out to be the killers."

"In mystery novels," Cathy pointed out.

"In real life, too." Nancy kept her gaze on Mildred. "Is this man an older guy? I notice you're blushing. Are you interested in him?"

Mildred's cheeks grew red. She lowered her eyes. "I, uh, might be, but that isn't influencing my judgement."

"Sure it isn't." Nancy laughed. "I've said it before, Cathy, these Buttercup Bend seniors see more action than us."

"That may be both of your faults," Michael said. "I see you worried more about Hobo than Brian when you came here."

For once, Nancy had no reply to that. Cathy knew that, since she'd been dating the assistant deputy, their relationship had been platonic because Nancy insisted that it might ruin their friendship.

"I'll never understand women," Steve said as Michael pulled up to Henry's house. As if expecting him, the old man stood by the open door. A light from a bulb near the entrance shone outside in the winter darkness. Cathy thought he may have seen their car. As Steve got out, Henry opened the door and stepped outside. Waving to him, he said, "Hey, there. I see you're with your friends. They can come in if they'd like."

Michael spoke out of the open window. "Thank him but tell him we can't."

Nancy said, "Speak for yourself. I haven't met him, and I'm sure Mildred would like an opportunity to see him again."

Cathy laughed. "She's right, Michael. We don't have to stay long."

As they all got out of the car to join Steve and Henry, Cathy noticed Mildred fluffing back her white hair.

Nancy said, "Don't worry. You look beautiful, Mildred. Henry won't be able to resist you." Cathy nudged her. "Leave Mildred alone, Nancy."

They stepped inside Henry's house. He invited them to sit in the living room while he made tea or coffee. "What would everyone like?"

Michael said, "We just had dinner, and we really can't stay, but thank you, anyway."

Nancy said, "Nice to meet you. I'm Nancy Meyers, their friend from Buttercup Bend." She held out her hand.

Instead of shaking it, Henry leaned down and kissed it in the European way of greeting. "My pleasure. I'm Henry Harris, a gardener at Oaks Landing Farm. I'm retiring next week, and I'm hoping that Mr. Jefferson will take my place." He glanced at Steve.

"Thanks, Henry, but Mavis tells me there's a lengthy list of candidates vying for that job. And please call me Steve. I'll be living with you here for a few days, after all."

Henry smiled, the small crow's feet by his eyes appearing. Glancing at Mildred, he said, "So nice to see you again, Mrs. Hastings."

Cathy held in a laugh when Mildred batted her eyelashes and said, "I feel the same, but it's Miss Hastings, Mildred to you."

On the way back to the farm, Cathy said, "You didn't have to rush us out of there, Michael."

"There was no reason to hang around."

Nancy said, "From what I saw, Henry is a gentleman. I've marked him off our suspect list."

Cathy was surprised. "I thought you were the one who said that most murders are committed by quiet people who seem nice."

"I know, but I can tell he truly is a great guy." She glanced over at Mildred next to her in the back seat. "I think he's going to ask you out, Mildred, or you could make the first move."

Mildred was looking out the window. Without turning to face Nancy, she said. "I don't think it would work out, as much as I'm interested. I'll be going back to Buttercup Bend soon, and Henry's house is here."

"So what?" Nancy said. "It's really not much of a distance,

and he said he's retiring. Maybe you can convince him to move. He seems all alone here."

Michael said, "Stop trying to match make them, Nancy."

Cathy knew that was her friend's favorite activity.

Mildred changed the subject. "Now that you've joined us, Nancy, where will you stay? Steve's with Henry, and Michael is at Chris' place."

"That's a good question. I haven't booked a room nearby. I was hoping I could stay at the house."

"I have an idea." Cathy recalled how Nancy had roomed with her in the past at Gran's house. "There's a queen bed in my room. We can be roommates."

"That's perfect." Nancy's voice held a hint of excitement. "We'll be able to confer about the murder and have slumber parties."

Cathy rolled her eyes, but Nancy couldn't see them from the back seat. "I think we're too old for that, Nance." Cathy was glad Nancy had given up pushing Mildred into a romance with Henry, but she also didn't want to encourage her about having another slumber party where they'd stay up all night eating popcorn and watching murder movies. The last time they'd had such a party, last spring, Nancy had also persuaded her to play a game in which they rated three bachelors in Buttercup Bend. The results were inaccurate and, she felt, unfair. It was something she dreaded participating in again.

"Sometimes you're no fun, Cathy."

"And sometimes you're immature," Cathy retaliated.

"Hey, girls," Michael said, "I'm dropping you off at the house and then driving back to Chris' place. He also gave me a spare key."

"You better hope Mavis doesn't spend the night," Cathy warned him.

Michael smiled. "Maybe Chris will spend it with her at her

place. It doesn't matter to me. I just need a place to sleep and give all of this some thought. Mavis may be my new boss, so I don't care what she does."

Cathy wondered if Michael's attitude had something to do with Steve and the others joining them for dinner that night. She knew he'd initially invited her and probably wanted to speak with her alone. As he pulled up at the house, she waited until everyone got out. "I'll be right in," she told Mildred and Nancy. "You go ahead." She handed Mildred the spare key Danielle had given her.

When they were alone, Cathy turned to Michael. "I'm sorry that we ended up with a group tonight. I know you seemed to want to dine with me alone."

His face was unreadable as he shrugged. "Oh, well. There's always tomorrow night." Unexpectedly, he reached over and took her hand. "Cathy, I've been very patient, and I want to give you as much time as you need, but I can't wait forever."

Cathy gulped. "I know. I'm sorry." She thought of Stacy and the attraction she thought she saw between them.

"You should also know," he continued, his dark eyes looking into hers, "not only did I find out that you were investigating a murder here with Mildred, but Steve told me about his proposal. If you choose him, I'll be hurt but not angry. He's a good guy."

"I'm glad you feel that way," Cathy said. It sounded hollow to her ears. "I don't know why I'm having this problem. I care for both of you."

"That may be the issue," Michael said. "You care for us but don't love either one." With that, he let her hand go and put it back on the steering wheel. Facing toward the road, he said, "Please get out, Cathy. I'm going to Chris' house now. I'll see you tomorrow."

CHAPTER TWENTY-SIX

Mildred and Nancy were in the living room speaking with Danielle and Mavis when Cathy came in. "We're all set," Nancy said. "Danielle thinks it's a great idea for us to room together."

Cathy was secretly hoping there'd be another room available since Nancy liked to stay up much later than she did and snored in her sleep, even though she denied it.

"Great!" she replied.

"You don't sound so happy about that," Nancy noted.

"I am." Cathy changed the subject "Did you tell Danielle yet about your idea for finding out who killed her mother?"

"What idea is that?" Danielle asked.

Nancy smiled. "You stage a reenactment of the dinner and invite everyone who was there that night. I think it's genius."

Mavis said, "It sounds crazy to me. First of all, Jodi won't come. Secondly, this is in the hands of the police now."

Danielle turned toward her aunt. They were seated next to one another on the couch. "I like the idea. Since Jodi's been questioned by the police, maybe she'll agree to come here to prove she's innocent. I doubt the police are working too hard on this case. They've released Stacy, but they told me they're going over everything and might interview people again, but at the rate they seem to move, it doesn't sound promising."

Mildred said. "Nancy thinks I should stand in for Doris. I don't mind doing that if it helps us solve her murder."

Mavis gave a short laugh. "All it will do is antagonize people, but I'll play along if you want to try it. I have nothing to fear because I'm innocent."

Cathy recalled the letter Mildred found in Doris' room and wondered if that was true.

Nancy clapped her hands lightly. "Then it's decided. When can we do it?"

Danielle looked at Mavis. "The police are still advising us not to let anyone in for hikes or farm visits. Luckily, it's winter, and we don't get crowds, but I think we should do this as soon as possible especially since Mildred and Cathy are only here a brief time more."

Mavis surprised Cathy by saying, "I agree. Betty won't be around very long either."

It was then that Cathy noticed the redness around Danielle's eyes. "Did Dylan find a place for your grandmother?" she asked.

Danielle nodded. "Yes. He's made all the arrangements. She'll be going next week."

Nancy said, "How about Thursday then? That gives you a chance to invite people and shop for whatever dinner you were serving that night."

"If we must do this, I wish we could get it over with tomorrow," Mavis said. Cathy noticed her hands were clasped in her lap, her long red nails biting into her palms.

"That's not possible," Danielle told her, "but we could move it up to Wednesday."

"Sounds good," Nancy said. "If you need any help, let me know."

Danielle stood up. "I can manage everything, Nancy. You, Cathy, and Mildred are still our guests. Now I'd like to call it a night. Dylan's upstairs putting Sheri to bed. I want to look in on them and my grandmother."

As she stood up, Mavis also rose. "I'm going to my room, too. Chris is with Michael tonight, so his place is off limits to me." She gave another short laugh.

Mildred, yawning, said, "I don't know about Cathy and Nancy, but I'm pooped. This has been some day." She looked at Danielle. "Your daughter is sweet, but she has plenty of energy and knocked me out."

"Thank you again for watching her, Mildred."

As Danielle and Mavis headed upstairs, Nancy said, "We should also go to our rooms." She glanced at Mildred. "I'd like to see that letter that Cathy mentioned you found and be introduced to the mysterious Betty."

Mildred showed Nancy the letter that Doris left in her drawer. After reading it a few times to herself, Nancy said, "I don't think this implicates Mavis. How do we even know Doris wrote this? It may not even be her handwriting."

"It was stuck under the drawer in her room."

Nancy rolled her eyes at Cathy. "It could've been planted. But even if Doris wrote this, it doesn't mean that her sister killed her."

Mildred, sitting on the bed, said, "Why don't you two ladies go next door and discuss this further? I'm very tired."

"Sure. I'll keep the letter with me. C'mon, Cathy. Let's go to our room."

Cathy wasn't looking forward to spending a night

discussing the suspects and the murder. She was also tired from her second day at Oaks Landing, but she followed Nancy to the room next door.

"Cute room," Nancy said. "I should go to my car and move my suitcase up here."

Danielle appeared in the doorway. "That won't be necessary. I already asked Dylan to do that. May I have the keys?"

"Thanks," Nancy said, taking them from her purse and handing them to her.

"He'll be up in a moment. Sheri's asleep, but he was just finishing tucking her in. I'll go give these to him."

When Danielle left, Cathy was relieved that Nancy, who'd left Doris' letter on the bureau, had decided to drop the discussion about it. "Can I meet Betty now?" she asked.

Cathy explained Betty's condition and told her that it wasn't a good idea. "Maybe if you ask Danielle or Dylan to introduce you, but you should keep it brief. They give her sedatives to sleep now, so she won't go walking the halls at night." She filled Nancy in about what happened the previous night.

Nancy's eyes widened. "Do you think she had a point about the killer being a woman working with a man?"

"She says a lot of crazy things, Nancy. It's hard to know what's true and what isn't."

Dylan arrived then, rolling Nancy's bag into the room. "Here you go, Nancy. If you need anything else, let me know."

"Thank you. Would it be possible for me to meet Danielle's grandmother?"

He took a breath, and Cathy didn't know whether it was from the exhaustion of lugging the suitcase upstairs or whether he was reacting to Nancy's request. "I'm sorry, but that's not a good idea. She's resting, and I'd rather not wake her."

Nancy nodded. "I understand. Thank you again for bringing up my bags."

After Dylan left, Nancy turned to Cathy. "Do you know where Betty's room is? You said you went with Danielle yesterday when she brought food to her."

Cathy recalled the incident with the tray and how Betty had insisted she wanted Pie, who turned out to be a horse in a movie. "Dylan told us not to go, Nancy."

Nancy squared her shoulders and looked Cathy in the eyes. "Are you a detective, or what? This woman may be the key to this mystery."

Cathy hated the way she felt that she had no choice but to give in to her friend's demands. "Okay, but only for a short time, and if she's sleeping, we leave her alone. Got it?"

"We'll see." Nancy walked to the door.

Cathy led Nancy to the room at the end of the hall. When they reached the door, they heard Betty talking to someone inside. "What big eyes you have, Grandma, and what big ears."

"Sounds like she's up," Nancy said. "and she thinks she's Little Red Riding Hood this morning."

Cathy tapped lightly on the door. "Betty, may we come in?"

A voice that sounded much younger than Betty, said, "Are you wolves?"

Cathy turned to Nancy. "You're right. She's having an episode. We better leave her alone."

"No." Nancy walked in front of Cathy. "No, Red, we're friends of your grandmother. Can we enter?"

Cathy had an impulse to pull Nancy away from the door, but it was too late. At Betty's invitation, Nancy had already turned the knob.

The room was dark, but there was light coming through the thin curtains. Betty sat up in bed. When she saw them, she said, "Where's the wolf? He wants to eat me. He's pretending to be my grandma."

Nancy, playing along, said, "We'll protect you from the wolf. We have a message from your grandmother."

Cathy couldn't believe how Nancy was egging Betty on.

Betty smiled. "Please tell me what she says. I'm on the way to see her."

Nancy walked toward the bed. Cathy stood behind her. She was afraid to witness her friend's interrogation technique on the poor, sick woman.

"Red, your grandmother wants to know about Doris Grady. She's holding a buffet in her honor on Wednesday at her cottage."

At the mention of her daughter's name, Betty looked down. She gripped her blanket. "No. She can't do that."

"Why not?" Nancy asked.

Betty looked up again, and Cathy saw fear in her eyes. She was about to stop Nancy from her questioning, when the old woman said, "because the wolf will dress up like me with a red cape and bring a basket with poison in it. Tell Grandma not to have the party. Please." Betty was begging now, her voice agitated and loud.

"Enough now, Nancy," Cathy warned.

"Listen to your friend." They both turned around to see Dylan in the doorway. He rushed in. "It's okay, Betty. You can go back to sleep. I'll give you another pill. You'll feel better in the morning."

As he approached the bed, Betty shrank back. "I'm not Betty. I'm Little Red Riding Hood. Leave me alone. You're a friend of the wolf."

Danielle, alerted by the commotion, came into the room. "What's going on here?"

"Your grandmother is having another episode," Dylan explained. "It was triggered by our guests."

Nancy said, "We didn't trigger anything. She was talking to the wolf in Little Red Riding Hood when we knocked on her door.

Danielle shook her head. "You should've asked me to introduce you, Nancy. Now you've got her all upset."

Betty began to cry. Sniffing, she said, in her own voice, "I'm sorry. Did I say anything bad?"

Danielle went to the bed and hugged her. "It's okay, Grammy. I'll stay here with you until you fall asleep." She turned to Dylan. "No more sleeping pills. They make her worse."

Dylan sighed. "I'm sure she has a way of not taking them, but whatever you say. I'm glad I found a place for her. Then we can get a peaceful night's sleep." With that, he walked out of the room, passing Cathy and Nancy.

"We should leave," Cathy told Nancy as Danielle took a chair by Betty's bed.

Back in their room, Nancy said, "I think we found important clues."

"What clues?" Cathy didn't understand a thing that Betty had said.

Nancy sat on the bed and patted a spot next to her. "I'll take this side tonight if it's okay."

Cathy joined her. "It's fine, but what were you saying about clues?"

Nancy smiled. "The wolf represents one of the suspects. Betty didn't want the buffet to be held because that person would pretend to be her and bring the poison. Now we have to figure out who she meant. Then there's Dylan." She paused, looked at Cathy, and said, "She said he was a friend of the wolf. That means she sees him as a villain. He could be the one she told you was working with a woman, but I don't think it's Danielle. That leaves Mavis, Jodi, or Stacy."

"Dylan wouldn't work with any of them, Nancy. He doesn't get along at all with Mavis. We already ruled Jodi and Stacy out, and no other woman was at that dinner except Danielle."

"It's not Danielle," Nancy said. "and we haven't ruled anyone out, so Jodi and Stacy are still suspects, as is Mavis."

Cathy decided it was best not to argue. She was growing sleepier by the minute. "We can talk about this tomorrow when we've both had some rest."

Nancy glanced at her watch. "Cathy, it's only 11 o'clock. If you want to go to bed, that's fine, but let me ask you one last thing because I'll be up a couple of more hours working on this."

Cathy sighed. "Okay. What do you want to ask me?"

"The poison in the basket. What do you make of it? Betty said the wolf would bring it."

Cathy got up. "I have no idea, Nance. I'm going to use the bathroom and get ready to go to sleep."

Before Cathy closed the bathroom door, Nancy said, "I think Howard made a bad choice in asking you to join our agency. It's obvious that the poison Betty mentioned represents the poison that killed Doris. What we need to do is find out who the wolf is and what he or she brought to the dinner."

CHAPTER TWENTY-SEVEN

The next day, when Cathy woke, Nancy was already up.

"You're up bright and early," she said, "Did you sleep?"

"Not much. I was thinking over everything Betty said when she was acting as Little Red Riding Hood. I also wonder if Danielle has gotten everyone to attend the dinner tomorrow."

Just as Nancy said that, Cathy heard Dylan's loud voice out in the hall. He was talking with Danielle.

"Why didn't you tell me about this last night? Your guests have caused nothing but trouble here, and I won't permit that dinner."

"Dylan, please. Nancy has a promising idea. It's worth a try."

"The only thing worth a try is allowing the police to do their job, not some amateur detectives who don't even live around here."

"If you feel that way, then don't participate. Mavis has

agreed to the dinner. She said she'll talk with my father today. I'm sure Chris will go along with it."

"Of course, he'll go along with it. He does anything you or Mavis asks him. I don't. I have my own mind."

There was quiet then, followed by footsteps going downstairs.

Nancy looked at Cathy. "Whoa! That Latin temper strikes again. I may be right that he's involved in Doris' murder."

"Just because he doesn't want to participate in the reenactment doesn't mean he's involved in the murder," Cathy pointed out.

"Well, we need everyone there." Nancy got out of bed. "I'm taking a shower and getting dressed. You can get ready after me."

"That's fine," Cathy said, falling back against her pillow. "I'm still tired. I might rest a little more."

Nancy was taking clothes out of her suitcase that Cathy noticed hadn't been unpacked. "You do that. Maybe you'll dream about the wolf."

After Nancy and Cathy were dressed, they headed downstairs. The smell of pancakes and syrup drew them to the kitchen. Danielle, Mavis, Chris, and Michael were seated at the table eating breakfast.

"Hi, ladies," Danielle said, "There are plenty of pancakes." She looked toward the platter at the center of the table. "I'll get you some and coffee." She stood up and brought two mugs to them. Cathy and Nancy were invited to sit at two of the four places that were already set with plates and silverware.

Nancy took one of the unoccupied seats, while Cathy ended up next to Michael. As she sat, he turned to her. "Good morning, Cathy." His tone sounded brusque, and he looked away before she could reply. Recalling their previous conversation, she understood why he was acting that way. "Hello, Michael," she replied.

As Danielle poured her coffee, Nancy asked, "Where's Dylan and Sheri?"

"Dylan took Sheri out for breakfast."

Mavis said, "He's upset over this reenactment thing. Poor Sheri. She loves pancakes."

Chris reached over to the platter which was closest to him and added another pancake to his plate. "I'm sure they'll be having pancakes at a diner. I don't understand Dylan. He's making a fuss over nothing. I'm not thrilled about this reenactment, but I don't see the harm in doing it if Danielle and Mavis are okay with it."

Cathy recalled what Dylan said about Chris doing everything his daughter and girlfriend wanted.

Mavis took a sip of her coffee and said, "Steve and Henry are coming soon. We need to see if they'll agree to this." She turned to Chris, "and you're speaking with Jodi today, right?"

"Yes Ma'am!"

Nancy said, "Mind if Cathy and I come along? I haven't met Jodi yet, and I'd like to be the one to fill her in about the reenactment."

Chris shrugged. "That's fine. We can go after breakfast. Are you coming, too?" He directed the question at Mildred.

"No. I think I'll just hang around here for a bit but thank you for asking."

Cathy wondered if the reason Mildred wasn't joining them was because she was waiting for Henry.

"One other thing," Nancy added, "Everyone needs to wear what they wore that night and bring anything they brought."

Mavis laughed. "You think I can remember what I wore last month?"

Chris smothered his pancake in syrup. "Of course you can't. You have such a large wardrobe. I, however, remember exactly what I wore."

"Easy for you," Mavis countered, "Men only keep a few shirts and pants." But Cathy could tell she was teasing him.

"How am I supposed to dress?" Mildred asked. "Does anyone remember what Doris wore that night?"

Danielle knocked over her coffee cup, spilling what remained of the liquid on the tablecloth. "Excuse me. I'm so clumsy," she said, wiping it up. "And I do remember what my mother wore. I remember everything from that night. It haunts me."

The silence that followed that statement was broken by the doorbell.

Danielle was about to answer it when Mavis stopped her. "I'll get it. I don't want you falling over your feet." Although that sounded like an insult to Cathy, she noticed that Mavis said it with a smile.

A few minutes later, Mavis led Steve and Henry into the kitchen. Steve held a bouquet of flowers. Cathy's heart jumped at the sight of them, but they weren't for her. Steve presented them to Danielle. "Henry took me to a flower shop this morning because I wanted to thank you for inviting me to breakfast. He said you used to work there."

"Yes. That was so sweet of you, Steve. Thank you." Danielle took the flowers and put them in a vase which she placed in the center of the table near the pancake platter. "Please have a seat and help yourselves." She nodded to Henry who looked dapper in his plaid shirt. He even wore a bow tie. The place next to Mildred was empty, so he took it. Steve ended up across from Cathy.

Henry said, "Those flowers are from both of us. If it wasn't winter, I would've picked them from my garden. As it turned out, Lisa was at the shop. It made my morning. I think it made Steve's, too." He grinned.

"Who's Lisa?" Mildred asked.

Danielle said, "I used to work with her. I should drop in and say "hi" some time."

"She's quite attractive, and Henry tells me she's single," Steve said, glancing at Cathy who nearly choked on her pancake.

"Are you okay, Cathy?" Henry asked.

She cleared her throat. "I'm fine. How old is this, Lisa?"

Henry smiled. "Around your age, young enough to be my granddaughter."

Cathy noticed that Mildred, who was holding her breath, let it out like a sigh.

"I almost forgot," Henry said, turning to her. "I brought you something from the shop, Mildred." He reached into his coat which he'd draped across his chair and brought out a single red rose.

Mildred's face turned as red as the flower. "Thank you so much. How lovely."

Danielle said, "I have a bud vase. Let me put that in it for you, and you can bring it upstairs to your room."

Nancy changed the subject. "Now that we're all here except for Dylan, Sheri, and Betty, I'd like to fill Steve and Henry in on our plans." She explained about the reenactment and waited for their reactions.

Henry said, "That sounds like a splendid idea. I've read Agatha Christie, so I can see how this may help us get to the bottom of poor Doris' death."

Steve wasn't as pleased with the plan. "It could be danger-ous," he said, spearing a pancake. "Maybe you'd be better to leave this up to the police."

"That's what I told her," Michael said, "but you know Nancy."

Cathy was still thinking about the flower shop girl Steve met that morning and Stacy, the vet, who Michael would see again at tomorrow's dinner.

CHAPTER TWENTY-EIGHT

After breakfast, Cathy and Nancy joined Chris in his truck, and they drove to Jodi's house. Before they left, Henry had invited Mildred to a classic movie. Cathy wondered where that was leading.

"Did you call Jodi and let her know we're coming?" she asked.

Chris nodded, his eyes on the road. "She's expecting me. I didn't mention you two were coming, but I don't think it'll matter. I just hope she agrees to this. Jodi is as stubborn as Mavis and Danielle."

Cathy didn't see Danielle as being stubborn, but she trusted that Chris knew his daughter well.

Nancy said, "Cathy, I think you're in trouble with Michael and Steve. You have competition."

Cathy didn't want to discuss her trouble with men around Chris and hated to admit to her friend that she was worried about it. "Steve and Michael are going back to Buttercup Bend at the end of the week and, hopefully, we will be, too," she pointed out.

"Right, and what will that prove? If I were you, I'd start making up my mind which one you really want."

"Nancy, please. I'm not you." But Cathy remembered what Michael said, that the reason she was taking so long to choose between him and Steve was because she wasn't in love with either of them.

Chris said, "Sorry to cut in, but I was in a similar situation as you, Cathy, with Doris and Mavis. It wasn't easy for me to leave Mavis for Doris. I hated to hurt her."

"Maybe that's your problem," Nancy said. "You're afraid of hurting Steve or Michael."

When Cathy didn't reply, Nancy asked Chris, "Do you regret marrying Doris? That didn't end well."

Chris sighed, his eyes straight ahead on the road. "Doris and I were happy for a long time. My wedding day and the day Danielle was born were the happiest days of my life. I regret none of it and would do it all again. Except this time, I would leave the farm and join Doris in Buttercup Bend."

"What about Mavis?" Cathy asked. She couldn't help but feel that Mavis, as Chris' second choice, would always mean less to him.

He gave a short smile. "I'm very fond of Mavis. But when Doris came back, well..." He realized he was driving too fast around a bend in the road and applied the brakes. Cathy and Nancy jolted forward. "Sorry about that, ladies."

"You were saying?" Nancy prompted him to finish his sentence.

"Nothing. It was a random thought, not worth mentioning."

Cathy realized that the letter Doris wrote before she died had hinted on a truth. Although she wasn't motivated to take up with Chris again, it seemed he was trying to win her back.

They arrived at Jodi's house. Chris parked and then turned to Cathy sitting next to him. "I have a piece of advice for you.

Look past the physical and into your heart. You'll make the right choice if you go with what you find there." He undid his seat belt and got out of his truck.

Jodi stood in the doorway, waiting for them. As they entered the house, Cathy recalled how she felt visiting the dark cabin last time. She had an urge to open the blinds and let the winter sun through. No wonder Jodi was depressed. She was there all alone with the painting of her cat above the fireplace reminding her of her loss.

"Thanks for seeing us," Chris began.

Jodi didn't invite them to sit.

"If you've come again to convince me to speak with Danny, you might as well leave now. The police questioned me and seemed pleased with my answers."

"I'm glad. We all know you're innocent. We never had any doubts."

"Danny did." Jodi faced them. Cathy noticed her eyes were red. Either she hadn't slept well the previous night, been crying, or both.

"For heaven's sake, Jodi." Chris raised his voice, and Cathy was surprised he was losing his cool, something she'd never seen him do so far, unlike Dylan who did it daily for the smallest reasons. "This has gotten old. Danny never meant what she said, and she's truly sorry. But you're so stubborn that you're pining away in this place." He waved his hands around the room. "It's just a matter of time before Mavis kicks you out."

Jodi laughed, but Cathy could tell she didn't find Chris' remarks funny. "You think I care? I'll leave this minute if she asks. Mavis is no better than Danny. She fired Henry and Stacy. It wouldn't surprise me if she was the one who knocked off her mother."

Chris raised his hand and seemed about to slap her when

Nancy stepped in. "Chris, stop. This won't solve anything." Cathy wasn't sure if Chris would've actually hit the girl if Nancy hadn't gotten between them.

Turning to Jodi, Nancy said, "I came up with an idea to solve Doris' murder. Everyone is going along with it except Dylan so far, and I'm hoping you will, too."

"What's your idea?"

Nancy explained about the reenactment. Jodi listened and then said, "Sure. I'm in."

Cathy was shocked. "You're willing to come to the house?"

Jodi nodded. "Yep. I'll be there tomorrow night wearing what I wore to the last one."

CHAPTER TWENTY-NINE

On the drive back, Nancy said, "Now we just have to convince Dylan."

"I'll take care of Dylan," Chris told her.

"What about Stacy?" Cathy asked. "I don't know if Danielle has spoken with her yet."

"I'm sure Stacy will have no objection," Chris said, as they pulled up to the house.

Walking in, they found Danielle alone.

"Where is everyone?" Cathy asked. She was hoping Steve and Michael would be there. She wanted to tell them that she was planning to make her decision shortly because it wasn't fair to continue leading them on.

"Mavis is shopping for tomorrow's dinner," Danielle said. "Dylan called and told me he's bringing Sheri to a play center. Mildred and Henry are at the movies. I think they're grabbing lunch afterwards. Michael said he was going to the animal hospital to tell Stacy about tomorrow's dinner, and Steve said he was visiting some local gardening centers. He may have gone back to the flower shop, too. He seems to have struck up a friendship with that girl Lisa."

Cathy felt as though Danielle had picked up a knife and stabbed her with it.

Chris said, "I also have to head out. Jodi has agreed to come tomorrow night. I'll speak with Dylan later and make sure he does, too."

"Thanks, Chris. Lately, I can't seem to persuade Dylan to do anything." Danielle's tone was wistful. Cathy heard the pain in her voice and knew how difficult it must be for Danielle, her grandmother being sent to a home, her marriage falling apart, her mother's murder still unsolved.

Nancy looked at Cathy. "I guess it's just us then. Let's make the most of the day."

"What do you have in mind?"

Nancy asked Danielle, "Do you mind if we go up and see Betty?"

"She's sleeping. Dylan gave her another pill against my wishes, but it's for the best. I don't think you should disturb her."

"She said some things yesterday that might be useful to us in finding out who killed your mother," Nancy pointed out.

"What things?"

"Do you know anyone who may have worn a red cape or coat and brought along something resembling a basket to the dinner?"

Cathy didn't expect Danielle to answer Nancy's crazy question, but, after considering it, Danielle said, "I don't know about the basket, but Stacy wore a red cape."

Nancy's eyes lit up. "Bingo. Make sure she wears that cape tomorrow."

As Danielle raised her eyebrows in puzzlement, there was a sound by the stairs. "Is anybody home?" Betty called.

Danielle rushed from the room. Cathy and Nancy followed her.

"Grammy, what are you doing out of bed?"

Betty rubbed her eyes. "I couldn't sleep. I had a strange dream. It woke me up."

Cathy noticed Betty hadn't changed into another personality.

"What did you dream, Gram?"

Betty shook her head. "I can't remember now, but Doris was in it." Tears formed in her eyes. "I miss her so much."

Danielle walked over to her grandmother and gave her a hug. "I do, too."

Cathy was touched by their show of emotion. She wondered how Betty would hold up during the reenactment.

The doorbell rang.

"I'll get it," Nancy said, since Danielle and Betty were still embracing.

Cathy watched as Dylan and Sheri came in, the two police officers who'd been at the house the day before stood behind them.

"They asked me to ring," Dylan said.

Sheri ran to Danielle. "We went to the police station, Mommy. I got to sit in the policeman's chair."

Officer Jones stepped forward. "We've been informed that there's going to be a reenactment of Doris Grady's murder tomorrow night at this residence. Is that correct?" He looked at Danielle who'd released her grandmother and told Sheri to go upstairs. "I'll be up in minute, honey."

"But Grammy's here. I want to talk to her."

Betty said, "I'll take you up, sweetie."

When they were gone, Danielle gave her husband an angry glance. "Why, Dylan?" she asked. "Why did you go to them?"

Dylan shrugged. "They have a right to know." He paused.

"I better go upstairs and keep an eye on Sheri. There's no telling if your grandmother is going to have an episode and frighten her."

After he left, Nancy walked over to Jones. "Are you ordering us to cancel the reenactment?"

The policeman shook his head. "No, but we plan to be there. It's not a bad idea, but it could turn dangerous."

"Must I remind you that we're detectives?" Nancy said, looking toward Cathy.

Danielle said, "Let them come, Nancy. It might be safer."

"And it might prevent the killer from showing herself."

Cathy knew that Nancy thought a woman killed Doris and that Stacy was now the main suspect.

"You'll have to take that chance," Jones said, "because we're coming."

After the policemen left and Danielle went upstairs, Mavis arrived carrying groceries. While Cathy and Nancy gave her a hand with them, she asked, "I saw a police car pull away. What's going on?"

Nancy explained about Dylan informing the police about the reenactment and that they would be at the dinner.

Mavis shrugged. "That may be for the best." When she finished putting the food away, she turned back to them. "Thanks for the help, and I have good news for you."

"What's that?" Nancy asked. "We can always use good news."

"I've decided to hire Steve. Since he gets along so well with Henry, he'll probably be able to room there unless he prefers to commute. In either case, I don't see the point in interviewing anyone else."

While Mavis considered this good news, Cathy didn't. "Have you told him?"

"Not yet, but I'm not done with the good news. I'm also hiring Michael. He won't be able to stay with Chris permanently, but I'm sure he can find a place nearby. The prices here are reasonable, and he'll only need an apartment."

Nancy asked, "What if they don't accept your job offers?"

Mavis smiled. "That's their loss, but it seems, between Stacy and that girl at the flower shop, they've made friends here already."

Cathy had an urge to scream. It would be a nightmare if she lost both Steve and Michael. Gran wouldn't be pleased either to lose her gardener and the veterinarian for Rainbow Rescues.

After sharing her news, Mavis said, "Well, ladies. I'm meeting Chris in a little while. I may not be around much today, but don't worry, I'll be cooking tomorrow night's dinner. The more I think about this reenactment, the more I'm excited about it. It should be quite a show."

"It's not a show," Nancy said, "or a play. It's a technique to uncover a murderer."

Mavis shrugged again. "Whatever. Have a great day." She headed for the door.

Cathy wondered if that meant Mavis wouldn't be offering Steve and Michael the job until tomorrow.

Nancy said, "I really hope, for your sake, that they don't accept, Cathy. But to be honest, you had your chance. It may be too late."

CHAPTER THIRTY

Cathy had a sinking feeling that Nancy was right. She felt a need to be alone to think over this turn of events. "I'm going for a walk, Nancy. I'd rather be by myself now. Mildred should be back soon, and Danielle will come downstairs with Dylan and Sheri."

"Go ahead. I still want to talk with Betty. She knows more than people give her credit for. They dismiss her because of her mental issues, but there are times she seems quite lucid."

"You shouldn't push her." Cathy felt bad that Nancy was provoking Betty. Her breakdown in tears was an indication of that.

Cathy took the path that she'd walked with Chris the day before when he showed her around the farm. All that remained of the snow was brown slush mixing with the dirt. The sky was overcast, and she felt drizzle in the air. It was cold enough to be considered hail, but she ignored it as she made her way forward. Passing the barn near the house, she looked for

Cricket, Rascal, and Piper, but the cats weren't around to greet her. She decided to look for them inside the barn. She found them nestled by a haystack near the horse stalls.

"There you are, guys," she said, plopping down beside them. Piper and Rascal came over to her, purring. Cricket stood behind them.

"It's okay, Cricket," Cathy said. "I won't bite." It took a little coaxing, but the gray cat finally joined her feline friends in allowing Cathy to pet her. "Good girl."

Cathy lay back against the haystack, breathing in the fresh hay and the scent of the horses. Feeling homesick and missing her grandmother and kittens, she let her mind wander to happier times. She remembered when Steve had asked her for a first date. He'd been nervous, jittery, his face turning red. They'd been in Rainbow Gardens the day after she'd found Maggie Broom dead. Then there was the night she made dinner for her brother Doug and his wife while Gran was out with Howard. Steve, Michael, and Brian had joined them with Nancy at Doug's house. When she brought the crockpot and other items home afterwards, Steve had helped her carry them. In the kitchen, they'd come close to kissing for the first time, but Nancy had interrupted them. Nancy ended up staying the night, and they had a pajama party where they rated the three men. The results had been crazy, but it made her more aware of Steve, Michael, and Brian and how she'd been avoiding relationships after her parents' death in the fear of again losing someone she loved. Now she felt just as afraid.

Rascal, as if aware of her anxiety, came closer and crawled onto her lap. She felt comforted by his purrs as she petted his black head. Her thoughts carried her back to the moments with Michael, the day she helped him deliver her brother and sister-in-law Becky's baby son in a rainstorm, the dances they attended at church, the way he made her laugh.

Her musings were interrupted by someone standing at the barn door. She didn't know how long she'd been there, but the sun had come out during that time and was now streaming in, blocking her view. She shaded her eyes to see who was there. A flashback to when she'd thought she was locked inside a spooky barn on the property of the new rescue center caused a tingle up her spine, even though the barn door stood wide open.

"Cathy, what are you doing in here?"

It was Dylan.

She stood up, dusting the hay from her jeans. The cats scattered outside as Dylan entered. "I didn't mean to disturb you. I'm checking on the horses. They haven't been ridden for a while, and I thought I might take one out. If you ride, you're free to join me."

Cathy didn't trust the change in Dylan's attitude after the way he'd behaved to Danielle. "I haven't ridden in a while." Another memory came to her, riding a horse next to Michael last spring when he'd invited her along to a dude ranch where he was attending a veterinary conference. They'd stayed in separate rooms at her request but had so much fun when he was in between meetings.

"It's like riding a bicycle. You'll do fine." Dylan walked toward her. She involuntarily took a step back.

"Are you afraid of me?" He shook his head. "No. You're mad about my ratting to the cops about the reenactment. Cathy, I'm not a villain. Everything I've done is to help Danny. I love her very much. I worry that this dinner party will push her over the edge. You have no idea how upset she was when Doris died. She fell apart. I thought she was having a breakdown."

"But it turned out she was right," Cathy said. "Doris was murdered."

Dylan sighed. "Yes. I regret that I doubted her."

"You're also taking her grandmother away from her."

"That's for her own good, too. You see how Betty is. She could be dangerous to herself and everyone in our house."

"You could get a nurse or someone with experience with people like her to come in."

Dylan shook his head. "Do you have any idea how much that type of care would cost?"

Money again. Cathy knew the farm was in trouble. Adding the services of a social worker or mental health professional might be too much of a strain on their finances. "There has to be something else you can do. It would mean a lot to Danielle."

Dylan suddenly raised his voice, his emotional side returning. "You need to stay out of this, Cathy. It's between me and my wife. I've already made the arrangements." He walked over to the stall next to her. "I'm going riding now. I've changed my mind about your coming. Why don't you go back inside?"

After Dylan mounted a black stallion and galloped away, Cathy decided to continue her walk instead of returning to the house. Her head still wasn't clear about Steve and Michael. If anything, it was more clouded about them, as well as the people at Oaks Landing. She didn't like Dylan or Mavis and felt bad about Danielle and Betty. The only other person she felt she could trust was Chris. What had he told her about looking into her heart to choose between Michael and Steve? She was trying, but there seemed to be something preventing her from doing that. Nancy might have been right that she was afraid of hurting one of them, but wasn't leading them on hurting them more?

The sun continued to shine as she made her way around the farm. When she came to Chris' house, she saw his truck in the driveway and decided to stop there to pay him a visit. But when she walked up to the door, she saw, through the curtains, three people seated at the kitchen table: Chris, Michael, and

Stacy. The three of them were laughing at a joke. Michael was laughing the hardest. She wondered why Mavis wasn't with them and was about to turn away when Chris turned his head and saw her. He smiled. "Cathy's here," he said, getting up from his seat to invite her in.

"Hi, Chris. I was taking a walk around the farm. I didn't mean to disturb you, but I saw your truck outside."

"I'm glad you came by. Michael and Stacy are here. Come on in."

Now that she was on his doorstep, she couldn't think of a proper excuse to leave, so she walked inside. She didn't need to stay long.

As Chris led her into the kitchen, he said, "We were talking about tomorrow's dinner."

Cathy found that hard to believe because she didn't think anything about the reenactment was funny enough to cause laughter.

"Hi, Cathy," Michael said. Stacy, next to him, gave her a bright smile and said, "Nice to see you again, Cathy." She noticed how straight and white her teeth were and how her blonde hair shone in the sun filtering through the kitchen window.

"Would you like coffee or tea?" Chris asked, after she was seated across from Michael and Stacy.

"No, thank you. I really can't stay long. I'd like to get back to the house soon."

"Lovely day for a walk," Stacy said. "I do two miles myself every morning."

Cathy could tell by the effect on her figure. Glancing at Michael, she remembered that Mavis was offering him a job. She wouldn't say a word about it. That might jinx his acceptance.

Chris sat next to her. "What do you think about tomorrow's dinner, Cathy?"

"I'm not sure. The police will be there, and it might not accomplish anything."

"They didn't seem to believe me," Stacy said. "They kept asking if I'd brought any xylazine with me. I don't know if they explained that it's a sedative usually used on animals such as horses to calm them down. If given to a human, it could cause death in a large dose. I don't usually carry any, but sometimes I do when Mr. Ed gets out of hand."

"Mr. Ed?" Cathy couldn't help but laugh. Then she remembered Dylan calling the Stallion he mounted, Ed. "That's the horse's name?"

"Yep. He's a favorite of Dylan's. Nasty temper like him, too."

"Did you have any with you that day?"

She paused, fingering her coffee cup. "I had some with me because, even though I was there to treat the llamas, Mr. Ed was acting up."

"Did you check your bag afterwards?" Chris asked.

She shook her head, and a blonde tendril fell across her brow. "I got home really late that night and was tired. I checked the bag the next day to prepare for another call, and it wasn't there. That's what I explained to the police. At the time, I didn't connect it with Doris' death because everyone said she had a heart attack."

Chris said, "We don't keep that drug in the barn. The police checked, even though I told them we didn't carry it on the farm."

Cathy found this interesting. She'd have to share it with Nancy. "I assume only a vet would be able get it?"

Stacy nodded. "That's correct, but the hospital was broken into once by an addict who stole a few vials."

"When did this happen?"

Stacy shrugged. "A few years ago. They caught the guy and retrieved what was left. It's not something that happens often around here."

Michael, speaking for the first time, although Cathy noticed he'd followed Stacy's words and lingered longer on her face than she would've liked him to, said, "You had your bag with you that night, right?"

"Yes. I told the police that. They wanted to take it into evidence, but it was a month ago, so..." she waved her hands, and Cathy saw her neatly manicured fingernails. She didn't strike her as following the stereotype of a country vet. She asked, "Did Michael tell you that Nancy wants everyone to bring to the dinner what they brought that night?"

"He told me all about that."

"And you're wearing your red cape?"

"My what?"

"Danielle said you wore a red cape to the dinner."

"I'm afraid I don't know where I put that. I was working on the farm that day, but I threw on the cape after I was done. I thought it would look festive for a holiday dinner. I'll check again and wear it if I find it."

Chris glanced at his watch and stood up. "I have to get going, folks. I promised Danny to take Sheri to the movies today. She wants to clean the house for tomorrow's dinner, so it's easier if Sheri isn't underfoot."

"What about Mavis?" Cathy asked. "I thought she was spending the day with you."

"Nope. I think she's getting her hair done, but I don't keep tabs on her."

Cathy found that odd. Mavis had already had her hair done and that wouldn't take the entire day. She also mentioned meeting Chris. Why had she lied?

CHAPTER THIRTY-ONE

C hris looked at Stacy and Michael. "You two can stay. Just close the door after you leave."

"Thanks, but Stacy wanted to show me a new ultrasound machine they got at the animal hospital." Michael pulled out her chair. Stacy gave him a smile. "Thank you, Michael."

"Would you like a ride back to the house, Cathy, or prefer to walk?" Chris asked.

Cathy needed to vent her frustration at seeing the developing relationship between Michael and Stacy, so she declined the ride. "I'd rather walk, thanks. See you back at the house."

Passing the llama and alpaca pen, Cathy was glad to see Lulu up and about. She looked brighter. "Hey, Lu," she said, walking over to the pen. The llama knew her name and came to the fence. Cathy reached in and petted her. "If things go right tomorrow, we'll find out who killed your friend, Doris. Once we do, Mavis will have time to test you and see if you're having a baby."

The llama looked at her through big, round brown eyes. It was as if she understood. Cathy felt that animals had special instincts. She gave her one last pat and continued on. Nearing the gift shop, clouds blocked the sun, and Cathy felt the wind pick up. It gave her a chill. She was tempted to try the door to see if it was open, but a closed sign hung in the window. She remembered the story about Doris being afraid to work there because she thought someone was stalking her. Although the farm was now closed to the public, a person could get in if they tried. Stacy spoke about a drug addict who stole xylazine from the animal hospital. She also said a vial was missing the day after Doris' death. These thoughts mingled together in Cathy's mind, but she dismissed them. Whoever killed Doris, if Stacy was telling the truth about the missing vial, had to have been at the dinner. Somehow, they'd found a way to put xylazine in her drink.

When Cathy arrived back at the house, Mildred opened the door. She noted the high color in the librarian's cheeks. "Hi, Mildred. Did you enjoy the movie?"

"I had a wonderful time. Henry took me to a park afterwards, and we had a nice walk. He's such a sweet man."

"Mildred, I know you like him, but remember that you're leaving at the end of this week, maybe sooner after tomorrow night."

"I'm aware of that, Cathy, but this isn't a fling. I don't believe in long-distance relationships, and I've told Henry that. He plans to move when he retires, and I have a feeling he's considering Buttercup Bend. I think he'd fit in perfectly there."

Cathy thought of Steve. Would that mean Steve would move to Oaks Landing? "Has he put his house up for sale yet?" she asked.

"He's planning to do that soon. It has a lot of memories for him of his wife but that's more the reason for him to let it go."

"Where is everyone?" she asked. "Have you seen Steve?"

"I haven't. Chris was here and took Sheri out. Dylan hasn't been back, and Danielle is cleaning upstairs. Nancy is helping her.

Cathy heard the low whirr of the vacuum cleaner from the top floor. Nancy wasn't known for her tidiness. "Nancy's helping Danielle?"

Mildred smiled. "I know that's a stretch. Whenever she comes to the library, she leaves books all over, but I think she's investigating more than cleaning."

"What about Mavis? I ran into Chris, and he said he wasn't seeing her today." She related the rest of what happened at Chris' house.

"Nancy will be interested in all that."

"What do you think?"

"I'm not a detective, but I'd say something's fishy if Mavis lied about where she went today."

Cathy considered. "There are a few possibilities."

Suddenly Nancy was there. Her steps downstairs had been hidden by the noise of the vacuum. "I agree, Cathy." She walked over to them. "Mavis could be hiding something about Doris' murder, or she could be seeing someone else besides Chris."

Cathy hadn't thought of that. "Did you find anything upstairs?"

"Why? Do you think I was snooping? I was dusting for Danielle."

Mildred said, "Cathy and I know you don't enjoy house-cleaning."

Nancy laughed. "Okay. I'll admit that I checked in the

rooms up there for anything suspicious. I also had a nice talk with Betty or, should I say, Amelia Earhart."

"Oh, no! What did she say?" Cathy's worry about how Betty would behave the next night intensified.

"She said she got lost and had to land her plane. I asked her about the wolf, but she stuck to character and said that she didn't know where she was. She thought it was the Bermuda Triangle."

"I hate to say this," Cathy said, "but I think Dylan's right about putting her into a home. I know it's hard for Danielle to accept, but her grandmother is very sick."

"I agree," Mildred said. "She needs help. I hope they found a good place."

"Maybe she should be excluded from the dinner."

"No, Cathy," Nancy said, "It's important that she be there. We need everyone who attended to be present."

"Stacy said she can't find her red cape."

"That's funny. When I was cleaning there was a red cape in Mavis' room.

Do you think it's the same one?"

"We can ask Danielle. Where did you see it?" Cathy was trying to figure out how Mavis would've gotten Stacy's cape.

"It was hanging in her closet."

"We can't ask Danielle about it because then she'd know you were snooping," Mildred pointed out.

"We could ask Stacy when we see her. She says she's looking for it." Even though she suggested it, Cathy wasn't in a rush to see Stacy because she knew Michael was with her.

Nancy said, "Why don't we go into town and check out a few places? We could eat there. Danielle's busy, so she won't mind. Lunch places are great for gathering intel."

Cathy laughed. "You're too much, Nancy, but you have a point. In small towns, gossip can often be heard in restaurants."

She thought of the Kafe and how Olivia and Hilda, the proprietors, chatted with the customers.

They took Cathy's car. Cathy remembered the small strip of shops that contained the animal hospital, flower shop, boutiques, fast-food places, and diners. Across from the shops was a small hotel. Cathy found a parking spot near the flower shop. Her heart sank when she saw Steve inside, speaking with the woman she assumed was Lisa. The girl, younger than she expected, in her early twenties, had long curly red hair. She wore a flowery blouse that went well with the bouquets she was arranging.

"Look at that," Nancy said. "Wanna get some flowers, Cathy?"

"I'd rather not." She watched Steve speaking animatedly with Lisa, smiling all the time.

"That looks like a nice restaurant," Mildred said, pointing to the left at a glass-fronted building that still displayed Christmas lights and a sign that said, "Oaks Landing Bites and Brews."

"That could be a bar," Nancy pointed out.

"Why don't we see?" Mildred asked.

But when they walked over to the restaurant, they received a shock. Two people were seated at a table toward the back. They were holding hands. Cathy gasped as she recognized Henry and Mavis.

CHAPTER THIRTY-TWO

Mildred mirrored Cathy's gasp. "That's Henry," she whispered.

Nancy said, "Oh, gee. You were right, Cathy. Mavis lied about seeing Chris because she's cheating on him and doesn't want anyone to know."

"I can't believe it," Mildred said.

Cathy's heart broke for her. "Let's go back to the house."

"Don't you want to see what they're up to?" Nancy asked.

"I've seen enough." Mildred turned around.

"There might be an explanation," Cathy said. "Henry seemed like such a nice man, not one who would lead Mildred on while having an affair with Chris' girlfriend."

"You forget that's what they say about killers after they catch them. 'He was such a nice guy.' It might be that he and Mavis are the man and woman Betty said murdered her mother."

"I wouldn't go that far, Nancy."

"Well, they seem to be plotting something. I wish I could be a fly on the wall."

"Not me," Mildred said. "If you two aren't leaving, I'll walk back, even though it's a distance." Cathy saw the glint of tears in her eyes. "Use my car, Mildred. It's easier for me and Nancy to walk."

"Thank you," Mildred said, taking the keys Cathy offered and heading toward her car.

Nancy said, "She needs time alone. I want to confront them when they come out of there."

It was at that moment that Steve walked out of the flower shop holding a bouquet. He stopped short when he saw Cathy and Nancy.

"Hi, Steve," Cathy said. "Are those for Lisa?"

"What? These are for you. Lisa's working. I was consulting with her about the flowers you might like. I felt bad that I only got a bouquet for Danielle this morning."

Cathy wanted to believe him as he passed her the flowers. "It must've taken you a long time to discuss that."

He smiled. "We got talking about gardening, and you know how long I can talk about that subject. Lisa's dad is a gardener. He's extremely popular, so he couldn't accept the job at Oaks Landing even if Mavis asked him."

That was Cathy's opportunity to tell Steve that he was already hired, but Nancy was pointing back toward the restaurant. "Cathy, they're on the move. I saw them go out the back door. Rats!"

"Who are you talking about?" Steve asked.

Instead of replying, Nancy raced off. "See you later, guys. I'll let you know what I find out."

Steve said, "We need to talk, Cat." He gestured toward a bench outside the restaurant. Cathy took a seat there, placing the bouquet in her lap. Steve joined her, turned, and looked into her eyes. She cast them down.

"Please look at me, Cathy."

She glanced up into his deep blue eyes.

"That's better. I want you to know that there's nothing between me and Lisa. I'm a very patient man. You have to be to wait for plants to grow." He grinned. "Michael is my friend, so I don't like to say things about him, but he's less patient than I am." He took a breath. "What I'm trying to say is that I'm not rushing you or giving you any ultimatums. I'm also not taking up with anyone until you make your decision. Do you believe that?"

Cathy nodded. Deep inside, she knew her jealousy of Lisa was unfounded.

Steve's smile widened. "Okay then. Let's have lunch." As he stood up, Nancy rounded the corner. Catching her breath as she joined them, she said, "I lost them. They parked in the back and got in Mavis' car. She drove off in that direction." She pointed toward the left. "We might be able to follow them, but we don't have a car since Mildred left. Steve, would you..."

Cathy said, "Steve isn't driving us on a wild goose chase, Nancy." She remembered when the two of them rode around with Steve searching for a poisonous plant in gardens all over Buttercup Bend.

Nancy sighed. "You're right. I'll confront Mavis back at the house. Are you guys good? Judging by that lovely bouquet, it looks like it."

Cathy smiled at Steve. "We are, and we were about to try out the Oaks Landing Bites and Brews. Want to join us?"

Over lunch, Nancy filled Steve in about Mavis and Henry and also mentioned Stacy's cape that she found in Mavis' room.

Steve, biting into his chicken sandwich, said after he swallowed, "I've been living with Henry, and I find it hard to believe he's seeing Mavis. He's not the type of guy to lead

Mildred on or allow Mavis to cheat on Chris." He paused, adding some of the coleslaw from the small container to his plate. "However, the thing about the cape is odd. Stacy said she couldn't find it. If she loaned it to Mavis, she should've remembered. And when would she have done that? She supposedly wore it to the dinner."

Nancy said, "I can't see Mavis stealing the cape. For what reason?"

"We need to ask Danielle," Cathy said. "She said she remembers everything from that night."

Steve agreed. "You should try to catch her before the dinner. I'll speak with Henry and find out what's going on with him and Mavis."

When they were done eating, Steve offered to drive them back, and they accepted.

At the house, they were surprised to see so many people gathered in the living room. Mavis was there without Henry, and so were Chris, Mildred, Dylan, Michael, and Stacy.

"Oh, Good! Steve is here," Mavis said, as they entered. "We're talking about the reenactment, and there's something I need to talk to you and Michael about."

Cathy's heart sank. Mavis was preparing to offer them the jobs.

"Where's Danielle?" Nancy asked.

"She's upstairs with Sheri and Betty. Mother is having another off day."

Dylan rolled his eyes. "When does she have an "on" day? I gave her pills, so she should have calmed down by now. I don't like Sheri seeing her like that, but I understand it's best she be out of the way while we talk about the dinner."

Cathy hoped that they would continue the conversation about the reenactment, but Mavis was intent on breaking the news to Michael and Steve.

"Before we resume our discussion, I'd like to announce that I've made a decision to hire Michael as our new vet and Steve as our new gardener if they'll accept, of course."

The men looked at one another. Steve said, "Thank you for considering me, but I'm under contract with a bunch of customers in Buttercup Bend. Even if I accept, I wouldn't be able to start right away."

"I can sweeten the pot," Mavis said. "Whatever you're making up there, I can double it."

Cathy was shocked. If the farm was in so much trouble, how could Mavis offer such a deal?

Michael said, "It's not a matter of money. Steve needs to think this over, as do I. We both have responsibilities that we can't just hand off. And although your offer is tempting," he glanced at Stacy, "I'll need more time to consider it."

Mavis nodded. "That's fine. We still have to get through tomorrow night. Speaking of which, is everyone set?"

Stacy said, "I am. I finally found my cape."

Nancy said, "That's funny. When I was helping Danielle clean upstairs, I noticed Mavis' closet was open. When I went to close it, I saw a red cape. I thought it might've been the one you were looking for."

Mavis laughed. "No, Nancy. It's not the same, but I admired it so much when I saw Stacy wearing it that I asked her where she purchased it and bought one of my own."

"That explains it," Nancy said. Cathy still thought it strange that Mavis, who said she hardly remembered anything from that night, could remember asking Stacy about her cape.

Despite her words, Nancy didn't seem happy with Mavis' answer either. She pursued another topic. "I thought I saw you in town with Henry today," she said. "But you mentioned meeting Chris."

Cathy saw Mavis, Chris, and Mildred's reaction to that

statement. Mavis gave Nancy an angry glare, while Chris looked surprised, and Mildred looked away.

"Sorry for that white lie," Mavis said, but she didn't sound sorry at all. She sounded mad. "I was filling Henry in about the dinner. He's a little hesitant about coming."

"I already did that," Steve said, "and he didn't seem wary about it to me."

Before Mavis could make a further attempt at an explanation, Danielle came downstairs with Sheri. "Grammy's asleep. Does anyone have any questions about tomorrow night?"

"Are the policemen coming?" Sheri asked.

"Yes, honey. They'll be here. Does that bother you?"

"No, Mommy. I like them. The fat one gave me a lollipop last time."

Since no one else had any questions, Danielle said, "I'm making a simple dinner tonight since Mavis is cooking tomorrow. Until then, you all can do what you want."

As people began to leave, Mavis called out. "Cathy, Nancy, may I speak with you a moment before you go?"

CHAPTER THIRTY-THREE

When they were alone, Mavis said, "I owe you two an explanation about Henry. I didn't ask Mildred to join us because it might upset her."

"She's upset already," Nancy pointed out.

"I'm sorry about that." Mavis glanced at her and then at Cathy before she continued. "First, I need you to understand about me and Chris. We go back a long time. I was once very in love with him. I still am, to a degree. But that love soured as I waited for him after Doris left. When she returned, nothing had changed. I realized that she was his great love and would never be anything less even after she died."

Cathy wondered for a minute if Mavis was confessing, but then she went on. "I hired Henry a month before Doris came back to the farm. His father had gotten too old for the job and decided to move to Florida. Henry wasn't that young either but was already doing landscaping around town. As I began to see my attachment to Chris was senseless, I started having feelings for Henry. But it's the same old story," she threw up her hands. "He wasn't interested in me in that way. He was still in love with his dead wife." She unclasped the hands in her lap. "I'm so sick of being second fiddle. I truly wish Mildred more luck with Henry. You can share my sentiments with her."

"So, you really were just speaking with him about the dinner," Cathy said.

Mavis reclasped her hands. "I was but that wasn't my main reason for seeing him. You see, Chris has asked me to marry him, and I don't know what to do. I prayed for years for this to happen but, now that it has, I'm not sure it will work. Danielle has enough marriage problems to offer me any advice, but Henry has always been a good friend. I was honest with him about my feelings, and I truly valued his opinion."

"What did he tell you?" Nancy asked.

Mavis smiled. "He said to listen to my heart."

Cathy found it ironic that Henry had given Mavis the same advice Chris had given her. "What have you decided?"

Mavis turned to her. "I haven't. I'm waiting until this darn reenactment is over."

Cathy told Mildred what Mavis said about Henry, and she brightened. She and Nancy had found her in her room crying, a soggy tissue in her hand.

"Mildred, you surprise me," Nancy said. "I didn't think you would cry over anyone. There are rumors around Buttercup Bend that you're quite the spinster."

Mildred sniffed, wiping her eyes. "I suppose the rumors are right. I never imagined, at my age, I would fall so hard."

"You need to be careful," Nancy said. "Men are cruel."

"Not all of them," Cathy said. "What about Brian, Steve, and Michael?"

"There are exceptions. We're lucky that three of them live in Buttercup Bend."

"Henry's an exception."

"I hope you're right, Mildred," Nancy said.

After dinner, which was as simple as Danielle promised, consisting of an assortment of sandwiches and salads, Cathy and Nancy went back upstairs to their rooms. Mildred stayed downstairs to help Danielle clean up, although most of the dishes were paper plates that only needed to be tossed.

"I think Mildred is trying to get more information from Danielle," Nancy said when they were in their room. "She's sharp. I think she'd make a good detective."

"She said librarians are curious because they're always searching for answers."

"Do you think she'd move here if Henry doesn't want to give up his place? There's got to be a library nearby. I thought I saw one across the street from the shops today."

Cathy considered that. "I'm not sure. Mildred loves Buttercup Bend, but she's pretty taken with Henry."

"What about Steve and Michael? Do you think they'd commute or find a place in Oaks Landing?"

Cathy didn't want to think about that. She was hoping they'd turn down Mavis' offer. "I can't answer that, Nancy. We need to focus on the reenactment and what will happen tomorrow."

CHAPTER THIRTY-FOUR

The next morning, Cathy woke to a commotion out in the hall. Dylan was yelling at Danielle. "Didn't you give Betty her pills last night?"

"I did, but you know how she fakes taking them. I should've locked the door. I forgot. I don't know how long she's been gone. Oh, Dylan, what are we going to do?"

"Calm down. We'll find her. I'll call Chris and see if she's by his house and then I'll check around here."

Cathy nudged Nancy. "Get up, Nancy. It sounds like Betty is missing."

Nancy turned over. "Sorry. I couldn't sleep last night. What? Betty? Missing?" She jumped up, causing the bed to creak. "Let's go see." She got out of bed and grabbed a robe.

"She could be outside, Nancy. It's cold. We should get dressed first."

"I'm not waiting. We have to help find her."

Cathy agreed, so she put on her own robe, a fluffy concoction that was nearly as warm as her coat. But, instead of donning her slippers, she took wool socks from the drawer and put on boots.

"You look ridiculous," Nancy commented.

"There's mud around. I don't want to ruin my slippers or shoes."

"Why do you have to be so sensible? You're holding us up." Nancy had her hand on the door.

They stepped out into the hall where Dylan was giving directions. "She could still be in the house," he pointed out. "Danny, you check to see if she's hiding somewhere. I just called Chris, and he's looking, too. He said Michael will also. Let me get my coat, and I'll go outside."

"Can we help?" Nancy asked.

Danielle, seeing her and Cathy standing outside their door, said, "The more eyes, the better. I can't believe she's not in her room. She hasn't done this since..."

Dylan cut her off. "I'm going now. All of you, take a different direction. I knew something like this would happen eventually. I wish I could've had the home take her sooner."

"Shouldn't we call the police?" Mavis, walking out of her room, asked. Cathy noted she was already dressed. Either that, or she'd slept in her clothes.

"Let's not involve the police if we can." Dylan stood by the staircase. "I'm leaving now. Call me on my cell if you find her."

A few minutes later, Cathy heard the front door open and close. "I'm so sorry, Danielle," she said. Danielle was still in her nightgown, her hair mussed, a tear sliding down her cheek. "I went to check on her this morning. I usually wake her later, but I had a horrible dream. A nightmare. She was in it. I can hardly remember it now, but it made me want to see her. This is all my fault. I usually check the door at night to make sure it's locked."

Nancy said, "It's okay, Danielle. Someone is bound to find her. But what did you mean that she's done this before?"

"There was one other time. It was right after Doris died. She disappeared."

"Where did you find her?" Nancy, ever the detective, asked.

"We didn't find her." Mavis was the one who replied. "She came home. We don't know where she was."

This surprised Cathy. "How long was she gone?"

"A few hours. She couldn't have been far because she didn't take a car."

Danielle said, "Oh, my God. Maybe she took one now. I have to go and check the keys by the door." Before anyone else could say anything, she literally flew down the stairs. A minute later, she called up, "The keys are still here, thank God. I'm going to start searching the house."

Mavis said, "I told her she should find another place for those. Danny is so stubborn. She doesn't accept the fact that my mother isn't in her right mind."

"It isn't easy for her," Cathy said. "If my grandmother was having those issues, I would also have a hard time coming to terms with them."

"I can't see Florence ever having those problems," Nancy said. "She's too feisty."

"It can happen to anyone, Nance. Dementia, Alzheimer's, mental illness, they can occur at any age."

Mavis glanced down at Cathy's boots. "Are you planning to join the search group outside?"

"Yes. I wish I had time to dress, but the boots will protect me from the mud."

"She's so practical," Nancy smiled. "I don't mind getting dirty or cold while that poor old woman is outside alone."

"I'll help Danny search the house and then will join you two outside. Split up, like Dylan said."

"Can I help you find Grammy, Auntie Mavis," a small

voice said, and everyone turned to see Sheri rubbing her eyes and clutching her teddy bear, bunny slippers on her feet.

"Sure. She may be playing hide and seek. You're very good at finding hiding places." Mavis took Sheri by the hand and led her downstairs.

Cathy remembered Mildred. "I'm surprised Mildred didn't wake up, Nancy. Should we get her?"

Nancy shook her head. "No. She's probably tired out from all the ups and downs about Henry yesterday. Let her sleep."

"Where should we look for Betty?"

"Dylan has a head start, but why don't you check the barn in case he passed it? She could've hidden in there. I'll look around near Chris' place in the other barn and near the llama pen."

Cathy was glad they had a plan. "Sounds good. I have Danielle's cell number, so I'll call her if I find Betty. Also, you, or course."

Nancy nodded. "Let's go then. The longer she's out, the further she might travel."

As Cathy walked toward the barn, she was surprised the barn cats didn't come out to greet her. She didn't call Betty's name because she didn't want to scare her off, so she quietly entered the barn. That's when she saw them. Mildred and Betty were huddled by the haystack that she'd occupied the day before. Each had a cat in their lap. Mildred was petting Piper, while Betty was stroking Rascal. Shy Cricket was waiting her turn for attention.

"Mildred!" Cathy exclaimed. "What are you doing in here with Betty? The whole house is searching for her."

Mildred smiled. "We were just talking. I left you a note on my bureau."

"I didn't go in your room. I thought you were asleep."

Betty said, "Are you mad, Mommy?"

As Cathy approached them, the cats ran off. She thought they'd recognize her and stay, but she knew cats could be skittery. Betty jumped up. "Come back, Kitty."

Nancy said, "She thinks that's the cat she had as a child. She was more coherent earlier, but she seems to have regressed."

"What were you thinking in bringing her outside?" Cathy blocked Betty's path because she was afraid she'd run after the cats.

"She came to my room. She said she wanted to talk with me. I should've woken you or Danielle, but she had something important to say and asked me to follow her. She led me downstairs and then here to the barn."

"You could've called me. I take it you took your cell."

Mildred shook her head. "No. I left everything in the room."

Cathy saw that she wore only her long nightgown and slippers that were now muddy. Betty was completely dressed with a coat over her clothes.

"You must be freezing. C'mon. Let's get her back in the house. I have to let Danielle and Nancy know I found Betty." Cathy took out her cell to call.

"Wait!" Betty said. "You mustn't call them. Please. The wolf's coming and bringing the poison in the basket."

"So that's what this is about," Cathy said.

Mildred got up. Cathy noticed it took some effort for her to rise from the floor and knew it was her bad knees causing her pain. "That's what she keeps saying. I think she's worried about the dinner."

"No," Betty cried. "Please. Let me stay here. I don't want to go. The wolf is bringing the poison."

"You have to come back with us, Betty." Cathy kept her voice firm and controlled. She took the old woman by the elbow. "It's okay. If you don't want to go to the dinner, you don't have to."

That relaxed her. She leaned into Cathy who led her out of the barn. Mildred followed.

When Danielle learned that Cathy had found her grandmother, she sighed with relief. "Oh, thank goodness. Thank you, Cathy."

Mildred apologized. "I should've insisted we stay in the house. I'm sorry."

"That's alright. I know you meant well."

"Maybe you should keep her in her room tonight," Cathy suggested.

Nancy said, "That's defeating the purpose of the reenactment. Everyone has to be there."

While Cathy agreed with that, she couldn't help worrying about Betty. She seemed so scared and confused. Another thought struck her. Betty's fears seemed to stem from the wolf who had to be Stacy and the poison that was being brought to the dinner. What if the poison wasn't in the wolf's basket but in her veterinarian's bag?

CHAPTER THIRTY-FIVE

Back in their room, Cathy shared her thoughts about the poison in the basket with Nancy. "Stacy said she brought the xylazine that night, but when she checked her bag the day after Doris' death, it wasn't there. Do you think that the poison Betty is so afraid of is the xylazine?"

"It's possible," Nancy said, "then we're back at considering Stacy our main suspect."

"Unless someone got into her bag."

"There's problems with that." Nancy counted off on her fingers. "First, that person would have to know that Stacy had the drug in her bag. Second, they would have had to take the drug out of the bag without anyone seeing. Third, they needed to get the drug into Doris' drink. That type of medicine is usually injected, and it isn't easy to open a vial without breaking it."

"Danielle said that she, Mavis, Chris, and Dylan had some training in administering veterinary medicine. Do you think any of them had the knowledge to inject the vial into Doris' drink?"

"Obviously not Danielle, but it's possible. I just think it's unlikely because, again, who would've known Stacy was bringing it?"

Cathy thought a moment. "What about Jodi? Didn't someone tell us that she worked part-time at the animal hospital? Could she have known that Stacy had it with her that night?"

Nancy sighed. "I think that's a stretch, but we can't discount any idea no matter how wild. But I don't think the reenactment will prove anything unless the person responsible is persuaded to confess."

"That's going to be difficult, especially since Stacy won't be bringing the xylazine."

"Who said she's not bringing it? I asked everyone to bring what they had with them that night. I'm making sure she brings it even if I have to ask Michael to convince her to do it."

"Please don't bring Michael into this."

"Why not? He's her pal now. I hope not more than that for your sake. But you still have Steve. He gave you that beautiful bouquet today and explained that he and Lisa were only friends."

"I feel better about that, but I'm worried that Michael has turned to Stacy because I haven't given him an answer."

Nancy shrugged. "That's his problem. It'll make your decision easier. Don't you know the saying about letting someone go and if they don't come back to you, they were never really yours?"

Cathy pulled off her muddy boots. "I don't want to talk about this anymore, Nance. I'd like to go back to bed. I'll have to clean these later."

Nancy glanced at the wall clock. "It's 4 a.m. I sometimes don't go to bed until this time, but I agree. Let's sleep on this. Tonight will be tough. Hopefully, we'll catch a killer."

. . .

The first thing Cathy did when she woke up again at 8 a.m. was to call her grandmother. She didn't tell Florence about the upcoming reenactment or the police's involvement, but she mentioned that she might be coming home at the end of the week. Florence already knew that Michael and Steve were at Oaks Landing, but she didn't apologize about keeping that from Cathy. "I wanted it to be a surprise. I hope you didn't mind. They all care about you, and I felt better that you and Mildred aren't alone down there."

Cathy admitted that she did, too. She didn't share the news about Steve and Michael being offered a job or the fact that both of them had made new female friends.

After she'd dressed and Nancy had finally risen, Cathy urged her to call Brian. "He might be worried about you," she said.

"He knows I can take care of myself. Besides, you didn't see him rushing down here with your boyfriends, did you?"

Cathy laughed. "You probably would've smacked him one if he had."

Nancy smiled. "You got that right, but maybe I should give him a ring." She took out her cell and tapped on his contact.

Cathy went into the bathroom to give her privacy. She brushed her hair and teeth. When she was satisfied she was presentable, she came into the bedroom. Nancy was no longer on the phone. She was getting clothes from her unpacked suitcase.

"How's Brian?" Cathy asked.

"He's good. He has no clue that Michael and Steve are with us nor Mildred. For that fact, he doesn't even think I'm with you."

"And you're happy about keeping him in the dark?"

"Not thrilled, but it's better than him knowing. I'm glad Florence didn't tell him."

"Maybe I'm being hypocritical by saying this, Nance, but I believe relationships should be built on trust. I know there are reasons why you're keeping this from him, but I think he'll be upset when he finds out that you did."

Nancy tossed a light blue tunic and jeans on the bed. She turned to Cathy. "It's like when you do something bad and your parent yells at you and then when you start to cry, they give you a sweet treat or another reward. I like the making up part best."

Cathy threw up her hands. "You're unbelievable. You take Brian for granted."

"And who's calling the kettle black?"

"Now you sound like Gran."

With that, Nancy grabbed her clothes and marched to the bathroom. "I'm taking a shower. You go down without me if you want or wait. I'm sure Mildred has already had breakfast. She's an early bird like Florence."

Nancy was right. The only person remaining at the breakfast table was Danielle nursing a coffee.

"Good morning, Cathy, Nancy. I hope you both got some rest. Everyone's had breakfast, but I can put eggs on for you."

Cathy noticed her eyes were red. "We slept a little, but it looks like you didn't. Don't worry about breakfast. We can grab fruit or cereal."

Nancy made a face as if she was upset Cathy turned down a hot meal, but she joined her at the breakfast counter by the fruit bowl. A few boxed cereals sat next to it along with a plate of muffins.

"I haven't been sleeping well since Dylan told me he found a place for Grandma. I also can't stop thinking about tonight."

"Where's Mildred?" Nancy grabbed an apple from the bowl and rinsed it in the sink.

"She took Sheri out to see Lulu. She feels bad about what happened last night."

"What about Dylan and Mavis?" Cathy asked, taking a blueberry muffin.

"They left. Mavis brought Chris and Michael breakfast. I have no idea where Dylan went. Before he left, he brought food up to Betty and made sure she took her pills, so she'll be asleep most of the day. I think that's for the best."

Nancy took a seat at the table. After taking a bite of her apple, she said, "It's good we're alone. I want to talk about the reenactment. I need to know where everyone was sitting that night."

"I thought you'd ask that." Danielle got up and took a paper from one of the cabinet drawers. "I drew a seating chart. I'm not as good as Betty and my mother were at art, but I think I did a decent job."

Cathy, sitting next to Nancy, glanced at the drawing. "I don't see Betty assigned any seat."

"No one was assigned seats. Everyone sat where they wanted, although they usually sat in their regular seats. Betty wanted to eat in the kitchen, but she was roaming around the dining room the whole time. I was keeping an eye on her."

Nancy seemed to find this piece of information interesting. "You were watching Betty?"

"Yes. Mother asked me to."

Cathy said. "I know you said she was starting to decline at that point but got much worse after Doris' death. When did her illness begin?"

"She was fine until about a year ago when my father died. I think that's what pushed her over the edge. A sudden trauma can do that. I've been reading up on it."

"Is that when she started to act out different personalities?"

Danielle glanced at Cathy. "That's right. It was Elizabeth Taylor primarily at first and then she started taking on other identities."

"What about before that? Were there any signs? How did she react when Doris came back to the farm?" Nancy took another bite of her apple, waiting for Danielle's reply.

"There was no warning. It happened suddenly. When my mother came home, Betty couldn't have been happier. Mavis, on the other hand, wasn't pleased."

"Because of Chris?"

Danielle shook her head. "That wasn't the only reason. Doris was always Betty's favorite daughter."

"She was Julia Child the night of Doris' death, correct?"

"Yes, Cathy." Danielle sighed. "I just want to get this over with. I cleaned all the rooms because the police may go upstairs during the dinner. Steve and Michael also have to stay somewhere."

"It's going to be difficult for Mildred," Nancy pointed out. "She's playing the part of Doris. You'll have to go over everything with her before people get here."

"I plan to do that." Danielle finished her coffee. "Are you ladies certain I can't make you anything?"

"No, thanks," Cathy said. "We're fine. Why don't you try to catch up on the rest you lost earlier since Betty's sleeping now?"

Even though Cathy knew Nancy would've preferred a larger breakfast, she said, "That's a good idea. Don't worry about us, Danielle. We'll manage."

After Danielle went upstairs and they left the kitchen, Mildred came in. She was smiling. "Good morning, girls."

"Hi, Mildred. Where's Sheri?" Cathy asked.

"I ran into Dylan, and he offered to take her out. He wants to keep her away from the farm until tonight."

"Maybe that's best." Nancy filled Mildred in about the seating chart Danielle gave her and the information about Betty eating in the kitchen but also spending time in the dining room with Danielle keeping an eye on her.

"I guess I'll have to wing it tonight then," Mildred pointed out. "I'm supposed to be Doris pretending to be Julia Child, right?"

Cathy nodded. "Yes. The only thing we know for sure is that Betty was present when Doris collapsed at the table."

Mildred said, "Could Betty have seen the killer put the xylazine into Doris' drink?"

Cathy thought a moment. "That's an interesting idea, and it makes sense. We need to check with Danielle about who prepared the drinks. I know Mavis cooked, but maybe someone else was in charge of refreshments."

"I'm sure the police went over all that, and they will again tonight. But getting back to your assumption," Nancy turned to Mildred, "if Betty was a witness, we need to find a way to get her to finger the killer."

Cathy laughed. "You're too much, Nancy. You've even begun to master detective lingo."

"She has a point," Mildred said. "The problem is that we can't always believe what Betty says. Also, she was traumatized by her daughter's death. Who knows how deeply she buried that memory, especially when you consider the person who murdered Doris is most likely a member of the family."

"You aren't sold on Stacy, Jodi, or Henry being a part of this?" Cathy asked.

Mildred shook her head. "No. I don't see them having

strong enough motives. Stacy may have brought the xylazine, but I don't think she was the one who used it."

"I'm not discounting anyone," Nancy said.

"Even Danielle?" Cathy had already written Doris' daughter off the suspect list, but Nancy insisted on including her. "She'd have ample opportunity, and you never know how she really felt about her mother leaving her and then returning to the farm so many years later."

Cathy had to admit that was a good point. It might even explain why Betty was protecting her granddaughter.

CHAPTER THIRTY-SIX

M ildred said, "Let's give this a rest for now. I was thinking about visiting the library this morning. I'm curious to see it, and we might also be able to research a few things."

Nancy finished her apple and threw the core away. "I'd love to read Doris' obituary. We can ask for a copy of that issue."

When they'd all put on their coats, Nancy offered to drive. Mildred sat in the front next to her, while Cathy took the back seat. They headed for town and parked in the same spot they'd occupied the previous day near the restaurant.

"After we check out the library, no pun intended," Mildred said, "maybe we can get lunch in Bites and Brews."

Cathy was surprised she suggested that, but she knew the relationship between Mavis and Henry had been explained.

"That's a good idea," Nancy said. "I'm dying to try the food there, and we didn't have much breakfast."

The library was across the street. It was a brick building that had been modernized inside. Cathy noticed a sign on the door for an opening for a full-time librarian. She brought it to Mildred's attention, but she hoped she wouldn't be interested. If she lost Mildred along with Steve and Michael, her best friends would be gone from Buttercup Bend.

Mildred said, "I should ask about it. You never know."

"First, let's get the paper from last month," Nancy said, walking through the electric doors.

An elderly woman sat at the reference desk. Cathy judged her to be no younger than eighty. Her white head was bent as she peered at a computer screen through oval-framed glasses that sat on her nose.

Nancy approached her. "Hello. We're visitors and would like some help."

The woman looked up and smiled. "Of course. Welcome to the Oaks Landing Public Library. I'm Mrs. Masters. How can I assist you?"

"We need a newspaper issue from last month. We're not sure which day. It would be after December 6."

The librarian stood up and nodded at Nancy. "We still have the paper copies of those. They're in the back. I'll get the issues from that week." She walked around the desk, and Cathy noted she used a cane.

"Please take a seat while I get them." She pointed toward the tables. None were occupied, but it was early. Although their request took longer than they expected, Mildred was the only one who sat down.

When Mrs. Masters returned, she carried a handful of newspapers and plopped them on the table. "Here you go. If you need anything else, please let me know. These don't circulate, but you're free to make copies." She indicated the copy machine by the desk.

"We can each take an issue," Nancy suggested, pulling out

one of the wooden chairs and taking a seat. She grabbed the top one off the pile.

Cathy sat down, and she and Mildred took their own papers. Cathy had chosen the December 8 issue of the *Oaks Landing Ledger*. It was published two days after Doris' death.

"It's in this one," she said. Mildred and Nancy looked up from their papers. "Read it to us," Nancy said.

Cathy cleared her throat and read the single paragraph. "*Doris Taylor Grady, sister to Mavis Taylor of Oaks Landing Farm, passed away unexpectedly on Tuesday night, December 6. She leaves her daughter, Danielle Diaz, son-in-law, Dylan Diaz, granddaughter Sheri Diaz, ex-husband Christopher Grady, and mother, Betty Taylor. A service will be held for her tomorrow night, December 9, at the Oaks Landing Funeral Parlor. The burial is scheduled for Friday, December 10, at Holy Oaks Cemetery.*"

"It doesn't mention a cause of death," Nancy pointed out.

"Not all obituaries do, Nance." Cathy didn't find that surprising.

Mildred said, "This doesn't give us much information. I'll tell Mrs. Masters that we're done with the papers."

As she got up, Cathy realized she'd volunteered to do that for an opportunity to ask about the librarian job. She watched as Mildred approached the desk carrying the newspapers. Mrs. Masters glanced at her. "Did you want anything else?"

"We're done with the papers, but I'd like to inquire about the position advertised on your front door." She dropped the issues in front of her.

"The librarian job? Yes, that's open. I'm retiring at the end of the month. I can't keep up with all the modern technology, and it's past my time here. We've been interviewing for the position. The Board is partial to young graduates who are into all the tech stuff."

Mildred smiled. "I understand that. I may be retirement age myself, but I'm still healthy and enjoy working at the Buttercup Bend Library. I've taken college classes to update my skills, so I think I'd be an asset here. May I apply for the job?"

Cathy gasped, and Nancy put her finger to her lips as if to quiet her. "Don't worry, Cat. She won't get it," she whispered.

Mrs. Masters reached into a drawer and withdrew a form. "Here's the application. Good luck to you. This is a small library, and we don't get too many patrons, but we get reference phone calls and interloan requests for books at other branches."

Mildred took the form, folded it, and placed it in her purse. "Thank you. I'll get this back to you before the end of the week."

As she walked back to the table, a smile on her face, she said, "Okay, girls. Let's go to lunch."

It was early for lunch, but they were all hungry, so they headed for Bites and Brews. After being seated by a waitress wearing a striped red and white apron, they glanced over the menus she handed them.

There were many choices, and Cathy had a challenging time concentrating. "Mildred, you aren't serious about taking that job?"

Mildred placed down her menu. "I might be if Henry isn't interested in moving to Buttercup Bend."

Nancy looked over her menu. "Aren't you known as the 'spinster' librarian? What changed your mind?"

"I never found the right man. Now I believe I have."

"You've only known him a few days," Cathy pointed out.

"At my age, a few days is enough."

Nancy looked back at her menu. "We won't argue with

you. Cathy and I have enough problems sorting out our love lives. Let's order. I'm starving."

"Do you know what you're having?" Cathy asked. Nancy always took forever to decide on her food choices.

"I think I'll go simple with the cheeseburger platter." She placed her menu on top of Mildred's. "What about you two?"

"I'm having the crock of French onion soup," Mildred said.

Cathy was still deciding. She finally selected the fried chicken sandwich with a side salad.

After ordering, their food was brought promptly. Cathy and Nancy devoured theirs quickly, while Mildred ate her soup with slow spoonfuls.

"Is that all you're having?" Nancy asked.

"It's filling, but I might also splurge on a dessert. What about you girls?"

Nancy said, "I should skip dessert, but I won't. That strawberry shortcake is calling to me." She indicated the glass case in which the desserts were displayed.

Cathy said, "I might go for a slice of that, too. What about you, Mildred?"

"I love strawberries." She signaled the waitress passing by. "Can we please have three slices of strawberry shortcake?"

"I'll get that for you right away. Coffee? Tea?"

They each asked for coffee and then Mildred requested the check. "It's my treat," she said, reaching into her purse. "I was the one who suggested this outing."

"We can leave the tip," Cathy offered and split it with Nancy.

Outside the restaurant, Cathy asked, "Should we go back now?"

"Wait," Mildred said. "Is that Henry's car?"

Cathy looked toward where Mildred was pointing. She recognized the gray Ford from when she'd been at Henry's house. "I think it is."

Nancy said, "I see him, and he's with Steve. They're in the flower shop. Let's join them and find out what they're up to."

Cathy no longer felt jealous of Lisa, so she had no problem following Nancy and Mildred into the store.

The men were at the counter talking with Lisa. Henry paused when they entered and glanced their way. "Hello, ladies. Did Danielle send you, too?"

Mildred walked up to him. "Hi, Henry. No. We were at the library and then had an early lunch."

Steve looked at Cathy, a smile lighting his face. "Hey, Cat. You can help. You're good with flowers. You always choose the right ones for Rainbow Gardens."

"Thank you," Cathy said, although she knew he was the gardener and should take most of the credit. "What can I help with?"

Henry answered her question. "Danielle has asked us to pick up flowers for tonight. We were lucky that they still had poinsettias." He indicated the two pots that sat on the counter. "It's not easy getting Christmas flowers in January."

Steve took out his phone, swiped it, and then showed it to Cathy. "This is Danielle's list. Dylan and Sheri are looking for the Christmas tree."

"Christmas tree?" Nancy said, "Why?"

"Danielle wants everything to be just as it was that night," Henry explained. "After Doris died, she got rid of the tree, the door wreath, and all the holiday decorations. Threw everything out. She was a real mess. Now she wants it all back."

"I think that's asking for too much," Cathy said.

Mildred smiled. "I don't think so. We should try to get as

close as we can to replicating the setting. I think it'll be fun decorating the tree, like a late Christmas."

Henry said, "You're so right, Millie. I have already offered to help. I'd love for you to assist me."

Cathy saw the face Nancy made, although Henry and Mildred were too occupied eyeing one another to see it. She often did the same when she caught her grandmother and Howard kissing.

Lisa said, "I'm afraid I don't have anything else on that list, but there's a big gardening center nearby if you want to check out what they have."

Henry said, "Yes. We have time. Please give us their address."

Lisa took a card out of the drawer under the counter. "Here's the card for Oaks Landing Nursery. It's about a mile from here. Should I ring up the poinsettias?"

Henry took the card, removed his wallet from his coat pocket, and handed her a credit card. "Danielle said she'll pay me back if I charge it," he explained.

Steve said, "Do you ladies want to join us, or do you have somewhere else to go?" He directed the question to Cathy, but Mildred answered. "We don't have other plans. Nancy, can you follow Steve and Henry in your car?"

Nancy nodded. "Sure. I'm good at tailing people." Cathy laughed.

CHAPTER THIRTY-SEVEN

As they left the garden shop, Steve holding the pots of poinsettias, Henry said, "There's room in my car for another passenger. Mildred, would you like to drive with us?"

Nancy rolled her eyes when Mildred accepted the offer. "I'd love to, Henry. Thank you." Cathy secretly wished she could ride with them, too, but Steve didn't ask.

The first thing Cathy saw when Nancy pulled into the nursery was Dylan and Sheri leaving the store. Dylan held a wreath. A Christmas tree was slung over his shoulder. Sheri was toting a bag that was bursting at its seams.

Henry, already parked, was walking up to them with Mildred at his side and Steve behind.

"C'mon, Cat," Nancy said, smiling. "Let's join the garden party."

She and Nancy joined the other five. "Funny meeting you here," Dylan grinned. Sheri said, "We got all the Christmas decorations Mommy wanted. I can't wait to decorate the tree. Do I get gifts again?" Cathy realized that Sheri's last Christmas had been disappointing to the little girl.

"This is only a make-believe Christmas, Honey," Dylan said, "but I did buy you that llama planter you wanted. You can consider that a gift."

She smiled. "It looks just like Lulu. I love it."

"I think we made this trip for nothing," Nancy said. "We might as well go back to the house."

Mildred said, "I don't mind looking around here. I love nurseries."

"I'll join you," Henry said. "Even though I'm retiring from gardening, I'm sure I can find something else for my house, even if it's a window plant."

Cathy found this statement worrying, as it meant Henry might not be considering moving to Buttercup Bend. She glanced at Steve. "Are you going with them, too?"

"No, but I'd like to check things out here. Would you want to come with me?"

Before Cathy could answer, Nancy said, "You go ahead. I'm heading back to the house."

"Do you need a ride?" Dylan asked.

"No. I took my car, but I'll see you back there."

As Nancy and Dylan walked to the parking lot, Sheri skipped next to her father, Steve turned to Cathy. Mildred and Henry had already gone inside the nursery. "There's really not much to see here this time of year, Cat, but I thought this might give us an opportunity to talk."

Cathy's stomach took a turn. She knew what was coming. He was going to tell her that he'd accepted the job here and would be leaving Buttercup Bend.

"Let's go inside where it's warmer." Steve led her into the

garden center. Mildred and Henry had disappeared from their view.

Inside, the only plants displayed were succulents, cacti, air ferns, and some hanging plants. There were watering cans, terra cotta pots, and bags of fertilizer. Steve walked over to a bench that sat near an indoor pond advertising a pond company. "Let's sit."

Cathy joined him on the bench. "I guess this is about Mavis' offer?"

He nodded. "Yes. I know you waited for her to tell me."

Cathy looked down. "Are you accepting the job?"

"I haven't decided yet. I'm waiting for all of this to be over. I'm not convinced that the murderer will be caught tonight. Either way, I'm going back to Buttercup Bend on Friday, and I'm hoping you are, too."

Cathy's heart lightened. "That's my plan. Nancy's also coming."

"Good. If I take the job, I won't move here right away. It all depends."

Cathy looked up into his blue eyes. "On me? On my answer?"

He smiled. "If you say 'yes,' we could move here together."

"But what about Gran, the rescue center, my school? I wouldn't want to commute an hour to college."

He waved his hand. "Hold on. I'm not asking you to do that. Not right away. I'm considering all possibilities right now."

Wasn't it like Steve to ponder everything? Cathy thought. It was also her way of thinking through things a thousand times before making up her mind. "Okay. What about Michael? Do you know if he's decided anything?"

"I haven't spoken with him." Steve got up. "Do you want to walk around or go back? That's all I wanted to say."

Cathy noted a tightness to his speech and regretted mentioning Michael. She didn't know what to say, so she just mentioned the obvious. "Nancy's gone, and you came in Henry's car, so we can't leave until Henry does."

"Good point. I don't know if there are any taxis around. We could try a rideshare company." He took out his cell phone.

It was then that Mildred and Henry came around a corner holding hands. "We almost forgot about you two," Henry said. "Are you ready to go back?"

CHAPTER THIRTY-EIGHT

enry dropped Cathy and Steve at the house. "I asked Millie over for afternoon tea," he said. "Would you two like to join us?"

Steve said, "Thanks, but I think I'll stay here until the reenactment. Danielle might need me to help set up things."

Cathy knew Henry had only issued the invitation to be polite. "I'll stay also. I need to talk with Nancy."

Henry smiled. "Alright then. We'll be back in time for dinner. If Danielle needs us, please let her know where we are."

"We'll do that," Cathy said, getting out of the back seat. She glanced at Mildred. "Have a good time."

As they entered, passing the wreath on the door, Cathy felt that they'd walked into a scene from a Christmas movie. Dylan and Sheri were placing ornaments on the six-foot tree they'd bought at the Oaks Landing Nursery. Christmas carols were playing from hidden speakers. She even smelled hints of pine, nutmeg, and spice.

"Merry Christmas," Steve said.

Dylan turned around. "Hi, there. Steve, you're a bit taller than me. Can you help put the angel atop the tree?"

"My pleasure." Steve walked over to them.

"Can I sit on your shoulder, Mr. Jefferson?" Sheri asked.

Steve laughed. The little girl was holding the angel. He bent down. "Get on board."

Sheri jumped on his back. "Daddy loves to give me horse-back rides," she said, "but he doesn't let me ride Lulu. That's okay. I don't want to hurt her."

"Don't hurt Steve either," Cathy said.

"No worries. She's very light."

Cathy watched as he stood up, and the girl placed the angel on the topmost branch of the tree.

"One more thing," Dylan said, as Steve lowered Sheri to the ground. "We need to test the lights. Can you switch them on, Honey?"

Cathy was surprised Dylan seemed to have gotten into the Christmas spirit when he'd been so against the reenactment.

Sheri ran to turn on the lights, and the tree came to life with multicolored bulbs. "Perfect. You can turn them off now, Sheri. We'll put them on again for dinner. Thank you, Sweetie."

Cathy asked, "Where's Danielle?"

"She's upstairs with Nancy," Dylan said. "They're doing some last-minute decorations up there."

"I'll see if they need help." As she started upstairs, she paused with her hand on the garland-covered banner when she heard Steve ask Dylan, "Do you know when the police are getting here?"

Dylan glanced at his watch. "They're coming about a half

hour before dinner. Danny told everyone to get here early. We still have about an hour. Mavis is over at Chris' place, but she made cocktails. They're in the kitchen if you want one."

"I thought we were reserving the drinks for dinner."

"These weren't on the menu. She thought we might want a few before the big event."

Sheri said. "Aunt Mavis made some for me."

"Mavis made some alcohol-free drinks," Dylan explained.

Cathy, halfway up the stairs, hoped Steve wouldn't have any of the concoction. Mavis was still high on her suspect list.

Upstairs, Cathy found Nancy and Danielle going through a box. Nancy noticed her first. "You're back. Good. Is Mildred with you?"

"No. She went with Henry for tea. Steve's here. He helped Dylan put up the tree."

"Rats!" Nancy made a face. "I need to talk with Mildred before dinner. I have to go over things with her."

"I'm sure she'll be here early." Cathy watched Danielle pull a mistletoe from the bag. "Mildred may be interested in this when she comes back with Henry."

"Let me have that." Nancy grabbed the mistletoe. "I'll hang it by the front door. Cathy, you have to get Steve under it or Michael when he gets here."

Cathy laughed. "That seems sneaky to me."

"It was up last time," Danielle said. "I put these things away after..." She paused, looking into the box. "I threw some of the decorations out, the ones I asked Henry and Dylan to find. I was so upset. It was the worst Christmas I ever had."

"I can imagine," Cathy said, "but did you have to be this accurate for the reenactment?"

Nancy answered for Danielle. "That was my idea, Cat. The setting is important to recreate."

"I hope you're right," Danielle said. "It's been a lot of work and brought back painful memories, but if we catch the person who killed my mother, it'll all be worth it."

Nancy asked, "Do you need anything else now? I'd like to go down and put the mistletoe up?"

"Everything's set. I should go down, too." Danielle opened a closet and shoved the box inside.

Steve and Dylan were still talking near the Christmas tree when Cathy, Nancy, and Danielle came downstairs. Sheri ran to her mother. "Look at the tree. It lights up, and Mr. Jefferson helped me put up the angel."

"It's very pretty," Danielle said. She turned to Steve. "Thank you."

Dylan said, "I'm going to try one of those cocktails Mavis made. I can use one before the cops arrive. Want to join me?"

"That sounds like a good idea."

"She made one for me, too," Sheri said, again for her mother's benefit. The three of them went into the kitchen while Nancy grabbed a chair, stood on it, and hung the mistletoe above the front door. "There we go," she exclaimed. "Cathy, Steve." She signaled them. "Can you two come here and test it?" She jumped off the chair and pulled it away.

Cathy saw the redness bloom on Steve's cheeks but, before either of them could make a move, she heard footsteps coming up the walk, the door opened, and Michael and Stacy walked through.

"Hey, everyone," Michael said. "We wanted to make sure we got here early."

Stacy, dressed in her red cape and holding her veterinarian

bag, glanced around, and said, "Oooh, it's Christmas again." Cathy's heart sank as she pointed out the mistletoe. "Mike, I think we walked under the mistletoe."

Michael turned around and looked up. Stacy put her arms around him. Cathy looked away as they kissed.

Nancy, nudging her, whispered. "You snooze, you lose."

CHAPTER THIRTY-NINE

A few minutes later, Mildred and Henry walked in followed by Mavis and Chris. Both couples took advantage of the mistletoe. Cathy couldn't even look at Michael, and she was disappointed that Steve didn't follow through on Nancy's suggestion to kiss her underneath it.

Danielle came out of the kitchen holding a glass of red liquid. Cathy thought she looked tipsy from the way she swaggered. "Did I hear people come in?" she asked.

Behind her, Dylan appeared less drunk, but maybe he could hold his liquor better. Sheri said, "Why is Mommy walking funny?"

Mavis smiled. "I see you enjoyed the drink I made."

Danielle shook her head. "I had the same drink as Sheri. I just feel a little dizzy."

Nancy turned to Mildred. "I have to speak with you. Come upstairs. Danielle has filled me in on what Doris did that night. You need to rehearse."

"What about Betty?" Cathy asked. "How are you handling her part?"

"She's sleeping," Dylan said. "We're not waking her until the last minute. I personally don't think it's a good idea to have her down here during dinner. She shouldn't have been at the last one."

Nancy said, "I disagree. Betty has given us clues. I realize they're not all accurate, but I think there's something to them. We also believe she knows who killed her daughter but is protecting them."

Mildred walked over to Nancy. "I'm ready to be briefed." She turned back to Henry. "I won't be long, dear."

But before Mildred and Nancy got to the staircase, the doorbell rang. "That must be Jodi," Mavis said. "She's the only one who isn't here yet." But when she answered the door, two policemen entered.

Nancy whispered to Mildred, "We still have time before dinner. I'll fill you in later. It wouldn't look good if we went upstairs now."

"Hello, Ms. Taylor. I must say you've done quite a job decorating," Jones said.

"Thank you, but the credit goes to my niece."

Danielle nearly fell as she walked toward them. "It was fun. I love Christmas."

Jones whispered to Reilly. "Is she drunk?"

Mavis said, "Danny is only lightheaded. I prepared those cocktails, and she says she only drank the mock ones I made for Sheri. I think she's just nervous about this reenactment."

Jones nodded. "Good because I'd rather everyone be sober for this. Please get rid of those drinks. The only ones you should have on hand are the ones that were prepared that night. Did you prepare those, too?"

"Yes," Mavis said, "but none of them were alcoholic. Danny even persuaded me not to spike the eggnog. She was a party pooper that night."

Chris said, "I brought a bottle of wine. That was served, too."

Reilly, next to Jones, was typing on his phone. Cathy assumed he was taking notes.

"Is everyone here?" Jones asked, looking around the room.

"Everyone but Jodi," Mavis said. "I hope she comes."

"I can call her," Chris offered, taking out his cell phone.

But just as he was about to tap her contact, Jodi rushed through the door. Her face was flushed, her red hair in her eyes. "Lulu's gone," she said. "She's not in her pen. Somebody must've let her loose. The gate was open. Luckily, the other llamas are still there."

"Lulu!" Sherri cried, "We have to find her."

"Don't worry," Dylan said, "You can look for her with me. She couldn't have gotten far."

Mavis put out a hand to stop Chris. "Wait! We just drove by the llama pen when we came. I saw Lulu, and the gate was closed."

"If Lulu was there when you arrived," Nancy said, "then the only person who could've opened the gate was Jodi."

"Why would I do that?" the girl asked.

"I don't know," Danielle said, sounding more sober. "You tell us."

Jodi shrugged. "Okay. If you must know. I did it. Lulu didn't want to go. She must be trained, so I gave her a treat. She finally took it."

Sheri began to cry. "Why did you let her go, Jodi? Please get her back."

Dylan said, "Which way did she go? You better come with us and show us."

"No one is going anywhere," Jones said. "We're here to reenact a murder, and everyone is upset about a llama?"

Reilly turned to Jones. "That little girl is sad. Can't you let them go? We have time before the reenactment starts."

Jones sighed. "Okay, but we're going, too."

Nancy said, "Jodi hasn't explained why she did this."

Jodi faced Nancy. "Why does it matter?"

"It matters because maybe you're the one who killed Doris and are trying to postpone the reenactment."

Cathy had thought of that, too.

"I did no such thing, even though Mrs. Diaz accused me and I still thinks she believes I'm guilty. The reason I let Lulu loose was because I don't want to be a part of this. It makes me remember what happened to Honey," her voice broke. "I knew I'd look guilty if I didn't come, but I had to find a way to put it off. That was stupid of me. I'll show you where Lulu went."

Jones said, "Mr. Diaz and his daughter can go. I'll join them, and you stay here and watch the others, Reilly."

When they left, Nancy took the opportunity to take Mildred upstairs and instruct her on what to do during dinner.

Danielle flopped on the couch. Cathy took a seat next to her.

"I have such a headache," Danielle sighed. "I'm so sorry I drank so much. I didn't realize how hard it was for me to do this. It hit me suddenly. Mildred looks nothing like my mother did, but all of this," she waved her hands, "It brings it back. I can understand how Jodi feels, but I don't understand why she still thinks I suspect her. I've apologized many times. I reacted so irrationally that night and now I have to do it again."

"I know it must be difficult, but you have to remember that this is only a reenactment."

Mavis walked over to them and took a seat on the other side of her niece. "Danny, we've all done things that we're sorry about. I should've known better than to make those drinks. I asked Chris to clear them away. Reilly went into the kitchen with him. I feel drained, and the dinner hasn't even started. I have the food in the crockpot and will be serving it soon, but I feel like you do. Even though it's pretend, it'll seem like my sister's still here. People think we didn't get along, but I loved your mother. We weren't alike in many things, but we were very close when we were young. I don't really know what happened. We grew apart. Maybe it was because of Chris or the fact she left the farm. The reason doesn't matter." She looked down at her hands that were clasped in her lap. "When Doris returned, I hoped we could reconnect in the old way, but she was distant. While she was in Buttercup Bend, she'd become a different person. She wanted everything back – the farm, Chris, even you."

Cathy knew that wasn't true because she'd read the letter that Nancy found in Doris' room, but she couldn't tell Mavis that. She wondered why Nancy hadn't shown it to the detectives.

Mavis was interrupted when Dylan, Sheri, Jodi, and Jones returned. Sheri was smiling and skipping. "We found her," she said excitedly.

"Lulu's back in her pen," Dylan said. "She was munching on grass on the trail she usually takes for hikes."

Jodi said, "I'm glad we caught her. I'm sorry I did such a stupid thing."

It was then that Mildred and Nancy came downstairs. Betty was behind them. A few minutes later, Chris and Reilly also entered the room.

Danielle stood up. "Gram, you're awake."

Nancy said, "She's okay. I spoke with her. She knows what we're doing, and she's prepared."

Jones said, "Then we should get this show on the road."

CHAPTER FORTY

"**B**efore we begin," Nancy said, "Danielle has shared everyone's movements with me that she remembers from that night. I had her set the dining room table with name cards in case people forgot where they sat. The main problem with reenacting this event is that while Danielle has a great memory, she only remembers what she saw and heard. She didn't witness the murder so can't guide us with that."

Jones said, "Excuse me, but I need to put down some rules." He glanced at Steve and Michael. "You two need to leave. Go upstairs. You weren't here then, so you shouldn't be here now." The men did as he requested. As he left, Michael blew Stacy a kiss, and Cathy's heart lurched. Jones then looked at Mavis. "Have you begun cooking yet?"

"The food's in the crockpot, but I should go check it." She left her seat on the couch and went into the kitchen. "Follow her, Reilly," Jones instructed. "I want you in the kitchen the whole time." Reilly nodded and left the room.

Jones turned around and pointed at Nancy and Cathy. "I'll

allow you two to stay, but I want you to keep quiet. Is that understood?"

Nancy said, "We're detectives. You're only here to support us."

Cathy was taken aback at Nancy's bold statement.

Jones met her gaze. "You're wrong. We're in charge of this jurisdiction. You're the ones who are here to support us."

"In order to support you," Nancy said, "we need to keep everyone on track. We want to recreate that night as accurately as possible. Danielle's gone through a lot of trouble with the decorations, and I've briefed Mildred who's playing Doris as best I could. I also spoke with Betty, but I still have to cue the others."

Cathy could see the wheels turning in Jones' head as he considered Nancy's words. "Alright then," he finally said, "you can speak with people, but you can't involve yourself or get in my or Reilly's way. Got it?"

Nancy smiled. "Yes, sir."

The expression Jones gave her was a cross between a smile and a sneer. He looked around the room at the others. "Let's begin. Please take your seats."

Danielle said, "I was helping in the kitchen when people arrived. I made the salads and brought them out. Gram and Sheri were with me."

"Go on. Do that."

Danielle took Betty's arm and her daughter's hand and led them into the kitchen.

Nancy said, "Everyone should hang their coats. There's a coat closet off the hall. Also, Danielle said that Stacy had left her bag on the couch."

"Why did you do that?" Jones asked.

"It's bulky," Stacy said. "I didn't want to bring it into the dining room."

"How come you didn't leave it in your car?" His fat eyebrows rose as he asked the question.

"I thought you already interrogated me. I had forgotten to leave it there. We're supposed to do exactly what we did that night, so I'm just keeping to the script." She walked to the couch and placed her vet kit next to a poinsettia pillow. Then she joined Chris and Henry at the coat closet.

Jones asked, "What about you, Ms. Johnson? Where's your coat?"

"I didn't bring one," Jodi said. "It wasn't cold that night. My sweater was warm enough. I hung it over my chair."

"Go ahead," he directed.

Everyone took their seats. Mildred was the last to claim her place. Mavis' chair was next to her at the head of the table. Chris was on the opposite side next to where Mavis would sit after serving dinner and directly across from Mildred. The chair on Mildred's other side was empty and missing a name card.

"Who's supposed to be there?" Jones asked.

"That was Danielle's seat," Nancy said. "She wasn't in it much. She said she was mostly in the kitchen keeping an eye on Betty."

"Hmmm." The detective's exclamation held a hint of suspicion.

Danielle and Sheri arrived then. Danielle carried a large salad bowl. Sheri held the serving spoons. They placed them in the center of the table.

"Where's Mrs. Taylor?" Jones asked.

"She's still in the kitchen. Mavis and Reilly are with her."

"I see. How is she acting?" Jones knew about Betty's condition.

"She seems fine. Better than I expected. She had a meltdown yesterday, but I think she's managing this well so far."

"How about you?" Cathy asked. She saw the strain on Danielle's face.

Danielle sighed. "I'll be better when this night is over."

Jodi asked, "Do we have to eat the salad? I don't have much of an appetite."

"That's up to you. I'd actually prefer no one eats," Jones said.

Chris said, "You'll change your mind once you taste Mavis' stew."

"I don't eat on the job and neither does Reilly."

Cathy asked, "Since Nancy is out here, may I go in the kitchen?"

Jones shrugged. "I don't care where you go. Just stay out of our way."

Cathy was thinking about Betty and how she believed the old woman had witnessed the murder. She hadn't mentioned to Nancy her idea of following Betty.

In the kitchen, Mavis was standing at the stove stirring the crockpot. Cathy smelled the aroma of garlic and spices. Unlike the officers, she was hungry and looked forward to eating dinner. Reilly was leaning against the refrigerator scanning the room. Sheri was on the floor playing with a doll. Danielle, sitting at the table across from Betty, looked toward her as she came in. "Cathy, are you joining us?"

"I thought I'd check on things." She glanced at Betty. "Hi, Betty. How are you doing?"

"I'm okay, Cathy. I'm confused about what I have to do."

"Gram, Nancy and I already went over everything with you," Danielle said in a tired voice. "You stay in here with me and have dinner. After we eat, Sheri helps me clear the dining room table. I thought you were helping, too, but I lost track of where you went. When I came back into the kitchen, you weren't here, but a few minutes later, you were seated at the dining room table with everyone. I decided to let you stay there, and Sheri and I took our places for dessert."

"What about the drinks?" Cathy asked. "And where was Doris at this time?"

Danielle sighed. "I have a hard time remembering that. I'm sorry. I wasn't paying close attention."

Mavis, turning from the stove after mixing the stew, said, "The drinks were in the kitchen. I'd made them. People were coming and going talking. Some brought their glasses in here for refills. I told the police all about that." She eyed Reilly as she spoke.

Cathy was surprised the officer didn't comment, but she continued asking questions. "And where were you, Mavis? Did you see who went into the kitchen?"

"I was in the dining room. I wasn't watching everyone, so I can't tell you."

"Did you see Doris? Did she go in the kitchen?"

She shrugged. "Possibly. Like I said, I wasn't watching."

"Did anyone else leave the table that you know of during that time?"

Reilly cleared his throat and gave Cathy a warning look. "Miss Carter, no more questions. Didn't Officer Jones tell you to stay out of the way? That includes talking with the participants in this reenactment."

"Jones said that we could talk to people to help guide them to remember what happened."

"That's not what you're doing." Reilly folded his hands over his chest. As he did so, Cathy glanced behind him at the counter where the drinks stood that Mavis mentioned. The glasses were lined up on a tray. She was tempted to ask who'd served them but kept quiet. She knew the night had just begun.

CHAPTER FORTY-ONE

Nancy walked in. "Danielle, I believe you bring the drinks out now," she said.

Danielle stood up, walked to the counter, and picked up the tray. "I'll be right back, honey," she said to her daughter who was whispering something about Red Riding Hood to her doll. Nancy asked, "Is everyone okay in here?"

"So far, so good. I think," Cathy said, although she wasn't happy that Reilly had silenced her.

Mavis mixed the stew again. "Dinner is almost ready."

Betty, hearing that, stood from her chair. "Do you need help serving it?"

"No, Gram, but I could use a hand taking the rolls out of the oven."

"I'll be happy to do that, but why are you calling me, Gram? I'm Julia Child, the famous chef."

Cathy feared that Betty was having another episode until the old woman smiled and looked at Nancy. "Did that sound right, Miss Meyers?"

Nancy nodded. "Very good, Betty. But I don't believe you

brought out the dinner rolls. Danielle said she did. She'll be back shortly."

When Danielle returned, Mavis had placed the stew on a large platter. Cathy was disappointed when she realized there wasn't enough for her and Nancy. Not to mention the men upstairs.

"Don't worry," Nancy said, reading Cathy's mind. "We'll order a pizza for us and the guys later."

Danielle took the vegetables out of the oven with a kitchen mitt and used a serving spoon to place a few on Betty's plate. Then she said, "C'mon, Sheri. We're eating now." Sheri jumped up and followed her mother into the dining room. Before Mavis joined them, she added some stew to Betty's plate. "We'll be right back, Gram," she said.

Reilly eyed Betty as she sat at the kitchen table. "Aren't you going to eat that?" he asked, and Cathy wondered if he was as hungry as she was. Jones said they didn't eat on the job, but it couldn't have been easy smelling the food.

Betty said, "I'm waiting for Danny. I can't remember what I'm supposed to do."

Nancy said, "You bring your plate into the dining room, Betty, and take a seat at the table. They left one for you, even though Danielle thought you'd be more comfortable in here. I'll bring you in if that helps." She turned to Cathy. "You stay with Officer Reilly and keep an eye on who comes in for drink refills. There's a pitcher in the refrigerator with the mix."

Cathy didn't like being left alone with Reilly and not able to observe what was happening in the dining room. She also realized that since she and the officer weren't around that night, they weren't recreating the circumstances that led to Doris' murder. "Nancy," she said, calling her back before she left, "This isn't going to work. If Reilly and I stay in here, the killer isn't going to come. In fact, I think they're well prepared to change their actions of that night."

"I'm aware of that, Cathy, but Jones ordered Reilly to stay in here. We already know that Doris came back for a refill of her drink. I've told Mildred to do that. Somehow, either in the kitchen or the dining room, the killer added the xylazine to that drink. I don't expect that person to repeat the crime. I most certainly hope they don't for Mildred's sake, but I think that if the others are more observant this time, we might be able to catch the killer. I've thought it strange, and I've shared my belief with Danielle, that none of the seven people at that dinner saw or heard anything. If you want, you can come with me and leave Reilly here. You might be able to help."

Cathy was relieved she could participate more fully in the reenactment. She knew Nancy was right because she felt sure that there was a witness to Doris' murder and that person was Betty.

CHAPTER FORTY-TWO

The atmosphere in the dining room was subdued. People ate in silence, which Cathy knew hadn't been the case last month. Jones, standing in the corner watching them, said, "Doesn't anyone have anything to say? What were you all talking about that night?"

Nancy, standing next to Cathy, said, "Go on, Danielle. Go through the conversations again like you did with me earlier."

Everyone's eyes turned to Danielle. She pushed her plate aside. Cathy noticed she hadn't eaten a bite. In a small voice, she said, "I can't."

"What?" Jones asked. "Speak up. What are you saying, Mrs. Diaz?"

In a louder voice that broke as she spoke, Danielle cried, "I can't do this." She jumped up. "I'm sorry, Nancy, but I made up all the things I told you. The truth is I don't remember any of it. The only time that sticks in my mind is when my mother collapsed."

"Then why did you go along with this?" Jones asked. "You took me and Reilly away from our work. We may as well leave."

"No!" Betty stood up. "I remember it all now. It's come back. I've been fighting it for too long. I know who killed my daughter."

The same eyes that had followed Danielle now gazed at Betty. Cathy watched the expressions. She knew that if Betty was telling the truth, someone at the table would have something to fear.

Dylan said, "I think you should go to your room, Betty. I knew it was a mistake having you here." He was about to rise from his seat, when Chris said, "Let her speak, or are you afraid she'll finger you as the killer?"

Dylan's eyes blazed as if he was ready to punch Chris. "She's a sick woman. She doesn't know what she's saying."

Mavis sided with Chris. "She sounds coherent to me."

Jones jumped in. "I'm not sure we can use her statement as evidence, but I agree we should let her talk."

Betty was about to open her mouth when Danielle said, "I'd like to bring Sheri upstairs with Michael and Steve. She shouldn't be around for this." She glanced at her daughter who was hugging her doll.

"The girl can go, but you have to stay," Jones said.

Danielle said, "It's okay, honey. You can bring your doll up there. I'll be up soon."

Sheri ran from the table. Cathy felt relieved that she'd been excused. Whatever Betty was about to tell them was sure to implicate a member of her family or a close friend.

After Sheri left, Dylan said, "I know you want to hear what Betty has to say, but if you can't use it as evidence, what's the point?"

Before Jones could reply, Chris said, "The point is that Betty might have witnessed the murder. You've seemed so intent on putting her in a home, feeding her pills to keep her asleep, all this against my daughter's wishes. I wouldn't put it past you that you killed my wife, too, and that's why you're so against Betty talking."

"Are you accusing me?" Dylan asked. He was standing now, his face red.

Chris didn't seem frightened of the angry Peruvian. Cathy knew it was because there was an officer present.

"Yes," Chris said. "You must be the killer. Cathy said Betty even identified you the first night she was here."

"She was having an episode then," Dylan said. "She thought she was Nancy Drew, and who knows if she's having an episode now." He turned to Betty. "Tell us who you are."

"I'm Betty Taylor," Betty responded in a clear voice. "Your grandmother-in-law. Danny's grandmother."

Chris said, "See. She's perfectly fine." Cathy watched as he turned to Betty. "Tell us, Betty, did Dylan kill Doris?"

Cathy expected Jones to intervene, but he just stood there waiting for Betty's answer. She heard everyone's intake of breath including her own. Danielle appeared close to tears. Still standing, she'd inched away from her husband as if ready to run.

Then Betty spoke in a calm, controlled voice. "No, Chris. Dylan didn't kill Doris. You did."

CHAPTER FORTY-THREE

At Betty's words, Chris paled. Mavis jumped up. "No. She's crazy. Dylan's right. She doesn't know what she's talking about."

Chris regained his composure at Mavis' support. He smiled, but Cathy could tell it was forced. "Alright, Betty. If I killed Doris, how did I do it, and why?"

Betty faced him. "You used the poison the wolf brought, and you did it because she wouldn't take you back."

"See," Chris said. "Dylan is right. She's having another episode."

Jones walked over to the table and stared at him. "Let her finish." He looked toward Betty. "Please explain what you mean, Mrs. Taylor."

"I'll be happy to do that, Officer, but I'd like to start at the beginning. Now that my head is clear, I think I can get it straight."

Nancy, speaking for the first time, asked, "What do you mean your head is clear, Betty?"

"I didn't take my pills," she said, "the ones Chris' doctor prescribed for me."

"I thought Dylan gave you the pills," Nancy said.

"I gave her the sleeping pills that the psychologist prescribed for her. Chris was the one who took her to those appointments. He's been doing that since before Doris' death."

At Dylan's words, Cathy thought that a lightbulb went off in Mavis' head the way her expression changed so quickly. "I remember. Betty was only having a few memory lapses, but after she started treatments, her episodes began. That's when Chris suggested I get her power of attorney and have her sign over the farm to me. It was before Doris returned."

"And the bank records the accountant showed me," Dylan said, "they weren't balanced. I thought a few figures were off, but now I see that someone was dipping into it."

"I gave Chris authorization on our account," Mavis said. "I was such a fool." She stood up and turned to Chris. "Did you kill my mother? Tell me now."

Jones stepped in. "Stop! I want to hear everything from Betty." He yelled out, "Reilly, come in here. I want you to listen to this."

Reilly rushed in from the kitchen. "Yes, Sir. What's going on?"

"I think we have a witness," Jones told him. He took out his phone. "I'm recording this. Don't anyone say another word. I only want to hear Betty."

Cathy saw that the smile was still pasted on Chris' face, but his skin had lost its color. He looked like a sick clown.

"Please continue, Mrs. Taylor," Jones said.

Betty looked around the room, avoiding Chris. "Chris, uh, Mr. Grady, suggested I accompany him on a hike with Lulu that morning."

"Lulu?" Jones raised his eyebrows.

"That's our llama," Dylan said. "She was Doris' favorite."

"I asked him why he hadn't asked Doris, but he said he thought I'd enjoy getting out in the fresh air. It wasn't very cold that day, and I do like walking."

Nancy asked, "Did he give you something to eat or drink on the hike?"

"No interruptions." Jones frowned at Nancy.

"That's okay. I want to answer that question." Betty turned toward Nancy. "Chris had a bottle of juice with him. He didn't drink from it, but he told me I should. It was at the end of our walk, going home. I was thirsty, so I drank it. It tasted odd. I was very tired afterwards and, when I got back to the house, I slept until dinner."

Reilly nudged Jones. "Sorry, Sir, but I'd like to ask a question. May I?"

"Go ahead."

"Wait!" Nancy said, "He can ask questions, but I can't." She gave Jones an angry look.

"He's on my team."

"I'm a detective."

Jones sighed. "Alright. You both can ask questions if they're pertinent. Go ahead, Reilly."

"Ladies first." Reilly glanced at Nancy.

Nancy turned to Betty. "Did you encounter anyone on your hike with Chris?"

"That was my question," Reilly said.

Betty smiled. "I should've mentioned that. We met Stacy. She said she had an appointment to look at Lulu."

Stacy, who hadn't spoken during dinner, said, "That's right. I met them. After Chris put Lulu back in her pen, I examined her. I also checked the other llamas and alpacas. They were due for shots, so I administered those."

"That's odd," Jones said. "I thought you came much later to the farm, around dinner time."

"I did," Stacy said, "on my second trip."

"Second trip? Why did you come back?"

Stacy answered Jones' question. "Chris told me that Dylan was having a problem with Mr. Ed, and I..."

Before she finished her sentence, Jones cut in. "Don't tell me. Mr. Ed is a horse."

"Yes." Stacy smiled. "Horses aren't usually kept on fiber farms, but Dylan likes to ride. He brought Mr. Ed back from Peru with Lulu, but he never completely tamed him. Occasionally, I would give the stallion a dose of xylazine to calm him."

At the mention of the drug that killed her daughter, Betty said, "It was in Stacy's bag. She hadn't used all of it. Chris put the rest in Doris' drink."

"Hold on," Jones said. "Are you implying that Stacy is an accomplice? Is that why she never mentioned this during our questioning?"

Stacy jumped up. "I didn't say anything about it because I knew you'd suspect me. After speaking with Chris that morning, I went to the animal hospital and got a bottle of the xylazine. Ed is really spooked by shots, so I got the liquid version. I fed it to him with a dropper. I was careful only to give him a few drops. I thought Doris had a heart attack, so I didn't check my bag that night. When I noticed the xylazine missing, I thought I'd misplaced it. I didn't connect it until the tox report on Doris' drink came back and then I knew no one would believe me."

Before Jones could question her further, Dylan said, "Mr. Ed was fine that day. Chris made that story up, so he could get his hands on the xylazine. He must've taken it out of Stacy's bag, added it to Doris' drink when she wasn't looking, and then disposed of it."

"He must've done that when he left to go to the bathroom right after dessert," Mavis said. She couldn't even look Chris in the eyes. This was the man she'd loved all those years, the man who'd asked her to marry him, the man who'd killed her sister.

CHAPTER FORTY-FOUR

"This is absurd," Chris said. His face had turned from white to red. "You have no proof of this except her word." He glared at Betty.

"You're right, Chris," Dylan said, "but I can get proof. I'll speak with Dr. Habib, Betty's psychologist. How much were you taking from the farm to pay him?"

"That doesn't prove I killed Doris."

"Let's hear the rest of Betty's story," Nancy suggested.

Jones nodded. "Yes. Please finish, Mrs. Taylor."

Betty, still composed, cleared her throat, and continued her tale. "I need to back up a little. During the summer, I'd been hiding my pills and not taking them. I slipped out when people were asleep and walked by the gift shop. I think Doris heard me once, but she didn't see me. I was snooping on Chris. I had a feeling he was up to something. I never cared for Doris' choice of husbands. To be honest, I was glad when they divorced but not pleased that Mavis insisted he stay on the farm."

Cathy realized that Betty was the stalker that had caused Doris to stop working nights at the gift shop.

When Betty paused, Jones said, "Go on. What did you hear or see by Chris' home?"

"I object," Chris said, jumping up as if he was in a courtroom. "This is still only her word, and it was months ago. What bearing could it have on this?"

"Sit down, Mr. Grady." Jones gave him a warning look, and Cathy noticed Reilly touch the gun in his holster.

Betty answered Jones' question. "He was with Mavis. They were having an argument. She'd accused him of taking up with Doris again, and he swore that they'd been together only once and that they were through. He sounded as if he was close to tears."

Mavis cut in. "Mother's right. What she's saying is true. I was angry with Doris. I'd never been happy that she'd returned to the farm. I was afraid she'd stake her claim to it as my older sister when I'd done all the hard work. I was also worried that she wanted Chris back. He'd started acting odd toward me, and then I caught him with her when he said he was busy one night." Her voice choked. "When I confronted him about it, he admitted it but said it would never happen again, and I believed him." She turned to Chris and said, "I was a fool to believe you." Chris turned his head and whispered, "I'm sorry but that still doesn't make me guilty of murder."

Cathy thought Mavis' words explained the note Nancy found in Doris' room.

Nancy said, "I think we're getting to Chris' motive now." She looked toward him. "Tell me, did you give up on Doris, or did she turn you down?"

"That's enough! I want a lawyer," Chris exclaimed. Nancy had hit a nerve. But Cathy knew that even if they confiscated Betty's pills and confronted the psychologist who aided Chris, that wouldn't be enough proof to arrest him for Doris' murder. For that to happen, he would have to confess. She said, "Now I see why Doris came to Buttercup Bend. She was escaping your control, Chris. I bet she hoped you were gone when she returned or that you'd changed. You, however, were hoping for something else. You thought she was finally coming back to you. When you discovered that wasn't her intention, you killed her. Why did it take so long for you to do that? Couldn't you see that you weren't man enough for her? The only one who cared for you was Mavis, and the reason you held on to her was to keep your claim on the farm." Cathy watched Chris' face as she spoke. He looked like a captured animal, but his gaze was on Mavis, not Cathy. "That's not true. I did it for her," he screamed. Mavis shrank back at his outburst, and Cathy saw Reilly reach for his gun, but Jones stilled his hand.

"I couldn't give myself to you until she was out of my system," Chris said, speaking to Mavis in a lower voice that now sounded anguished rather than angry. "I knew she'd come back. I waited and, yes, I thought she'd come back for me. But she hadn't. When I finally convinced her to sleep with me, she said it would never happen again and gave us her blessing. That was a kick in the face. She didn't understand." His voice cracked as tears streamed down his face. "I knew the only way I could be happy with you was to kill her."

"You're the one who's sick, not my mother," Mavis said. Her eyes no longer held fear. That was replaced by pity.

Jones turned to Reilly. "Cuff him and read him his rights. Even the best lawyer won't be able to get him out of this." He turned and gave Cathy a smile. Nancy whispered, "Good job, Cat."

As they led him away and he passed his daughter, Chris said, "Danny, you'll come bail your old man out, won't you? Remember, Doris abandoned you."

Danielle watched him go without a word.

CHAPTER FORTY-FIVE

After the policemen left with Chris, Dylan said, "That was brilliant, Cathy. You fired him up enough to get him to confess."

"I took a chance. I had no idea it would work."

Danielle covered her face with her hands. "I can't believe he killed her. All these years, he was my only parent. Poor Sheri. How can I tell her?"

Dylan, at his wife's side, placed a hand on her arm. "I'll take care of that, honey. We can say he left. I'll think of an explanation. She can learn the truth when she's older." He looked across the table. "I should apologize, Betty. I thought I was only giving you pills that would help you sleep, not hallucinogens."

"I know that, and you're still my favorite grandson-in-law." She winked.

Nancy said, "There are still a lot of unanswered questions. The one that bothers me most, Betty, is when you saw Chris put the xylazine in Doris' drink, why didn't you stop him?"

Betty sighed. "I wish I had, but after that drink I took in the afternoon and my evening dose of pills, I wasn't thinking clearly. I thought I was Julia Child. When I saw Chris add xylazine to my daughter's drink, I believed he was adding syrup or nutmeg like what was in our eggnog. Afterwards, even when I wasn't drugged, I had nightmares and saw flashes from that night, but I didn't realize what he'd done until this evening when the fog lifted."

"I can understand that," Cathy said, remembering how she'd felt after the accident in which her parents were killed. "When you experience something traumatic, your mind blocks it out to protect you from the horror. It's known as PTSD."

"And the pills didn't help," Dylan added.

"About the pills," Cathy said. "If Chris was able to get them off that doctor, Habib, how come he didn't use those or something less detectable to kill Doris instead of the xylazine?"

"Because he wanted to frame me," Stacy said from the end of the table.

Nancy said, "He didn't succeed at that because my reenactment worked." She looked pleased with herself. "Now I think it's time we go upstairs, bring Michael and Steve down, and tell them what happened."

"I need to go up, too," Danielle said. "I have to check on Sheri. I should put her to bed."

"I'll go with you." Dylan joined his wife. "We can both read to her tonight. There's no need to tell her until tomorrow that she won't be seeing her grandfather anymore."

Cathy, watching them head to the stairs, felt a flutter in her chest. It looked like Danielle and Dylan were on the way to repairing their marriage. She and Nancy followed them.

When Nancy explained everything to Steve and Michael, she emphasized how Cathy solved the case.

Steve smiled, "I'm not surprised. Cat is one smart lady."

Cathy felt a blush touch her cheeks.

Michael said, "I'm glad Stacy's in the clear." Cathy was disappointed that the vet was uppermost in his mind.

"I think we should order that pizza now," Nancy said.

Downstairs, Mavis, Stacy, Jodi, Mildred, and Henry were still seated around the dining room table. Mavis was staring blankly ahead. Cathy imagined what a blow her lover's guilt had been.

Mildred said, "I'd propose a toast to Cathy for catching the killer, but I'm not sure people would be interested in drinking right now."

"I would be," Mavis said, "but not this non-alcoholic stuff. I want something stiff."

Henry walked over to her and patted her on the back. "Oh, dear. I know how hard this is for you, and I'm sorry. I wish I could help."

Jodi said, "He was the only one I trusted. I guess my instincts suck. I need to apologize to Danielle. It's awful to lose her mother and then her father this way."

Michael pulled an extra chair from the kitchen and sat next to Stacy. "Are you okay?" he asked. "I heard that Grady tricked you into bringing the xylazine."

"I'm angry at myself for not figuring that out. I should've checked my bag afterwards. That was a careless thing to do knowing how dangerous that drug could be in a high dose."

"It's not your fault." Michael placed a hand on top of hers. Cathy looked away.

Nancy said, "Pizza will be here soon. I ordered two boxes."

"Thanks, Nance. I'm starving," Steve said. He'd also pulled up a chair to the table. He glanced at Cathy. "While we wait, I have some news. It's not as front page as what happened here tonight, but I think it might be of interest. Mike and I had a talk upstairs." He looked toward Mavis. "We're not taking the jobs here. We appreciate you considering us, but our place is back in Buttercup Bend," he paused, "with Cathy."

Cathy felt relief wash over her, but it was short lived because Stacy said, "Mike told me he wasn't taking the position and invited me to work with him at his animal hospital. I've accepted and am excited."

"Congratulations!" Steve said. "Mike has always had too much work to manage there despite Brody's helpful assistance. Having you on staff will be an asset."

"I'm looking forward to easing his load and helping out at the rescue center, too," Stacy said, glancing at Cathy who pasted a false smile on her face.

Mildred said, "I've come to my own decision. I don't know whether the Oaks Landing Library will offer me the job I applied for, but I don't care. My place is also in Buttercup Bend."

Henry, who had rejoined her, said, "I've been meaning to make some changes myself now that I'm retiring. I think a move might be what I need, and Buttercup Bend sounds like the perfect town in which to spend my golden years." He smiled.

Mavis said, "I understand about you all wanting to make new starts elsewhere, but my place is here on the farm. It always has been. I have my niece and her family who I know will continue to support me, and I plan to keep supporting them, too. There are quite a few young men interested in the gardening job, and I'll find a new vet somehow. Now that Chris isn't stealing from us, I should be able to offer them more." She took a breath and continued. "Danielle told me yesterday in private that she's expecting another child. Since Chris will be in jail, moving into his house will give Danielle's family more room. The new gardener can take Henry's place, and I hope Jodi will stay with us." She glanced at the young woman.

"I sure will. I'm prepared to start working again. I can help in the gift shop and with the animals. I love the llamas and have missed them very much, especially Lulu." She looked at Cathy. "I've also decided to adopt another cat. As much as I loved Honey, I realize that there are many pets who need homes and someone to care for them. I plan to visit the local animal shelter and choose one or two cats. I'll be spending time with the barn cats, too."

Nancy said, "That's a great decision. I adopted Hobo after I lost my beloved Popeye, and I've never regretted doing that. I still think of Popeye, but I know he would be happy to see me with Hobo."

The pizzas arrived. Steve and Michael brought them to the table and opened the boxes. Everyone took slices including Sheri who came down with Danielle and Dylan. "She couldn't sleep," Danielle explained. "I heard you say something about pizza and figured she was hungry."

"Yummy, pizza!" Sheri said, grabbing a slice. Dylan quickly placed a paper plate under it. Sheri didn't seem to notice a change in her parents, or maybe that's what her smile meant. Cathy was glad that Sheri also didn't seem to notice her grandfather wasn't at the table. "I'm going to have a baby sister or brother," she said, her eyes bright and a smile lighting up her face.

After everyone congratulated Danielle and Dylan, Jodi walked over to Danielle. "I want to apologize for how stupid I've behaved. I'm through feeling sorry for myself. We all lose people we love, whether they have fur or hair, whether they die or move on in other ways. I accept that now. What you said that night was from a place of pain. I should know what that's like. I should've accepted your apologies. So please let me help you now around the farm. I'll also be happy to babysit, so you and your husband can have date nights." She smiled.

Danielle hugged her. "Welcome back, Jodi, and thank you."

Everyone was eager to lend Danielle a hand cleaning up. Although most of the pizza was gone, there was still a lot of Mavis' stew to put away and the serving items. Cathy was surprised when Michael, carrying salad bowls, walked over to her. "Follow me into the kitchen," he said. "I have something to tell you."

Cathy glanced at Stacy who was talking with Steve. "Aren't you waiting for her?"

"No. It's you I want to see."

Cathy grabbed a few glasses and followed him. After handing the dishes to Mavis who was rinsing them and placing them in the dishwasher, Michael motioned Cathy to a corner. "Maybe we should go outside," he said. "It's noisy and crowded here." He took her hand and led her from the room. She felt a jolt at his touch but then remembered Stacy.

Neither of them had grabbed coats. The outdoor air hit Cathy with a chilly blast. "This won't take long. I know you're cold." Michael looked into her eyes. She saw something there that warmed her. "I know there's been a lot of apologies today, and I want to add mine. I've been trying to push you into acknowledging your feelings for me by pretending a relationship with Stacy, but all I'm doing is pushing you away."

When Cathy began to reply, he stopped her. "Don't say anything yet. I have more to tell you. I spoke to Steve while we were upstairs. He was having fun with Sheri. He'll make a great dad one day. I think I'm better with animals." He smiled. "Steve made me see how stupid I've been. For a man with a doctorate, I hated to admit that. But that wasn't enough for me to give up my act. I saw your face and the hurt I was causing you. It wasn't worth it. No matter which of us you choose or when you do, I want you to know that Stacy and I are just friends, colleagues. I'm sorry if I made it look like more than that. I also owe her an apology for leading her on. She already suspects my feelings for you. She knows we have history." He paused, "I still hope she comes to work with me. She's an excellent vet, but if that makes you uncomfortable..." he waved his hands. "That's about it, Cathy. I'm sorry for being such an idiot."

Cathy kissed him. It was short but sweet. "I accept your apology, Michael. When I took this trip with Mildred to help Danielle find her mother's killer, I'd planned to take time to think over my true feelings for you and Steve. I wanted to come back to Buttercup Bend with an answer. I still plan to do that. Now that the case is closed, Nancy, Mildred, and I can go home at the end of the week."

Michael smiled. "That doesn't give you much time."

"I've taken enough time. At first, I thought the reason I couldn't make up my mind was because I didn't love either of you enough to accept your proposal. But then I realized that's not true. It's because you're both my friends, and I don't want to hurt one of you or lose that man's friendship."

"You'll never lose my friendship, no matter what you decide."

"You say that now, and I'm sure Steve would say the same. But knowing I turned you or him down will make a difference. It has to."

"Cathy, I can't talk for Steve, but I know he's mature enough to move on. So am I. You have nothing to fear and everything to gain, but there's one other thing I hate to admit." He looked away.

"What's that?" Cathy waited. She felt the chilly air enter her lungs as she held her breath for his answer.

"Either of us will make a great husband. If you choose me, you'll also have free vet care for your kittens."

Cathy laughed and blew out her breath which formed a ring of smoke. "But if I marry Steve, I'll have a beautiful garden."

CHAPTER FORTY-SIX

When Cathy and Nancy were in bed that night, before turning off the lights, Nancy asked, "What did Michael want with you when you went outside?"

Cathy hadn't realized Nancy had seen them, but she should've known. Nancy didn't miss anything. "We had a talk. He told me he's not interested in Stacy. They're just friends."

Nancy smiled. "So, is he the one?"

"I don't know yet, Nance. I should, shouldn't I? I promised him I'd make the decision when we got home."

"Cat, do you remember when we played that game the night I stayed over after your dinner party with Steve, Michael, Brian, your brother, and his wife?"

Cathy laughed. "How could I forget? It was crazy. We rated the three men. I can't even recall who we gave the highest scores. It seems ages ago. We weren't even dating them then."

Nancy sat up in bed and plumped her pillow. "What if we play another one? To help you make up your mind?"

"No!" Cathy screamed. "That game meant nothing. You

can't put a rating on your feelings. Take Mavis, for example. She wasted her whole life on Chris. What if I make a mistake? I could choose the wrong man."

"You're thinking too much, Cat. And if you want an example, look at Chris. He was obsessed with Doris. He had a woman who loved him, but he threw it all away. Now he'll spend the rest of his life in jail. Talk about a wrong decision."

"That has nothing to do with me. I'm not a killer. I'm not obsessed with anyone. But I keep thinking about Chris' advice to me to ignore the physical and look into my heart. He may have had a point."

"What are you saying? That you find Steve and Michael attractive but need to ignore those feelings to know who you really love?"

"I don't know." She sighed.

"So how are you going to decide by the end of the week?"

Cathy switched off the lamp on her bed table. "I'm sleeping on it."

Cathy was in a garden. The most beautiful flowers of all types and colors were in bloom. How could they be blooming this time of year? she thought. And where am I? She walked down a path bordered by deep blue larkspur and recognized the gate to Rainbow Gardens. Opening it, she stepped into a field of red, pink, yellow, and white roses and smelled their scents everywhere. Multicolored petals floated around her on a gentle breeze. She followed them to two gravestones between which a man sat kneeling. The stones were the graves of her cats, Floppy and Oliver, who'd crossed Rainbow Bridge at different times in her life. Even though Oliver's ashes sat in an urn in her bedroom, she'd still wanted a place to visit him and leave flowers.

When the petals led to the man, she saw it was Steve. He

turned but didn't stand. "Cat," he said. "You've come. I knew you would." He held a bouquet of red roses in one hand and a ring in the other. It was the ring he'd tried to give her at Christmas. He moved so that he was now kneeling on one knee. He offered her the flowers and the ring. "Will you marry me?" he asked.

She wanted so badly to stay in that place and to float away with the petals and Steve. But the wind suddenly picked up. Steve dropped the flowers and the ring. She reached out to grasp them, but they disappeared along with him. A blanket of snow now covered the ground. She saw a building a few feet away and, to get out of the cold, she approached it. As she reached it, she realized it was her rescue center, Rainbow Rescues. There was a man standing at the door. It was Michael. He held her kittens, Harry and Hermione, in his arms. "Come, Cathy," he said. "Let's bring them inside where it's warm. They've missed you."

Cathy followed him inside where she was greeted with meows and purrs from the cats in the cat section of her rescue center. Michael handed her Harry and Hermione and then took a ring from his coat pocket. It was the ring he'd offered her on New Year's Eve. "Marry me, Cathy." She was about to take the ring, when she remembered she still had an armful of felines. She looked down at her kittens, but they suddenly disappeared. So did the cats in the center. Michael was still there, but the ring had turned to dust. When he wiped it from his hand, she had a strange thought that it was cat litter. He smiled and said, "Choose wisely, Cathy," and then disappeared.

She woke with a start. The dream was gone, but she now knew her answer. "Wake up, Nancy." She nudged her friend who was curled up next to her with the blanket over her head.

"What's going on?" Nancy murmured in a sleepy voice as she turned over and popped her head out of the blanket.

"I had a weird dream, but it helped me make my decision."

"What?" Nancy sat up quickly. She now seemed wide awake. "That must've been some dream. Who is it? Who are you choosing?"

"I'm not letting you know yet."

"Are you kidding me, Catherine Marie Carter? You woke me up to tell me you've figured out whose marriage proposal you're accepting and then you won't say who'll be the lucky man."

"I'm sorry, Nancy, but it wouldn't be right. I'm not saying a word until we're back in Buttercup Bend and then you'll be the third person I tell."

"The third? Excuse me."

"Steve and Michael have to know first."

In the dark room, Cathy still managed to see Nancy's pout. She sighed. "I'll figure it out, even if you don't say. I'll watch you with them and look for signs. I'm good at that."

"I plan to be as neutral as possible. I'm not giving it away."

Nancy turned over. "We'll see. I'm going back to sleep."

CHAPTER FORTY-SEVEN

True to her word, Cathy didn't give Nancy any clues to whom she'd chosen. On the day they were leaving Oaks Landing, they learned that Chris would be in jail until his trial and that it was likely he'd spend the rest of his life there. Dr. Habib would also see jail time. Dylan had cancelled Betty's admission to the nursing home, but he'd registered her into a detox center. When her treatment was done, she'd return to the farm and stay with Mavis in Chris' house.

After breakfast, Cathy asked Nancy if she wanted to join her on a last walk around the farm. Nancy declined. "You go. I'm still packing."

"Packing? I only saw you pull things out of your suitcase the whole time we've been here."

Nancy smiled. "Don't you know it's harder to get clothes back in a case after they've been worn? Besides, Danielle gave me a few things as a thank you. A couple of them belonged to Doris but were given to her by Chris. Danielle and Betty didn't want to hold on to them. They want to start a new chapter in their lives."

Cathy felt disappointed that Nancy had been rewarded instead of her. She wondered if Danielle had given Mildred anything, but she couldn't ask because Mildred had left shortly after breakfast to spend time with Henry before leaving.

Outside, Cathy took the path toward the llama pen. She wanted to say goodbye to Lulu whose pregnancy had recently been confirmed after she was tested by Mavis.

Considering the decision she made after her dream, Cathy felt happy with it. She knew it would make one of her boyfriends sad, but she also knew she'd listened to her heart, so it was the right thing to do.

She found Lulu munching on grass. She opened the gate and walked over to her. "Good morning, Lulu. I've come to say goodbye. I hope to be back to visit you, but it might not be until after your baby is born."

Lulu looked at her through her big brown eyes. Cathy felt that animals were in tune with people's emotions. It seemed that Lulu knew what she was saying. She gave her a quick kiss on the head and turned away. As she did, Cathy caught a movement behind her. She turned to see Danielle. "I'm glad I caught you, Cathy. I wanted to speak with you alone."

Cathy caught her breath.

"I didn't scare you, did I?"

"No. I didn't hear you coming." Cathy closed the gate and gave Lulu a last wave.

"I saw you leave the house. I gave Nancy a few things last night that my father had given my mother." Cathy noticed she didn't use Chris' name.

"She told me. I didn't see them, but that was nice of you."

"I've also given Mildred something, but I owe you the most.

If it wasn't for you..." She paused. "Well, here it is." She took a dark blue jewelry box from her pocket.

Cathy's hand shook as she took it. "You really didn't have to give me anything, Danielle."

"Open it. Please. I want you to have it."

Cathy lifted the lid. It revealed an emerald-cut diamond ring. "No! I can't take this. If you don't want it, you can sell it and use the money toward the farm or your new baby."

"It's my mother's engagement ring. When she divorced my father, she didn't give it back to him but put it away. It's a symbol of his betrayal, and I want nothing to do with it. For you, it could mean saving more animals and money toward your wedding." She winked and added, "Don't worry about the farm. Now that he's gone, we'll be okay and so will my baby since things are good between Dylan and me again. We owe you that, too."

"I don't know what to say."

"Thank you is good enough, Cathy."

When Cathy and Danielle went back to the house, Henry was giving Mildred a hand loading her and Cathy's luggage into Cathy's car. Steve and Michael were helping Nancy with her bags. Stacy and Jodi were there to see the five off. Henry gave Mildred a light kiss on the cheek and promised her that he'd see her again soon. Stacy didn't hug or kiss Michael, but she told him that she'd arranged a meeting with a realtor in Buttercup Bend and would start work once she was settled in her new place.

Sherri ran from the house behind Danielle and hugged Mildred. "I'll miss you, Millie," she cried. "Please come back again."

"I will. I want to see your new brother or sister and Lulu's baby, too."

Sherri smiled. "Mommy and Lulu are both having babies. I'm so happy. I can't wait."

Jodi watched from the barn where she sat playing with the barn cats. Nancy and Cathy walked over to her. "I see you're practicing for your new kitten," Nancy said.

She smiled as she dangled a cat teaser in front of Cricket. "Yep. I can't wait."

Cathy said, "I'm sure you'll find the right cat for you. If you have any problems, you can always come to Rainbow Rescues."

Danielle gave Cathy, Nancy, and Mildred big hugs. "Thank you again for everything."

Betty, next to her, said, "I'm thankful, too. My daughter can now rest in peace because of the three of you."

Steve and Michael, having finished loading Nancy's car, walked back to them. "You can follow us, ladies," Steve said, "but if you lose us, just let your phone's GPS guide you."

"I think we should meet at Gran's when we all get to Buttercup Bend," Cathy suggested. "She'll be relieved to know we made it back safe. I can't wait to see her and my kittens again."

The men got into Michael's car. They waited until Cathy and Mildred boarded theirs. Nancy's car was behind Cathy's. She spoke to her through the window. "I know why you suggested we go to Florence's house. That's where you're breaking the news, but I already figured out who you chose. I saw how you looked at him."

Cathy laughed. "You're bluffing. I looked at both of them the same way."

Nancy avoided her gaze. "You're right, but won't you at least give me a clue?"

"You'll know soon enough."

With a sigh, Nancy walked back to her car and got behind the wheel.

As the three cars drove away, Dylan, Danielle, Mavis, Jodi, Sheri, Henry, Betty, and Stacy waved. Cathy felt glad Doris' murder had been solved but also sad that she was leaving the farm and the new friends she'd made.

CHAPTER FORTY-EIGHT

S ince Cathy called Gran from the car when they'd exited the parkway and were stopped at a light, Florence was waiting for them at the door when they arrived at her house. Howard stood behind her, and the kittens, appearing as though they'd grown in the past week, looked on with wide eyes from the sidelines.

As soon as she entered, Gran embraced her. "I'm so glad you're back, Catherine. I wish you'd given me more notice, but I still managed to put out a few refreshments for you and your friends. Doug and Becky are in the kitchen with the baby. Your brother is helping himself to the food already, and Becky is making sure there's some left for us." She smiled.

Nancy, behind Cathy, whispered in her ear. "Looks like your whole family is here for you to make your announcement."

"What's that, Nancy?"

"Nothing, Florence, uh, thank you for having us."

"Well, come on in. All of you." She waved Mildred, Steven, and Michael inside. "We have a lot to catch up on. Cathy said something about your solving the case. I want to know all about it."

Howard, who'd taken their coats to put away, said, "Please, Florence, let your granddaughter breathe a moment. She's had quite an adventure."

"I suppose you're angry with me and Cathy," Nancy said.

"No," Howard corrected her. "I'm not mad. I understand you wanted to do this undercover, but I expect a full report. Brian is at the station. I'm sure he'll want to see you as soon as possible, but I don't know if he'll feel the same way as I do when you explain things to him."

It was then that Harry and Hermione came warily forward, sniffing Cathy's slacks. "I guess I smell of the farm," she said, "but it's me, guys." She picked them up and hugged them. "You've gotten so big. I've missed you very much."

"They were fine," Florence said, "and, yes, I believe they've grown since you've been away."

"How did you manage to get everyone here so quickly and food, too?"

"Doug and Becky were already here when you called, as was Howard. I'd invited them to breakfast. Becky brought over muffins, and there's still a lot left, if Doug hasn't consumed them all."

"We had breakfast at the farm before we left, but I wouldn't mind one of Becky's muffins." Cathy's sister-in-law was a great baker, although Doug often cooked their dinners after his work at the post office. Her brother, despite his huge appetite, was skinny as a toothpick.

"The kitchen is too cramped for everyone, so please sit in the dining room," Florence directed, as they followed her, the kittens trailing alongside Cathy.

After they were seated around the dining room table, Cathy, Mildred, and Nancy took turns recounting their adventure and how Chris Grady was now behind bars for the murder of his ex-wife.

"Oh, my," Florence said, "that's quite a story. I'm glad you were able to help Danielle. She sounds like a nice woman. I'm sorry about what happened to her mother and finding out her father killed her."

"It's sad," Nancy agreed, "but there were some bright points. Mildred met a boyfriend." She looked across the table at the librarian whose cheeks turned red at her comment.

"I guess you could call Henry that," Mildred said. "He's a widower, a sweet man. We make a nice match. He's looking into moving here after he retires from working as a gardener. He was a librarian before that. We have a lot in common."

"I'm happy for you," Florence said.

"Seems like love can be found at any age." Howard winked at Florence.

"Talk about love," Nancy said, munching into a chocolate muffin, swallowing, and wiping her mouth with a napkin, "I think Cathy has something to tell everyone."

Cathy hadn't expected Nancy to say that. Her heart beating fast, she felt and saw all eyes turn upon her.

"I, uh..." she stammered.

"You shouldn't have put Cathy on the spot," Steve said. "If she has something to say to me and Michael, I think it should be in private."

"I agree," Michael said. "Is there somewhere we can go to talk?"

"Howard has been helping me convert the spare room upstairs to a craft room," Florence said, "It's empty now except for a few chairs." She turned to Cathy, "Go ahead, dear. Take your time. There's no rush, and you don't have to make any announcements until you're ready."

Nancy frowned. Cathy knew she was disappointed because she was desperate to hear Cathy's decision.

Michael and Steve followed Cathy upstairs. The room was unfurnished except for two folding chairs against the wall and the paint cans, rollers, and shelving hardware that stood next to them. On the opposite side of the room was a bin containing yarn and Florence's sewing machine. Cathy glanced out the window from which she could view the bare oak tree that was covered with a thin coating of snow.

Steve pulled out a chair and opened it. "Sit, Cat. I can stand."

Michael opened the other chair. "I can stand, too."

Cathy felt a laugh bubble up in her chest. Both men were offering her chairs. "You two sit. I'd rather stand."

When they hesitated, she said, "Believe me, you're better off sitting for what I have to say."

After glancing at one another, they took their seats at the same time.

Cathy looked from one to the other and drew in a deep breath. "I know I've taken a long time to make up my mind which of you I want to marry. It was hard because I love both of you and you're both my friends."

When they started to speak, she waved her hand. "Just listen. I have to explain. When I say I love both of you, I only love one as a friend. I had a dream and woke up realizing which one that was and who I love enough to spend the rest of my life with. I know I'm going to hurt one of you, but I also know it'll free you to find the person who's right for you. I'm honored that you both proposed to me. I was surprised and not prepared for that, but I'm ready now. I'll be right back." She left them murmuring together as she went to her room.

When she returned, they stopped as soon as they saw her, their eyes focusing on the two jewelry boxes she held.

"These are the rings you gave me. I'm returning one. I'll let the person I've chosen place the other on my finger." She approached them.

To find out who Cathy chose, check out the forthcoming book, THE CASE OF THE WHALE WATCHING WEDDING PLANNER," Buttercup Bend #4.

ACKNOWLEDGMENTS

I'd like to thank the staff at Next Chapter Publishing, especially Miika Hannila whose vision for marketing, distributing, and promoting books worldwide in various formats has allowed my novels to appear on both virtual and real bookshelves. I'd also like to thank Petteri Hannila for my manuscript layout and the Next Chapter design team for their incredible covers. I also want to acknowledge my fellow Next Chapter authors. I'm honored to be a part of this talented team of writers. Thanks also to my author friends, my husband, daughter, and all those who have encouraged my writing, especially my readers who make all the hard work worthwhile.

A special thank you to Tabbethia Haubold of Long Island Yarn and Farm (www.liyarnandfarm.com) for a tour of her farm where, by seeing her pregnant llamas, I was inspired to add Lulu's pregnancy to the book. Another special thank you to Andrea Parent-Tibbetts of Clover Brooke Farm (https://clover brookefarm.com/) for the information she provided about llamas, fiber farms, and her barn cats, Piper, Rascal, and Cricket whom I featured as the cats at the fictional Oaks Landing Farm.

Last but not least, I owe thanks to Virginia Healy who won my newsletter's book naming contest by providing the title of the third Buttercup Bend mystery and Linda Herold who won my llama-naming contest by suggesting "Lulu" as the name for the llama.

If you enjoy this book and any of my others, I'd be grateful for a brief review on any book sites you prefer and/or your blog.

ABOUT THE AUTHOR

 Debbie De Louise is an award-winning author and a reference librarian. She is a member of Sisters-in-Crime, International Thriller Writers, the Long Island Authors Group, and the Cat Writers' Association. She writes two cozy mystery series, the Cobble Cove Mysteries and Buttercup Bend Mysteries. She's also written a paranormal romance, three standalone mysteries, a time-travel novel, and a collection of cat poems. Her stories and poetry appear in over a dozen anthologies. Debbie also writes articles for cat magazines. She lives on Long Island with her husband, daughter, and two cats. Learn more about Debbie and her books by visiting her website at https://debbiedelouise.com.

To learn more about Debbie De Louise and discover more Next Chapter authors, visit our website at www.nextchapter.pub.

Printed in Great Britain
by Amazon